PENGUIN BOOKS

MIRROR, MIRROR

GW00361208

RESALE FOR CHARITY ONLY

Mirror, Mirror

MARIA ALVAREZ

PENGUIN BOOKS

PENGUIN BOOKS

Published by the Penguin Group
Penguin Books Ltd, 80 Strand, London WC2R ORL, England
Penguin Group (USA) Inc., 375 Hudson Street, New York, New York 10014, USA
Penguin Group (Canada), 90 Eglinton Avenue East, Suite 700, Toronto, Ontario, Canada M4P 2Y3
(a division of Pearson Penguin Canada Inc.)
Penguin Ireland, 25 St Stephen's Green, Dublin 2, Ireland (a division of Penguin Books Ltd)
Penguin Group (Australia), 250 Camberwell Road, Camberwell, Victoria 3124,
Australia (a division of Pearson Australia Group Pty Ltd)
Penguin Books India Pvt Ltd, 11 Community Centre,
Panchsheel Park, New Delhi – 110 017, India
Penguin Group (NZ), 67 Apollo Drive, Rosedale, North Shore 0632, New Zealand
(a division of Pearson New Zealand Ltd)
Penguin Books (South Africa) (Pty) Ltd, 24 Sturdee Avenue,
Rosebank, Johannesburg 2196, South Africa

Penguin Books Ltd, Registered Offices: 80 Strand, London WC2R ORL, England

www.penguin.com

First published by Fig Tree 2007
Published in Penguin Books 2008
1

Copyright © Maria Alvarez, 2007
All rights reserved

The moral right of the author has been asserted

Typeset by Rowland Phototypesetting Ltd, Bury St Edmunds, Suffolk
Printed in England by Clays Ltd, St Ives plc

ISBN: 978-0-141-02861-3

www.greenpenguin.co.uk

Penguin Books is committed to a sustainable future
for our business, our readers and our planet.
The book in your hands is made from paper
certified by the Forest Stewardship Council.

'I am not I: pitie the tale of me'

from Sir Philip Sidney,
Astrophel and Stella

It was a woman's shout, then a man's, cut short by a slamming door. Flicking the blind aside, I put my eye to the gap.

Silence. No one. Only bare branches twitching. And lamplight bathing everything – terraced houses, parked cars, the slither of sullen night sky – in a gaudy orange film. Perhaps it's me, perhaps it's just the sudden waking.

I can hear a loud tock-tock of heels from the opposite corner. She's tall, young, in jeans and narrow black leather jacket; long hair, a dark, burnished gold. She casts a quick glance behind her, and now up, it seems, towards me.

We lock gazes and I step back, slightly stunned. She halts, turns and retraces her steps. A car door shuts somewhere close by. I remain snagged at the window, shivering to the distant roar of an aeroplane.

Voices again – coming from the same corner. Now she is coatless, bare-armed in a tight sparkling vest. A long denim handbag swings furiously from her shoulder as she speeds up her clunking, high-heeled pace. Close behind follows a man, fair shorn head rising from a black parka, face thrust out like an angry fist.

I can make nothing of their hoarse shouts as she comes to an abrupt stop on the pavement, directly opposite my window. His reaction is to push her hard with a flat palm, mid-chest. It's a laboured, sideways fall, in which she manages to strike her forehead against the roof of my car on the way down, cigarette clutched in her left hand.

Balance recovered, she leans against the car and stays with her back to me, smoking, watching, as he gropes about in her

I

fallen denim handbag, flinging makeup, hair brush, mobile to the ground. Finally, some object is found and stuffed into an inner pocket of his parka. As he slings the bag into the gutter by her feet, he turns a slow semi-circle around her, as if unable to tear himself away.

At this point, she utters something – something devastating because even from here, I see his tautening mouth, the ominous rise of his hand. But he moves away – giving my car door a stiff kick – before marching back round the corner. A car engine gnashes to a start; only now does she turn, touch her forehead and stare at the blood gathered on her finger.

The tilt of her head provokes a smudged recollection and the sensation of tiny hot shards coursing through the top of my skull. Full of urgency, I lift the blind and open the window to the slap of icy air.

'Are you all right?' I ask.

Her head swivels round with ceremonious slowness.

'You'd better come in,' I say, noting a fleeting little smile on her lips.

The chill slices through my skin as I tie my silk dressing gown tightly at the open door. She approaches at a sullen gait, fixing me with a calm, beatific look. Close up, her pupils are dilated, hopping with manic life in that mess of smudged eye shadow. Dark daub of blood on her brow, the mouth nearly purple with cold.

'Come in, it's freezing,' I say to her. A sudden movement; her body falters. I steady her by her shoulders, help her over the threshold, but it's a job; she's tall in those boots and marble-cold to touch.

I lead her into the sitting room, on to the corner of the sofa nearest the door, lighting the lamp beside it. Collapsed back, the arc of light strikes her with a kitsch dazzle. She is all antique sheen, her dirty-gold mane merging with the sparkling camisole. There's a secretive ecstasy in the curling ends of the mouth. In a daze, held by the icy-blue gleam of her skin, I literally have to shake myself into waking, action. I decide to do what they do in films: walk quickly yet calmly to the kitchen, assemble a medical kit of sorts to clean and dress the wound, and grab Jake's Armagnac (he never drinks it). Back at the sitting-room door, I hear her say, 'The cunt took my fucking fags.' She is transfigured: crouched, rummaging in her handbag. 'Can't believe it. Oh, here they are.' It's an affecting voice, a voice thick with wood smoke. She shoots me a manic grin, oblivious to the thin line of blood trickling down to her eye.

'Drink this. Let's clear up your forehead.' Standing behind her now, I guide her head back. She gulps down her drink, woozily submitting to my hands smoothing back her hair.

'By the way, I'm Christabel Fellner,' I say.

'This is all really freaky. I'm Tina.' She has jolted her head back, but I press it back down, noting slanted eyes, half-moons of pale green glass. 'Try to keep still.' She responds with a gravelly giggle.

Time floats drowsily in the silent lull. I clean the wound gently; there's not much more blood. I notice her eyebrows are russet-coloured, with a sprinkling of faint gold at her temples. The hair smells of bar fug and silt, and of sweetish singed plastic like a burnt doll. I push down a bandage with firm finality, letting go of her head.

'There, just a graze, though you should get it checked out.'

'Hate doctors.' She helps herself to a good swig of Armagnac while reaching for a cigarette and then clicks at a long lighter with a trembling hand. A high flame shoots up, coming to rest a millimetre from her eyebrow; I hear the tiny fizzing of hair. Cigarette lit, she follows with a lengthy, self-absorbed exhalation into mid-air. 'Yeah, well, fuckit.' The tips of her long, bony fingers are grey with the grime of a long, hard night.

'How do you feel?'

3

By way of response, I am met with a straying, doleful gaze, a swift don't-careish hunch of the shoulders. And it is here that I begin to be – charmed, tenderized.

'Do you live close by?' I hand her an ashtray from the coffee table and turn, sitting towards her, suddenly flushing with self-consciousness at being in my dressing gown with a stranger.

'Nowhere. It's his flat. He took my keys, didn't he?' The accent is all young urban layering, hard to place: the ubiquitous estuary mockney, a hint of Jafaican. But the aspirated 'h', the occasional swooping consonant, sound the caricatured airs of a diva.

'Is he your boyfriend?'

'Carl? Caaarl?' The sound is a spit of derision. 'Hate him. Hates me.'

There follows a dismissive drag on the fag. 'He's lost the plot. Won't leave it. Tonight, right . . .' Moving round to fix me with that pale-glass stare, she stabs at the air with the cigarette for emphasis. 'Tonight he was like, really on to me with this sleazeball in the car; so he could like, watch . . .' A knowing laugh cuts the narrative short. The long eyes narrow and glaze over. 'Yeah, well, you don't wanna know. I'll call old Charlotte, she lives ten minutes away.'

Now she clambers over the coffee table, mouth fretting at ash-heavy fag, and swoops towards the hallway worrying at her mobile, a sleek, silvery, flip-top affair. I can hear much impatient stomping up and down the hall corridor. 'It's me, Tina! Carl's flipped. Totally. I'm locked out. Answer the phone. Okay, ring me asap. Jeezus.' I can make out a long sigh of annoyance – at the inconsiderately sleeping friend. But it sounds an overblown note. Why did she go out to ring? It occurs to me, instantly, that she may have faked the call. I look across at the time, glinting greenly on the DVD machine: 05.14. I had no idea it was so late.

Back in the room, she has sobered up enough to sense my agitation. 'I'll just have to turn up and buzz the fuck out of her buzzer.' I am flashed a shark-like smile with a row of tiny, glinting teeth. She edges closer. 'You know me. I work in The Castle, round the corner.' She blows smoke shamelessly into my face. 'You came in for a meal three weeks ago. It was a Friday . . . Ever so slinky in black, slinky black hair – your plate, you didn't touch anything . . . just puffin' and drinking, all mysterious – and pissed off.' She holds out her cigarette hand, flips it deliberately into a gesture, my exact 'troubled-and-smoking' gesture. I start, as if chancing on a dissonant, angry self in a reflecting window. 'This one's different, I thought to myself, different,' she continues, exhaling roughly, 'not like the rest of the wives. If you cut them, they'd have organic cranberry juice for blood.' An abrupt automaton's cackle erupts from the direction of her half-closed mouth.

Absurdly, I seem intent on injecting a tinkling drawing-room tone. 'So, don't you enjoy your job?'

'First regular job for, like, three centuries. Tryin' to bin all that shit.' She gestures at the window, by which I take her to mean the earlier drama. Now she turns, pulls herself up straight with a skittish amusement. 'How about you? Do you enjoy it?'

'Enjoy what?'

'Your job, your life.' I see her arm is sweeping graciously outwards in a parody of my own. There's a ticking sound from the direction of the dark fireplace. I finally answer, 'Good question. Not since I gave up smoking.' She holds out her lit fag to me and I take it and pull on it. Our ensuing laughter cuts itself suddenly short, arrested by the night's silence.

'I don't really have a job at the moment,' I tell her.

I am now being assessed with drunken boldness, the tips of those creaturely teeth chewing contemplatively at her lower lip.

'You alone here then?'

'Yes. No. I mean, my husband works in LA.'

Now she swoops forward, hand extended. Her index finger begins slowly to stroke the chain around my neck, coming to rest on the pendant diamond in the middle. 'Bet he gave you that.'

'Yes, yes.' My neck smarts at the strange touch. I lift my hand automatically to stop hers, flinching in confusion. She removes her own hand calmly, smiling opaquely. I say, 'I must have forgotten to take it off.' I feel peeled, exposed.

'So why did you ask me in then?' A lilt in her voice tightens the net of edgy intimacy around us; I try to shake it off with glibness.

'You did hurt yourself. Well, the truth is, it was concern for my car. You fell on it and your boyfriend kicked it.'

'But I could be anybody.' She shoots me a sideways leer.

'You didn't look too dangerous. Just a vulnerable, cold girl.'

'Girl? I'm twenty-five.' The voice is thickening, clotting. 'I saw you, looking at me out there, it was you, up there . . . and . . . I knew, like from the start . . .' She halts for breath. The moment stales. Oh yes, she was right. What the fuck is she doing here? I get up, gingerly, my unease somehow deepening at the sight of the vulnerable, skeletal bones on my feet.

'Listen, I'll call a cab and lend you some money.' She stays seated, long pale arms crossed in her lap. Having fetched my purse from the kitchen and called a cab, I hand her twenty pounds; far too much, but she plucks it from my hand with a breezy air of entitlement. I say, 'Now, the cab's coming straight away . . .' Her glance has fixed on my white-knuckled grip on the purse defensively held to my midriff. Our eyes meet in a charged exchange. Out of guilt, or fear, I add impetuously, 'I'll lend you a jumper.'

'If you like . . .'

'It's fine – for God's sake, you work round the corner.'

6

Rushing upstairs, I grab the first suitable thing, a red cardigan, from the bedroom, realizing too late when I'm back downstairs that it is one of my new Christmas presents from Jake. Expensive cashmere. Hermès. Far too small, delicate, inappropriate. I could have given her one of several hoodies hanging by the door. Never mind: I want her out. I open the front door to an inky sky being beaten into fast grey whorls. A gust blows from nowhere. Spindly branches clack and poke about. Her hair flies back and her eyes, her mouth, all follow, slanting, as she puts on the cardigan. She's shouting through a column of air.

'Pay you back, pay you back.'

'Whenever.' I close the door with difficulty against the heave of wind. Through the spyglass I note the girl's forlorn backward gaze in the receding taxi. By contrast, the mouth, otherwise petulantly full, is pressed into a thin line of intent.

Back inside, I am struck by the stilled air. I – we – have been here nearly two months, and the house still feels inscrutable, a little contemptuous of us even. I hear again the gravelly catch in her voice, my neck pricking at the memory, the chain intolerably scratchy. I fumble for ages to unclasp it and sling it back in its box in the drawer – as Jake always reminds me to do. Then, the slide into the new bed I have chosen. Plain, simple mahogany.

Sounds invade: random creaks, the odd snapped gust punctured by the whistle of a distant police siren. My heart twitches in its cage – the diazepam, disturbed in its course. I feel for the bottle on the bedside table in the dark. Another won't kill me.

I

The television is showing a news flash. Hundred-mile gales in the north, paralysed transport services, cars blown off the road, bridges closed down, damaged power-lines, trees devastated.

The winds have reached the south and parts of the city. The images show loose fragments of buildings, house fronts slashed like the flimsiest of silk, a steeple blown off a church, like the work of some bored hooligan deity. Looking out of the bay window, I see no overturned cars, no roofs savagely swept away. Only one of the pavement cherry trees has suffered a half-lopped branch. In the glass, my reflection merges with a matted tangle of twigs huddled in a corner. Other lines weave in, arabesque fashion. A face forms there with exaggerated, slanting features. Oh dear me, last night. I switch channels. Soldiers scurrying around Baghdad like rubble sculptures, rubble stick-men. London. Another police search in some bedraggled block of flats.

Ah now, that's better – *Home Invaders*, the new morning rival to *DIY Brigade*. Josh and Daz are arriving at a new house on whose doorstep waits a quivering housewife. A mini-squad of iconic masculinity, indistinguishable in their khaki combat gear from the newsreel soldiers, they set to work after a quick flirt and a cup of tea. Here they are, thundering into walls with power drills, masculine thighs straddling the floor as corner fittings are prised out with grunting expertise.

These are the sort of shows that zip me through the mornings. *Rural Bliss*, *Restoring Follies*, *House Swap–Life Swap*, *Top Pads*, *Renovation Renovation* – the illusion of rebirth through the cult of interiors. Dark, handsome Josh is now demonstrating to the newly appeared husband how to make shelves that stay up. Josh holds up a long screw and a long plastic rawlplug and inserts screw in plug. 'These two need each other.' He grins at the camera. 'Otherwise, it's a case of this.' His large paw on the bookshelf behind him causes it to flop down – the husband's goatee beard twitches. The TV flashes up a sign: '*Wall Colour: Deep Boudoir Red*'.

It's barely a week since I called a halt to my own Home Invaders, to their endless screeching drill, my mind fraying with their sodden cigarette butts floating in the loo. So the house is only half habitable. Kitchen, front sitting room, bathroom and my bedroom form one region, stripped and smoothed of history, bare rectangles for hearths, a sanctum of white and glass. But the old house remains in the nicotine-hued hallways, the two spare bedrooms, dining room and disused attic.

It had been empty for months before we bought it; some man living abroad had inherited it from his mother. I feel the old woman's brown breath in the cloistral hallway, her tread on the balding carpet-stair. And here, in the old dining room, so dismal I'm almost fond of it. The room needs exorcizing of a congealed, overcooked pall. A huge patch of damp dominates one corner, in the shape of a crab with an outsize claw sprawling over the window. The yard outside is in the permanent shadow of the wall to its right, and on its other side by the street corner. I'm still startled in my tracks by the rodent-like shuffles of people passing unseen beyond the wall. And here in the other corner, the only item of furniture, my mother's high-backed Jacobean chair. Even the stacked boxes are succumbing, their cardboard edges curling and merging with the gristle-coloured marble of the fireplace surround. Nails prod dimly through the floorboards like miniature mines.

I leave for the gleaming contrast of the kitchen in shiny new metal and pale wood, the partitioned French windows

9

framing the chaos of garden outside in multiple screens. The wind has done some stealthy work: a bush has been stripped bare, leaving thin, toothless combs for branches, revealing a convolvulus curled tight about its newly naked core.

Back from this view, the mess in the hall needs even more immediate attention. I cannot leave it in this state for Kim, my new cleaner. She'll never stay. I hoover and scrub away the clinging dust of the decorators – all to little effect. The smell of dust is pervasive, as if the house were built on some vast, cindery desert. I finally give up, surprised by the suddenly darkening afternoon light, and go upstairs. Stepping out of the shower, I realize I am a violent pink from scrubbing myself and wonder exactly how long I've spent in there. These recurring distortions of time, needle-stings of anguish.

In the bedroom mirror, I force my gaze to meet me full on. Portrait of a Pointless Woman. At thirty-eight. It has a numbing clang to it. (Bring on the ringing toll of forty.) On good days I can 'pass' for less but still, my relationship with mirrors is becoming anxious, glancing. And to think of how I used to gobble up mirrors. Well, the thrill is gone, baby. It's not vanity, not as such. All right, well, perhaps. But vanity aside, there's something else to it, a blind panic at any visual scrutiny. As my face fades, the veil will slip to reveal it: that huge, psychic blister silently building underneath. Only in anonymity can I shed skin, flesh, age, self. But today, I make an effort; I'm paying a long overdue visit to Suzy, old friend and near neighbour, and this is what it reduces to: dressing up to others' expectations. I should have spared Jake and married a gangster property tycoon with hair implants. Cocaine for breakfast; Kristal for lunch, followed by a monumentally ravaged decline. Anything but this blanching, this drip-drip effacement.

Making my way downstairs, I grow clammy recalling the girl on the threshold, as if I'd literally sleep-walked through the incident.

The sky is low, drizzle slashes thinly on cheek. My breath forms plumes which die quickly in the icy air. Most early afternoons, I've taken to prowling around this becalmed neighbourhood of Ladbroke Park, savouring the cosy novelty of its neo-suburbia. The bare stumps of the harshly pruned trees, the placid streets, all so different from last summer by the copse in the country, dank foliage and dank earth encroaching. A disaster, that experiment. No use dwelling on it: I've escaped all that. Here, I – we – (Jake is hardly 'here') will find balance in the limbo of this satellite world, under the eiderdown of the smoke-grey clouds.

There's a lightly emotional pull too, a tentative family connection, my father having spent part of his childhood a mile to the north. They must have arrived, my paternal grandparents, Polish Jew and cockney – what, nearly sixty years ago. At some point, when their business prospered, they'd decamped to a larger house, further out, the one I knew. I'd been seven when they'd died soon after each other. Though their faces have long since faded, still, I hear the warmth of their voices, grown alike through the years – or perhaps it's my memory that joins them in one sound. Still, I hear their fond, plangent awkwardness around my father, their brilliant son Leo, the art historian, married to a lapsed Catholic and visiting them always in his black, Bohemian sweaters. Not in denial, I prefer to think, so much as in aesthetic retreat from his roots. My aunt, his sister, is also dead. Apart from her children in Chicago, there is no other family on that side, so many potential branches having strayed, or perished. But then, I'm hardly close to my own brother, or to the remnants of my mother's querulous bloodline and their withered genealogy. What a furtive thrill would overcome me, after she died, when I lied and told people I was an orphan.

I have a photograph of my father, little Leo, a wiry boy in tweed gazing with shrewd coyness at the camera in a garden.

Even then, in the tilted head and impish curl of lip and forelock, that assumption of seductiveness, the cosseted aura. He has not yet visited me here in the new house or shown me the house where he lived, if it still stands. But then, he affects not to know, scoffing at the idea of revisiting such Pooterish horror.

These terraces, built for clerks and shopkeepers, have already seen several waves of immigrants in the last century – from Ireland, the Caribbean, Pakistan. But recent booming property prices have brought a different species. Priced out of the grander, stuccoed central localities, comforted by the presence of other Ruperts and Mirandas, they – I have yet to think of myself as we – continue to arrive in sleek silver hatchbacks and MPVs. These are tucked in rows of new parking bays marked out by freshly painted white lines. I notice one of the street's few remaining eyesores, the crushed-nosed rusting red saloon, has vanished overnight. A curious thing this: the more the new arrivals attempt to impose their tasteful individuality on their property, the more the houses, previously scarred by different degrees of dilapidation, end as serial images of one another, their windows like port-holes in a well-oiled ship. There's a joke, a local myth. They arrive to breed only to find their desire drain efficiently away down the well-maintained copper pipes.

'It's everywhere,' Suzy tells me of the passionless torpor of the unions as she reels off a growing list of examples. 'It's in the air.' But there is no real air except the soft sighing through the cherry trees. Not even today, the night's gales having glided through fitfully, late for somewhere else. Clouds float motionless. Inclemency seems to bypass Ladbroke Park, baffled by its satellite status, neither city centre nor real suburb.

Suzy's house is the other side of Main Road, on a corner of the Park, the area's dinky pastoral heart. The street names – Hopeglade, Mornington – promise painless lives, cheery avenues to painless deaths. I glimpse the Park, which I've yet to visit. Encircled by low black railings, one can see through to the other side, to the pert two-storey houses, their low contours scaling down all, sky, trees, humans, to their own dainty proportions.

We are in Suzy's neo-industrial kitchen where gleaming pots and pans hang obediently in a rectangular formation over the central cooking range. Only jars of expensive oils and spices are allowed an artful disarray on two stainless-steel shelves. The steel worktops reflect back our faces with clinical precision. Suzy's large-boned frame fizzes metallically around the place, under the stern watch of a forbiddingly rectangular white vase at the windowsill, stuffed with spiky wintry foliage.

'From your garden?'

'No, darling, haven't you noticed the new florist's by the tube station? Next to the new organic deli.' Her mock-astounded glare never fails to bring to mind those Lely portraits of Restoration ladies, all urbane pragmatism behind coy, bulbous eyes. In fact, Suzy is growing nicely into her Restoration character, the blithe drollness in her voice bringing every subject, lofty or sad, down to the same rolling foothills of gossip. It works its way into her face, a deadpan irreverence pulling down the lines around her mouth into a bemused moue. In stillness – a rare thing – her mouth settles into a depressed arch.

As she prepares coffee, she starts in on her usual comic plaint, the chaos and strife of juggling her work as a freelance art director, motherhood and play – though her life is as regulated as her precision-layered glossy dark locks. On the table lies a large biblical leather diary – a thick codex of organic traders, bikram yoga teachers, contemporary dance tickets, children's dental appointments, private openings, dinner in new restaurants with old friends, lunch in old restaurants with new contacts.

It appears her husband, Nick, has forgotten to order something or other from Real Soil, the organic delivery people. She offers up some hilarious examples of his convenient lapses of memory. I recall the multiple doomed love affairs of her youth with cute Jamaican dub DJs, each break-up heralding another avant-garde hairstyle: yellow-and-green mohican would give way to surly-fringed Juliette Greco beatnik. And how, on the stroke of her thirtieth birthday, the mettle of her breed had set in and bagged the obligingly suitable Nick. As she reopens the fridge, she lets out a melodramatic groan, both hands on hips. 'No milk. And yes, of course, you guessed it, the butter's gone too. She gets through half a pound of organic butter in two days!' 'She' is Olga, her taciturn au pair.

'She might have other uses for it,' I suggest.

'She's far too busy throwing up to get buggered.' The last word bounces jauntily in the air; Suzy sighs with lengthy emphasis. 'Oh well, it'll have to be the soya milk.' As our cackles subside we move into Suzy's large sitting area, open-plan, though ingeniously sectioned. I am shown the new black leather sofa unit. 'Black is a much better colour with children around,' she says as she ushers me down. Recently I've had the sensation that all Suzy's utterances to me are speared with strategic hints; might this be about my childless state? But now we've moved on, with Suzy's customary deftness, by way of sofas to our mutual friend Zara Marshall. 'She's completely lost the plot, the new house is all garish post-punk – purple sofa, pink and black everywhere. Poor old Tom – now she's decided she wants to live in Goa . . . and – as if heroin weren't enough, she's apparently moved on to crack.'

By way of contrast to her environmental minimalism, Suzy collects friends like a collection of cherished, cracked antique dolls, about whom she likes to confer darkly. She and I are the last of the old college gang in town, drawing closer as people do on large tables as departing diners begin to leave salient gaps. Ours is an elastic friendship, stretched on a tacit pact against unwelcome truths – yet fondly loyal. My cracks appeal and appal; if nothing else, they must enhance her own hold on virtue.

'Last time she invited me for a girlie supper,' she continues, 'and she wasn't there! No one. No lights in the house. No message. Nothing.' Suzy's patrician nose snorts with indignation. 'And when she's feeling bad she just dumps it all on you, for hours, on the phone. In the end, you have to let them fall. Hope they pick themselves up again.' By way of punctuation, she gets up to rearrange two twigs in another austere vase. 'I mean, she does have a three-year-old child.'

I feel the mischief of my father in me: 'You've just given me an idea on research. "On Contemporary Vanitas: the iconography of early-twenty-first-century interiors."'

'I wouldn't mind being a student again,' she sniffs, 'if I could afford it. Anyhow, I thought you'd already done a PhD or what have you.'

'An MPhil, which, you may recall, I left half-way through.' I add a hint of despair, to veil the flatness. 'You're right. Here I am, like some empty, privileged hausfrau from another era, doing up the house.'

Suzy's cup chinks with efficient irritation against its saucer. 'Well, babe, the pills might be helping but – you need something. If not a job or a baby – a – a project. A dog – a Jack Russell. You like Jack Russells. How's the house?'

'Oh, I got rid of the builders. They were quite literally doing my head in.'

I am thrown a tart frown, dramatically despaired of, and let off, though not without a caution, my attention being drawn to a pair of black art deco ashtrays on the coffee table in the shape of female dancers. 'Kitsch or what? Nick hates them. Bloody architects. But there has to be some compromise in a marriage.'

I take my leave, tickled, as I always am, by the unintentional comedy of Suzy, her genius for illustrating the grave with the mundane. At least her affinities reveal a tireless pedalling at life – so much more human than my own sniggering evasions.

Back out on Main Road, walking rapidly through the charcoal air, I am caught by a bust of a child in green glass in the window of the junk shop. With its blankness of eye, hairless head, it brings to mind a dream from last night. Fragments surface and collide with the uncanny softness of mercury. I was in the gallery, in The Big Room, with Paddy, my old boss. Then I was alone, with a sculpture which had just arrived; I didn't want to look into its blank eye.

Thank God we opted for a larger house on this scruffier side. I would have throttled myself in all that pleasantness. But what use the barrier is at the end of my road, I'm not sure. Perhaps to discourage entrance from the pitted, traffic-guzzling, shop-strewn Broadway, a section of a long old Roman road leading westwards out of the city. Grimy men with jumpy dogs cross over in the afternoons to the corner shop, a family-owned 'dairy' and newsagents run by Ali and his family with resigned good humour. Here, in the cramped interior divided by a long tall shelf creating two single-file rows, presence is heard rather than seen, in sonic variations. The gentle clack of elderly teeth; the scrape of coins in children's sticky hands; the fractious jangle of maternal car keys. Today, it is silent as I buy the paper. At the counter, Ali tells me he is planning a month's holiday to Pakistan, letting his sons do the work.

'So they don't get so lazy, hey, Reza.' He elbows the abashed, fluffy-moustached teenager beside him, whose gaze skids off in alarm along the counter. I tell Ali I've just been to the Park.

'Ah, the Park.' His deep eyes rise upwards from his round, dimpled face and prophet's dark beard. 'For a few weeks, the

16

beautiful blossom comes on the trees, glorious. Like a dream come true. Then, it's over.' He chuckles. 'Each year the blossom comes too early, each year it leaves too early.' Our laughter falls off. Young Reza's eyes snag furtively on a mini-skirted, leather-booted blur passing the shop window.

Back outside, I glimpse my car and recall the girl's boyfriend kicking it. Oh yes, a neat little dent, a thin black line at its centre. So I didn't dream it up. Frankly, I don't give a toss, but Jake will. Nothing escapes the rigour of Dr Jake's medical scrutiny. Yes, what had truly baffled Suzy was my marriage to him, as if I'd committed a cardinal sin of miscasting. We're still tentative after the rural fiasco. Clearly, quite clearly, it's no accident he jetted off with supersonic haste to LA. I wonder, does he think he made some terrible mistake? Had he formed a notion of some endearingly dizzy creature, only to have caught a glimpse of the slavering monster behind the jungle foliage? But he would never let on; his tact is heroic. The real luxury Jake affords me is that of shade.

The dried fungal whiff of the walls as I re-enter the hall: the scent of solitude. There we are, in the wedding photograph. My heavy mask of bridal makeup, his long neck anxiously stretching from his collar, baffled eyes aimed up at the middle distance, as if at some unaccountable development in the sky. His hands removing his tie that night, his clean clinician's fingers, like fine instruments. At home, as in his practice, he washes his hands, those fingers, with sacramental regularity. I seem to conjure him up as a lovable alien. His pride is veiled, his obsessions and rituals intense. When he sits on lawns, it is with trepidation, as if the grass beneath him will seethe and heave and throw up unimaginable reptiles. And yet he can tend to the horror of a burnt or disfigured face, look death in its dull eye.

Jake was such a rarity in our circus of artists, gallerists, hacks, curators, liggers, drug dealers, bar jockeys and tenuous celebrities. The fact of his being a real doctor filled us with immature glee, so that if we'd overdone it on the drugs we'd say, 'Oh, come on. Let's call Doctor Jake and ask him for a script to come down.' It became a clarion call, a panacea for all occasions. As a dermatologist he was hardly in a position to help, but we'd call him out of sheer mischief. Jake would sigh fondly, cataloguing my litany of symptoms; slowly extracting admissions of half-recalled excess. At gallery openings I would turn to find him, just behind, his gaze in hasty retreat. He'd stand there, silent in the loud banter, with his air of hushed sanatoriums and careful vigil, or bemusedly scanning some arcane installation art. He'd put business our way at the gallery; he knew wealthy consultants, fund managers with serious bank accounts. But what exactly drew me? My sick soul clung to his white-coated ministrations. And something else, that acute, droll tact of his, screening a secretive obsess- iveness, an antiquated courtly ardour. Love proffered and never retracted. Later, he told me he had waited for me for three years, bided his time.

Like all beginnings, it began with departures. I had just left the frantic, self-enclosed world of Paddy's gallery. I remember waking up with the now familiar red-hot dread pressing on my chest. And then it came to me, Jake's clear, unblinking stare, the way he spoke gently to me, through my illness, as if words were fallen rocks to be negotiated on the road. Once I came to from some near-blackout to glimpse an unusual convulsion. His face looked down on me but his thoughts had startled in their tracks. With visible effort, he brought himself back to calmly meet my gaze. I knew he'd heard something, half-spied my inner phantoms; I'd been muttering something as I came to. 'What was I on about?' I asked. He examined me slowly, carefully weighing up the possible consequences of his words. At length, his expression arranged into one of theatri- cal blitheness, he said, 'You were ordering another Brandy

Alexander.' With the solemnity of a guarded heart in thrall to love, he stayed, unflinching, true.

I called him. We had lunch. Outside the air had the citrus tartness of early April. Slipping into a breezy persona, I thought the answer is to will, just to will, a new beginning. We strolled past old Greek restaurants and dank delis, past the pub where my father once drank with old-style artists who fought over one another's mistresses, fought over unpaid debts, made up with another round. A young postman had rushed by, his slate-grey uniform mocked by his tall toucan hairstyle – all bright red dyes. And I'd felt a pang, a full stop in my centre.

It's late at night. I surf the net for a while, trawling ebay. A minor compulsion. I never go so far as to buy any of the old tat. Well, yes, I lie – once, when I bought the whole shebang from one seller. Three garden chairs; a disused saw; a prehistoric-looking claw hammer, good but chipped and faded porcelain, an awful watercolour, a bashed-up thirties wood veneer side table. Some eleven items in all. There were a few other takers for the auctions; perhaps, like me, they scented death. I like to think it was the image of a penniless widow. But that wasn't it – nor the five glasses of wine. There was an automaton quality to my clicks of the computer. When they arrived, I almost didn't open them, but they'd been touchingly well wrapped. My eyes ran over the nicks and welts, the chips and scratches and rust, until they came to the final item: the most knackered of the striped canvas garden chairs, its bottom sagging, its backrest warped with the imprint of its absent owner. Out came hot, automatic, silent tears, as if out of two leaking taps. No emotion at all. The next day I phoned to have it all removed. I look now, but I haven't bought anything since that peculiar spree. I put it all down to idleness and its peculiar distortions.

2

I'm instantly warmed by the kitsch chiaroscuro of the restaurant's dark brown wood, fat orange candles and jazz photographs. She doesn't appear to be working tonight. Relieved, a little deflated, I try to entertain Jake out of his jet lag. He refuses wine; I order a bottle of Gigondas for myself and tell him about the plumber, astoundingly named John Leak.

Jake smiles absently, his usually clear grey eyes red-rimmed from the long flight, his equine face waxy in the candlelight. By way of comfort, he fingers his flat mobile phone. His passion is for the ultra-smooth aesthetic: the thinnest electronic gadgets, the sleekest minimal lines, geometric abstract art, as if by way of compensation for all the weals, cysts and nodules, the hairy epidermis and infected subcutis, the burns and base cells. One might say his life's mission is a perpetual smoothing-out. In another life he would have made a good ironing lady. He believes, with uncynical certitude, that even the lucrative, purely cosmetic side of his practice offers an ideal, a release from the tyranny of the flaw.

He buys me Chanel, vintage St Laurent, mainly in black or navy; silver or platinum jewellery (never vulgar gold), a few diamonds – the Cartier engagement ring and the Graff pendant. At first, we shopped rigorously and often. And then his gifts began to suffer more and more violent accidents. Some inner hooligan in me revelled in cigarette burns, nail rips, claret stains. It perturbs him that I bother only in occasional manic spurts to spend his ready credit on acupuncturists and glycolic facials. I'm somehow not conforming to expectation, not revealing my desire. Lately, he's taken to inspecting me as he does now – aslant, discreetly alert to the as yet uncatalogued flaw, the shivery psychic mole once briefly glimpsed, which will, given patience, one day reveal itself entirely to his scientific eye. To be smoothed, cured.

Her voice, all honeyed grit. 'Hello there.' A smile of conspiracy plays on her lips as she comes to take our order. I straighten up, realizing with a stinging jolt that she is wearing the red cardigan.

'Hello, yes, thank you,' I cut in briskly, afraid she will talk. 'My husband is starving!' Jake has given no appearance of noticing. And what might she notice? His fine physician's brow? More likely his compulsive, precise reordering of the cutlery. We order our food, he asks for a pomegranate juice. One dismissive glance suffices to assess him before she saunters away – the eyes of the men, all except the preoccupied Jake's, swivel on furtive stalks towards her.

She returns with deliberate slowness, forgetting the juice. A game evolves in which I send her off needlessly to fetch and carry each time she appears, and she responds with frequent intrusions, deliberate mistakes, menacing solicitousness. The game pivots around the unmentionable, the other night. I wonder why I don't just tell Jake, entertain him with it. But he wouldn't find it remotely entertaining. I'd be nudged solicitously in the direction of some five-star funny farm. Yet during one of Tina's appearances at the table I think I can see a muscle pulsing in his cheek.

There, in the large gilt mirror directly opposite me, I catch her looking over. I register that antique glint to her colouring, follow the line of her shoulders, the way her torso (longer, more solid than mine), the pert breasts (fuller than mine), inhabit the lustrous wool. Briefly, we lock eyes. She rolls the sleeves of the cardigan up to her elbows in a slipshod gesture before pinching the front of the garment, letting it go with a sluggish, hot-and-bothered ping. She is wearing a dark mauve bra beneath. An agreeably sluttish colour. My own look in the mirror, I note with surprise, is cold, appraising, calculating. We are sharing a game that Jake can't possibly enter.

The candle on the table splutters, dies out, leaching Jake's long face to hollows and bones, as he concentrates on slicing at his poussin, his fingers clamping the cutlery. He blinks, mouth gawping with soft alarm. She brings another candle. But the light is altered, harsher. I listen half-distractedly to myself talking about the house, how I've delayed the building work. Jake, who can see little reason why I would prefer this to a more expensive, white-stuccoed postcode which we can well afford, finishes his rigorous chewing, cutting in quietly. 'Is it going to help you? Why don't we just call in an interior decorator?'

A cold key turns the foggy-drunk mood in my head. 'I don't want to live in some rich interior-decorated ghetto.' The beetroot has leaked everywhere, soiling the rest of my food. I push my plate away in disgust.

He nods down at the plate. 'It might be an idea to eat though,' he says breezily, 'just to prevent you slipping into a coma and fading gently away.'

'I thought you got off on me pale and lifeless. God, I'll get a job, chuck the pills.' It shocks even me a little, my reproach, the ungrateful jibe. I breathe hard, trying to contain the signs of my ancient temper. I take hold of his right hand and the caress turns into a consolation, a pat.

He clears his throat, watching my hand. 'I don't think that's wise. But it might be a good idea to change your medication; especially the SSRIs, well, we know they don't suit everyone. I don't need to tell you that drinking on them hardly helps. I've spoken to Schuster Vanderhoos, consultant psychiatrist . . .' He glances up, warming to his theme.

'Why on earth would I want to entrust myself to someone with a name like Schuster Vanderhoos!' I snap. She's begun to clear our plates. She clears up badly, brusquely, leaving crumbs. We both sit, silently gathering our moods until she returns to lay the cutlery for Jake's pudding. I stare at the dully glinting glass, at the crumbs. I light a cigarette from a packet in my bag. Jake notes this with discreet surprise and inspects his unused pudding fork, polishing one prong interminably with his napkin. I gulp down some more wine. 'You wanted to rescue me and it's too hard, isn't it? Damaged goods.'

He looks quickly down at his watch, then quickly up, his brow making an appreciable effort to smooth itself of encroaching irritation. 'Let's discuss this when we're both less tired.' For the first time this evening, his dimmed grey eyes, swimming in redness, catch mine directly before turning back to the fork in his hand, as if scorched.

He says quietly, 'I realize it doesn't help with my being away . . . you just didn't seem to want me around, in Suffolk.'

'It was the space, the place, driving me mad.'

'Anyhow, let's hope this is the answer.' Hand shielding his mouth, he emits his customary cough by way of discreet finality.

'It would help if you stopped talking to me with so much bloody clinical tact!' She is behind me, standing, with the pudding. I wait for her to leave. Jake hesitates, folding his napkin carefully, twice, three times, on the table. Back at the bar, her glassy eyes flash narrowly. My hand lifts, knocking my full wine glass; it thumps down, rolls and clatters, ringing against spoon, water glass. Splashes of red fall on to his lemon tart. A fast-spreading dark pool begins to form a rose-red clot on his napkin. I put on my jacket and leave, and feel the heat of her gaze on my back.

The front door closes quietly. Footsteps approach, enter the sitting room, where I stand, in the darkness. The crinkle of his jacketed arms as they encircle me from behind. He smells of business-class cabins. His voice is thickly soothing, muttering into my neck. 'If we get the funding for those extra clinics, I'll need to be there quite a lot for a while. You could come over . . .'

'I really can't cope with the thought of LA right now. All those gloriously sunny mornings, driving off in a cabriolet to see Schuster Vanderhoos.' I smile, turn, kiss his square, smooth brow. 'The brow of a gentil knight,' I say. He takes something tenderly from his bag. A box. He has bought me a gift, another gift. A digital camera. I hope, silently, it won't drown or get crushed to a pulp too quickly.

Jake sighs. 'Paddy's gallery's on the brink of bankruptcy.'

'Oh God, no. I should ring him.'

'Most of the big artists have left. Including Eva. She wasn't happy after you left, she told Paddy. You rediscovered her, it was you, brought her career back to life.'

'Did I? I guess I must have been useful once then.'

He reaches for my arm. 'Much, much more than useful.'

I look down. 'I'm –'

'Sshh . . . don't apologize.'

'What on earth makes you think I was going to do that?' I quip.

He grins, a little too hopefully.

'You go on up,' I say, releasing my arm. 'You're shattered. I'll watch TV.'

'Are you still on the diazepam, to sleep?'

'Yes, but I'm reducing it,' I lie.

Coming closer, breathing labouredly, he runs his index finger delicately down the side of my neck, his gaze following it, as he carefully composes a thought. 'It's weird, you barely see Paddy these days.' He lets his hand drop.

No longer used to sharing a bed, I had to take two pills to sleep, and this morning I feel unearthed, gliding over the pavement. Here's the restaurant and the pub, chairs atop tables, funereally empty. She and I last night, pulled in together by the same murky current, conspiring. Conspirators share the same intentions; but I doubt that we do.

I skirt quickly past the people queueing for the bus, outside the Baptist church, its weekly slogan announcing, 'Neither have I silver nor gold.' There's no food in the fridge; and certainly none of Jake's food. Organic raw nori, miso soup. Cold-milled flax seeds. The new delis don't stock his favourite wheat-free pasta. I try in vain in Sainsbury's in the Broadway. A youngish woman, heaving huge mounds of thighs in loud combats, her trolley filled with parachute-sized frozen-food bags, continually blocks my way in one aisle. Angry dark roots show from straw-dry bleached hair. Two round children throw themselves around the trolley like detaching body bags. I think of Jake, Suzy, Nick, addicted to shedding toxicity from their bodies. I think of Tina, her gravelly voice as she says, 'They've got organic cranberry juice for blood.'

I leave the pitiless lighting of the supermarket, drive to one of the chic organic grocers in Portobello where they dispense only the holistic, the gluten- and toxin-free. Another parking ticket. Soon, Jake will suggest that we 'get someone' to run the house. I'm all for it. There's just not enough time in the day for taking the medication. Suzy phones on the mobile, her voice harbours news.

I drive straight on to her house. I find her, legs up, on the L-shaped sofa, stroking Marie Antoinette, the cat's blackness dissolving into that of the black leather except for a pair of unblinking lime-coloured slits.

'It's such bliss,' she says, 'the children are at art workshops. I can actually hear myself speak. So. And how is Jake? How are things?' Once, walking through woods filled with huge colour-blocks of bluebells, I had stupidly confided in her about sexual matters.

'Things are better.'

There's her customary preamble, a fondly told anecdote about the unfortunate effect of three cocktails on a mutual friend two nights previously. 'Nick and I were left eating alone, a very rare thing these days. It was rather nice. In The Castle.' Now we come to the meat of the matter, artfully sliced in. 'By the way, the girl, the waitress . . .' She waits for me to enlighten her. I pretend bafflement.

'Tina, that's her name,' she continues, after a pause, 'she told us you rescued her. Couldn't stop asking us about you –'

'How does she know we're friends?'

'She saw us together in there, once. Nick filled her in on you rather shamelessly, the art world, your famous father, the trail of broken hearts . . .' Suzy titters archly at Nick's daftness.

'God help me.' I secretly doubt it was Nick doing the talking.

'He said she's smitten.' She turns to gauge my reaction, mischief blazing in those Lely eyes. As if catching herself laughing in church, her voice registers concern. 'So what happened?'

I feign tedium. 'Oh, she was rowing with her boyfriend outside my house. It was quite aggressive, she got hurt and he left her high and dry. No money, no keys. The fact is, they managed to bash my car in the process.'

'She said it was in the middle of the night –'

'God no, she's exaggerating.' Immediately, I regret this lie, so much more telling than the truth.

'Nick fancied her rotten . . . She's a beauty. A bit Slavic-looking . . . like, who was that actress in *Crash*? The Ballard thing. Peculiar name? Met her once.' She chuckles darkly. 'I teased him about it, I mean – we're all nearly forty now, we must seem ancient to her.'

Marie Antoinette's glossy black being is focused on a sparrow frolicking with yesterday's ciabatta in the terraced garden. Suzy falls silent, following the cat's gaze. Then she lets out a portentous sigh. 'You know, I'm going to give up the medi-

tation – everyone's given it up and I see what they mean,
I need something more focused –'

'Kick-boxing?' I suggest.

The door slams, Suzy's children thump in, the putty-
featured Olga sauntering lazily behind. The younger boy
begins his whining to blot out the words of the fragile, older
one whose albino looks, no eyelashes, result in a disconcerting
nakedness, as if he were missing a layer of skin. As I leave, I
note Olga's astute, laconic way of blocking Suzy's questions.

In the car, I brake suddenly to avoid running over a woman
who leaps out on to Main Road. Annoyed, I open my window
to shout at her, but think better of it when I see her face –
sucked in, like the dried-out core of a pear, framed by a lank,
hennaed mane. Petrified in the style of her youth, she is trailing a long Goth coat, grey-shiny with wear. Something is
flustering her. Her dog, a pit bull terrier, is straining violently
at his leash. I hear a pleading 'Boris, please' through the open
window. Finally, Boris deigns to lift his thuggish neck and
strolls casually across.

Once on the pavement the woman begins tugging at some
deep coat pocket, pulls out a mobile phone. 'Yes, yes, hello.
Oh. Tina.' A presentiment rolls through my mind. I look up
towards The Castle. A shadow flits across the window. Tina.
She must be working today. She was there, watching.

Jake spends much of the day in the sitting room, fingers
splayed tenderly on his laptop, emailing, studying business
plans and new research on basal cells. At night we dine with
some friends of his, two catatonically dull couples. Back in the
car, I moan about one of the wives. 'Did you hear her, droning
on throughout the main course about "interiority" and "lack
of subjective space"? Why couldn't she just stick to Hampstead
versus Knightsbridge pedicurists, like the other one?'

'She was probably trying to "bond" with you.' He raises a droll eyebrow.

'Oh sure, I'm the guru of consciousness-raising, the Simone de Beauvoir of the Knightsbridge sistas.' I light a cigarette by way of punctuation. He opens the window all the way down, letting in a thick smack of cold air as he steers my car with silky strokes into our street.

'I realize her vocabulary must have grated on your sophisticated ears.'

I turn to him, gleefully brandishing my cigarette. 'Oh, so *I'm* the pseud now. Anyway, she was a bloody imposition.'

After he parks, he inspects the dent on the door. 'Have you seen this? What happened?' He straightens up, concerned.

'No idea. What do you expect? It's out on the street, whereas yours is endlessly having beauty treatments in the garage – like your Bel Air patients.'

Still no sex, for nearly three months; tension stretches between us like an unhealed ligament. And more and more, the sense of a concealed, sidelong scrutiny as he continues to dispense his discreetly ardent devotion. At the door, as he leaves for the airport, he hesitates as he inspects the liverish clouds before squeezing my upper arm with an arcane glint in his clear eyes. 'I've left you a new skincare range in the bedroom. I hear it's the only one with adequate levels of titanium oxide. For blocking out the sun.' He waves a mock-stern finger at me. 'Cancer.'

Back in the kitchen I take the two glass 'ffarmacy' bottles (the new fashion in cosmetics is for austere medical packaging) and bin them.

The house feels overheated, toxic. I pull on a coat and head out. Even for a winter weekend there are few people scattered in the muted air of the Park. Inside the tidy black railings, everything is neat, round, bordered: self-contained pens (playgrounds, tennis courts, café, mini-golf) around a smooth, plate-shaped area of grass, bounded by a path. Visible through every side, the protagonists of the scene, the impassive, smug fronts of the terraced houses. Up from my left, a long row of benches lines a small path like black dashes. At the far bench, a couple in matching shiny black parka jackets sit with their hoods up, clutching their cigarettes low, unaffectedly, as people do when they smoke outdoors, unobserved. With their back to the Park, they look both secretive and exposed. There are no arbours, no pockets of intimacy, just neatly parcelled green space, a space afraid of its own shade.

I glance over to the eastern side, to a playground behind barbed wiring painted a nursery-jolly red. But no laughter, no childish screams carry over. The cold is spiteful now, or perhaps I was too fitful to notice before. I decide to leave, but passing the animal farm, I am intrigued by the wrought-iron door, the thick, enclosing foliage, the sense of something, at last, hidden from the eye.

I look through the gate but can see little except a few twigs and brambles surrounding a skinny acacia tree. Propped stiffly to one side of it is a straw man, or rather a sealed papier mâché variety, clothed in yellow and black park-keeper's dark jacket and black trousers. Black hair has been painted on him, along with two thick sideburns. He has two conkers for eyes, one of them askew, a badly scrawled, exaggerated moustache, and a label container for a mouth, painted red. His clothes flap loosely around what must be a thin wooden pole for a body and he is lurching forward, as if his grotesque head were pulling over his insubstantial body down into the earth. He looks every inch the cheesy park rapist. How delightful for the little ones.

The sky bruises, quickly falling. The couple in matching black parkas are ahead of me, entering Main Road, which is already lighting up in the dusk. Cars are snorting in impatient queues. Headlights come on. Further along, my vision is caught by the two parkas again, inside the off-licence, their hoods now off. It's Tina and the guy from that night. Carl, she called him Carl. I can't look away. She is out of my sight, busying herself deeper in the shop. Carl is nearer the door. Through the window I spy a broad, pale brow. His hair is a fair, crewcut halo, the face all stony, primitive reductions. The effect is of strength, but with a coiled grace which makes me think, improbably, of some half-forgotten image, of a young Bolshevik. He has a soldier's cupped-handed way with smoking. As if on constant guard, his eyes, two hard brown pebbles, swivel round towards me, his jaw following studiedly behind.

Ashamed, in case they mock me later for following them, snorting into their damp post-coital pillows, I turn and enter the local library. Picking out books blindly, I stumble on a history of the area's early Edwardian days. Schools, manor houses, stores, all vanished to make way for the grids of neat terraces. Faces, trapped in the amber of the halted past: a draper's boy, all pinched neck, looks out in that peculiarly stiff, antique trance. Others show children with hoops, behind them the wrought-iron bandstand. I am caught by one of two women sitting in the foreground; behind, to the right, a man in a light suit sits alone on the edge of a park bench, his legs crossed punctiliously. He seems to be gazing, entranced, from some private incarceration up at their vast, oblivious hats. A sigh escapes me like a bubble. Why this overblown sentiment at the sight of the anonymous, the still, the irrevocable? And such numbness elsewhere. Perhaps because I've lost the present in myself; and the past.

Inside The Big Room at the gallery it is hot, bright and crowding as arrivals swiftly fill the gaps between the disparate groups. Faces swell redly, their mouths uttering, sipping, as if in perpetual suck. Successful artists and rich collectors hatch round one another in rare cultures. One, a conceptual artist with a reputation for plagiarism, coils around one circle with the silent alertness of a python, beer bottle clasped yob-style in his hand by way of disguise. Suzy and her husband Nick stop to talk to someone; I edge away. Paddy is nowhere. I see a few welcome people: an old artist friend, Eva Hussein; and there's Zac, the installation assistant, but they are surrounded and I can't make it across the human wall, past the infamous living legend, the painter of cadaverous flesh with his high-nosed sardonic glare. A tall man comes up, bespoke pinstripe suit, thick grey crest of wavy hair. He is gently febrile as if from an extinct species of greyhound.

'Ah, Christabel. How are you getting on?' he asks. His voice crackles warmly. I know him, like him, but cannot place him.

'Fine, fine, I'm married now.' I can find no words to soothe his awkward incongruity among the heehaws and squawks. I beam, hand motioning in the direction of the drinks table, steal swiftly past another potential greeter. Now I recall the man – Adam Hoffman, Royal Academy, my father's old colleague. My sweater itches around my neck.

Some peace, some calm. I head for Paddy's office and as I take a cigarette from a packet on the table, Paddy strides in. 'Hey. Caught you,' he says, 'sneaking out for a fag.' There is clumsy intimacy in our embrace. We do away with polite catching-up.

'Thought I'd enter the old den, too old for these shenanigans.'

'Nah, just lost the habit, you old tart. Miss it?' He lights our cigarettes.

Pause. 'Nope.' We both giggle.

'Back in the land of the living, hey?'

'Well, hardly. We've chosen to live in Ladbroke Park.'

'Sounds like a residential home.'

'Yes, for the retired wives of dermatologists.'

'Doctor Jake away?'

'Jetting back and forth, examining the folliculitis and fibrous growths of half of Bel Air.'

'I hear he's setting up a chain of clinics over there, with some new American partner.'

'Well, not a chain exactly. Three. But yes, that's the idea, state-of-the-art anti-wrinkle, anti-acne, anti-flaw. But you know Jake, his guilt will add to the workload. He's taking on some residency there, helping the poor and genuinely ill by way of balancing the moral books. And before you ask, no, I haven't succumbed to all the free collagen and Isolagen yet.'

Paddy begins a clownish scrutiny of my face, behind which there is some keener inspection going on.

I sit, swivelling on the chair, and say incredulously, 'Bloody awful in there. Who are half these people?' It used to be our catchphrase, a routine, in the middle of openings, to which Paddy responds, as he always did: 'Dunno, thought you'd bloody asked them.'

He points at my cigarette. 'I thought you'd given up.'

'I have! But only in months without an "r" in them. Hah!'

'You'll have a hard time of it in the summer then. May, June, July, August . . . oh my God, all over your lovely suede trousers.' Paddy has somehow spilt his drink on me.

He goes out to fetch a cloth from a waiter, begins wiping slowly at my trousers.

'Are you that desperate for a surreptitious feel of female body-parts?' I ask him.

'Oh no, I've got a blow-up doll called Sandra. Much hotter than you,' he replies, relaxing his elbow against a shelf, one hand in his pocket. How admiring, envious even, I am of his knack, the tease without spite.

'Actually,' he continues, 'one of the photographs out there has blow-up dollies and in theory they all have the same banal expressions. Except, after a while, you begin to notice differences between them.'

'Do you? Isn't the whole point that you begin to fantasize the difference, just as we imagine our own uniqueness, our thinginess?'

'Thinginess, ha, I like it.' That Paddy gesture, the compulsive scraping down of his hair with his open palm. He catches my eye, holds it for a beat while I laugh at his futile efforts with his hair. 'You know, Thing, the thing is you don't really want anything, or not the usual things,' he says after a pause.

But he's wrong: if never having to want is wanting, then I want something badly: to breathe the ether of a pure present – a necessary delusion, in my case, but a trap.

For three, four years it had worked; he'd made me a director. I'd even bought a watch. The pull of paternal influence had steered me clear of contemporary art. Now, some of it had begun to excite me; I no longer sounded like a bad copy of my father. All I am, or have, seems to me like the spoils of cheating at cards. Not then, though, not for a while at least. But it couldn't last. The blackouts began. Jake entertains some explanation involving cocaine, serotonin, neurons. He urged me to see a neurologist, an eye specialist, to have tests done, to seek a specific diagnosis. All futile, of course – how could I ever risk that sort of intrusion?

'So. How's tricks?' I ask him, recalling Jake's gloomy news.

Paddy crosses his arms in front of him as he leans back on the wall, his suit an eccentric take on 1940s spiv, a dark blue chalk-stripe, waistcoat, blood-orange shirt with no tie, one cuff undone and flapping eloquently through the sleeve of the jacket. 'Well, Zara Marshall knocked Eva Hussein off her stool last night in The Empire, right at the bar after fourteen tequila slammers. Eva's new show's a little too "everywhere" for Zara's liking, even though, or perhaps because, Zara can't be bothered to do the fame stuff. No damage done. Well, Eva broke the strap on her Fendi handbag.'

'How quaint. I meant you – how are things with you?'

'Oh, fine, fine.' He fingers one cuff, straightens up. 'Better go back in – my public awaits me. Let's do something. Soon. You never call me.'

That discomfiting look again. If I didn't know Paddy better, I would think it accusatory. I extinguish his cigarette stub out of habit, and stay smoking, surveying the yellow Post-its on the computer. 'Torture Fest. Drilling 4 p.m. Monday'. (A dental appointment.) 'Apocalpyse Now. Accounts meeting, Thurs 10 a.m'. There is only one painting on the wall, from the famous series of gloss paintings by Jim Dunn; although, such is Paddy's recent luck, that by the time Dunn won the Turner last year he'd already gone over to the snazzy American gallery. I wonder why he keeps it on the wall: as a reminder of glory or failure? It never ceases to amaze me, Paddy's talent for cheerful self-flagellation.

Back in The Big Room, the overlapping voices have meshed into a metallic roar. Occasionally, people make a show of looking at the work, noses briefly pecking at the wall. The photographs are vast, detailed, hyperglossed in surface. My eye falls on one. A view through a shop window, rows and rows of mannequins and blow-up dolls, all with too-real flesh tones, all arranged like produce for sale, dwarfing and mechanizing the people, the shoppers, behind. It's a well-trodden theme. The detail, the microscopic attention, the sheer scale, the repetition of their blank stare. I shouldn't have looked; why did I assume I was cured? It begins lurching forward from the wall with the low humming, the fast-spreading glare, then the bleaching out, the familiar dig-dig of a silent drill behind my eyes, the clamminess in my brow. I turn before the black dots appear – I can't bear any glance. They will see; I'm peeled, I have no skin.

To my relief, a crimson-faced Suzy complains it is too crowded (for which I read, there are few of her acquaintances present, provoking the nearest Suzy gets to an existential crisis). We climb into a black cab and slip away.

At last I'm back, comforted by the whispering gurgle of rain in runnels. Ladbroke Park acquires melancholic density with night. The drizzle and phosphorescent light lapping at the terraces, the mist straying in fine shreds from the Park, remind me of a film I once watched with Paddy, both of us entranced by the fogbound wartime setting; the passionate, stilted dialogue of the unfaithful lovers. That night, we made love with a parched, hostile urgency. It never returned, as if we'd made a wordless resolve to disallow it. And then, of course, I was about to marry Jake. It doesn't stop, the pip-plop, pip-plop. Is it rain? The guttering? The radiators are bled, but one noise disappears and new ones come up from the entrails of the house. No matter. I'm trailing off now to my trusty Halcion netherworld.

Then three loud knocks, rattling the entire house. A woman's cough. I am rooted to the upstairs landing; sensing, knowing it is her. Above me, a light bulb hums; the house cocks its hostile ear. More knocking, followed by the tearing of paper, the twang of the letter box, the receding squeal of trainers. A brown wages envelope lies on the mat. Her name has been crossed out; replaced by mine (misspelled) – 'Christabelle'. Inside, a folded note and ten pounds. (Wasn't it twenty I gave her?) 'Sorry I took so long – your cardigan awaits you in The Castle, Milady.' The whiskery fluency to the script intrigues me (I'd expected underlinings, babyish calligraphy, circles for dots), as does the impudence of defrauding me of ten pounds. Not even so much as a thank-you. On impulse, I open the door and scan the nocturnal street. It's empty.

4

Days of wind, sun and fast-moving clouds, soft squalls of rain as if April had invaded February. I'm goggle-eyed from reading newspaper reports of freakish changes in nature, habitat loss, spring arriving in midwinter. Daffodils are already in the parks; the birds trill out neurotic songs, not bothering to migrate south, the common sparrow is disappearing. My days merge into one another in runnels of unspecific time, yet during the nights I wake, gasping from the gluey folds of fugitive dreams. Occasionally, voices outside will bring her to mind. I suppose, that day in the Park, I was tailing her – obliquely.

The neighbourhood has become a place of watching out, of being watched. Adrift and idle, the intrigue suits my spoilt nature – he spoiled me, my father, literally, not in any overfond way; as long as he was left to his perusal of the pictorial plane, so long as the au pairs were full-lipped, Jimmy and I could wreak havoc. He'd only threatened discipline as the result of the curt school note about my 'ungovernable temper' and 'pernicious influence', held in his quivering hand. Up to then, what with Mother's death, I'd virtually got away with murder.

Looking about, it's not surprising that the idea of her sparkles so luminously. I'm already regretting this move – not that I'd admit it to Jake. New establishments are constantly appearing, all replicating what's already there in pointless superfluity: another new deli, another new café charging a kingdom for a croissant; another chi-chi new gift shop or healing centre or estate agent's. The writing is on the wall for the old bric-a-brac shop, its lame old plastic soldiers, scarred china vases, and my favourite pieces, the spare-time creations of some long-dead glassmaker: figures of horses and birds, a walking-stick, the child's bust. There it is, staring with its vitreous seer's eyes at the gift shop across from it, a bazaar of pricey ethnic knick-knacks with twenty-three varieties of scented candle.

Ladbroke Park is supposedly multicultural. Flocks of veiled girls from the Islamic school wait with agitated self-effacement at the bus stop. In the current climate of torpid emergency, of endless sirens and security scares and traffic diversions, I have heard the enraged despot in the white drunks as they grudgingly hand over their coins to Ali. But that aside, such neighbourliness as there is, across class or race, seems at best discreetly unfettered. Each to their own. And each day affluent white women disgorge fumes and tempers as they drive their children to private schools. It's one of these I'm poised now to become; that I shudder at becoming.

But none of it explains why I'm always clamped in a spiny anxiety when I pass The Castle, never going in and retrieving my cardigan. Not that I care about the cardigan, but there's some underhand agency marking out a time with missed beats, jangled rhythms.

This morning. A heartlessly beautiful winter's day, clean and cold. Quickened by the alpine air, the highness of the heavens, I was browsing in the junk shop, holding a musty old menologium. I heard muted running, someone halting, and quickly swinging round, in panic . . . 'Got you.' Growing instantly bashful, she first peeped into my book, then followed my distracted inspection of the child's glass head in the shop window. She looked altered, fuller, rose-gold. We seemed to talk as if deafened, over roaring waves.

'Yes, yes, fine, come round with it later,' I say to her.

Back home, I find myself phoning Paddy at the gallery for the first time in more than a year. His chocolatey drawl, half street junkie, half don, like a familiar incantation. We discuss some possible areas of work for me.

'You sound distracted.'

'Mmm. I am. I have a new distraction, a young waitress. I let her into the house in the middle of the night . . . I didn't know her.'

He responds with his familiar whispered thrall. 'What does she look like?'

'Ravishing –' I recoil at my own easy regression with him, playing the libertine conspirator, shaping the intrigue, but carry on, denying him too many details. 'She's moving slowly in, centre-stage.'

'What does she want?'

'I don't know.'

'Why did you let her in?'

'I don't know.' I laugh tauntingly. 'That's the point.' Three heavy knocks at the door. I hang up, leave him for once without feeling those tiny chimes of loss. He picks this up somehow, falters his goodbye.

There she stands, in the doorway, framed by the feathers of her silky black parka hood, her old-gold glint illuminating the dusk. My red cardigan held high, like a flame in one hand, a bottle of wine in another. The blinding strobe of those eyes – as always, making her seem like statuary. My very own statue of liberty.

'The bell does work, you know,' I say.

'Hate bells.' No hello, straight in, boots clacking on the wooden floor. 'Do they call you Christabel?'

'God, no. My friends call me Christy or Chrissy.'

Her face comes very close to mine. 'I'll call you Belle.'

'That's my family nickname.' I feel weightless, empty and full, brushed by electric fingers. 'Come in.' She walks into the sitting room and absently moves her hand along the edge of the mantelpiece as if claiming the room. She turns, brandishing the wine. 'Gigondas. Remembered you liked it.' She insists on fetching the corkscrew, glasses, pouring. 'Have a drink, chill.'

'Do make yourself at home,' I say, since she is already sprawled on one sofa, arms folded behind her head.

'Yeah,' she intones, as if in a reverie, 'after that night I just thought . . .' She slides her hand along the air fancifully '. . . your voice is so tuneful, like musical glass. It clinks up and down, like doin' the scales . . .'

'Have you been drinking?' I'm hearing back my cutting voice in the room.

'Just two – after my shift.' Her tone is impudent with the obvious lie. 'Had a toke though, want some?' There's much rooting around her bag until a half-smoked joint is produced and lit for me with reverential flourish. Beyond the odour of coconut and bar fug, she has a flinty whiff, of lead, pencil cases, school; the past.

'How are things? Is your life less turbulent?'

'Turbulent?' She mocks the word before reddening remorse-fully. Sigh. 'Well, I'm staying with a mate, old Charlotte. I feel a bitch for saying it, but she's a couple of oranges short of a Jaffa . . . She was well into the brown, and in NA she met this Albanian who flogs illegal fags up the Broadway, you know, by the bus stop near Superdrug. Maybe he thought she was rich, dunno – he could tell she was posh even though he's been here for, like, two minutes. Anyhow, he talked really heavy, you know, just like she likes, about being a refugee, the Afghan war, the Iraqi war, fucked her twice, and buggered off. She's still off the scag but bouncin' off the walls. The dog made sure he scared him off. Boris, her pit bull psycho.'

I recall the woman crossing the road.

'I think I've come across them.' I laugh at her melodramatic glare. 'You're like a walking exclamation mark.' Tina's face bristles, wondering whether to be flattered or insulted.

'I believe I saw you. With Carl.'

She scratches her nose. 'I believe you did. In the off-licence. I see you nearly every day. Wondered why you hadn't come in. I turned it round in my head . . .' She slips into solemn, clairvoyant reflection. 'I thought . . . it's not the time.'

'So you're back again? With Carl.'

'No, no, it's not like that. Thing is, I've known him ages. When I move on he takes it bad. His mum used to run off. Well, that's one excuse for his general arseholiness. I start thinking of going to college, he starts hassling me. He's a head-fuck.'

'Not to mention hitting you, leaving you in the middle of the road drugged out of your eyeballs.'

A secret knowledge flutters around one corner of her mouth, which is stained, a touch obscenely, with the red wine. 'God!' A hand is cupped over her head. I recognize my intonation and gesture, no trace of conscious mimicry. There follows a labyrinthine narrative of muddled chronologies and digressions, about an on-off stormy love affair with an Aaron, thwarted by this Carl, through whom they'd met. Aaron had a 'wicked' band, a recording contract. 'We were backwards and forwards like a yo-yo. But Carl kept stirrin' it, broke us up.' So, she had no choice, see, no money, moved into Carl's. The captive.

I sense she must have revelled in her role as the object of love and division for both men. 'Triangles can be dangerous – especially when one of the angles collapses,' I say.

Tina's little teeth bite at her bottom lip with incomprehension. 'You mean like it's losing two people?'

'Well, desire is kickstarted by triangles.' I flap my hand. 'Oh, forget it. Tedious bollocks.'

'You talk just how I imagined.' She begins to take me in as if after a long absence. 'Suits you, the winter. I was thinking that this afternoon, you're a silvery person, Moon, not Sun. Enigma. Shadow. Definitely.'

'Oh God . . . I suppose you're going to try to divine my star sign now. Please DESIST. So. What are you going to study?'

'Access course.' She sits up. 'Just applied. Today. History of Art and English.'

'Ah, my subject, history of art. But then, Suzy must have told you that. She said you were very curious about me.'

Tina does a demure blush, lowering her head to reveal that always-askew middle parting. 'I did know –' An arm rises up, in confusion; a hand grasps at the side of her head, slowly stroking it for meaning. 'I was thinking along those lines . . . my friend Charlotte's an artist, well, was, and then, after meeting you again, today . . .' She does a little act of daring herself to look up, face me, gulping a little. That dramatic timing, the flagrant use of eye – all learned before she could gurgle. 'I posted it, the application.' I can hear someone else's voice (not my own this time) in the syntax, the accent. It's as if she's a pure mingling of others, a receptacle for pilfered voices. She looks around pointedly, deliberately puncturing my thoughts. 'So how come you don't have paintings in here or sculpture?'

'It's too much; they pulsate, they drag you in.'

'But your job?'

'Oh yes, those pretentious press releases. Quote: "unsettling us into new reconfigurations of the everyday, resonating with the invisibility of the familiar".'

Her fingers grip hard on her joint, as if clinging to my glib words. 'Listening to you, God, I feel a real idiot starting college. At my age, I'll never catch up.'

'Don't – you make me feel like an old crone.'

'You don't look it. You're gorgeous.' Flattery will get her everywhere – she walks over to sit on the other end of my sofa. 'Something happened, Belle – the way you knock yourself.'

Funny that, how befriending someone requires the tricks

of the con, the slick, fast intimacy of articulating a name; the suggestion of some privileged, intimate knowledge of the other. But her translucent gaze, her hungry intrusiveness; it turns some key in me. I tell her about the tall gallery, in white, concrete and glass, the charged, exalted hush of the best artworks. How I was addicted to the contrast, the buzz of the change-overs, working on the new installations with Paddy and the artists until the early hours. How at night, the job filtered into the warm veins of bars, into impromptu moments when, almost magically, an idea or a deal would seem to shape itself out of the cigarette smoke and the banter. I tell her about the exhilaration of the real artists, about the gossip, the greed, the fraud.

I weave hurriedly again through the teeming streets, the sensation of pure movement rushing through my blood. My mind would feel newly minted, intoxicated by the fast rhythms and the pink neon of Soho. I recall my small flat with the long windows, how I made friends with the coughing hookers and the students. At night, we would all stare out of the windows in drugged wonder at the lit-up church. 'It clanged and clanged on Sundays. I loved that double toll. And the more I listened, the more I realized that repetition is a consolation, a way of answering the unanswerable.'

Tina smiles patiently. 'And then?'

'Oh, I had blackouts. For some obscure reason, they came on when I tried to look, especially looking at the art. Ridiculous really. At first, I could see but not look properly. My vision would skate. Then it got worse, a line would exaggerate itself, vibrate, hum. The image would flatten and whiten, and encroach, come towards me . . . then the rush, like a nest of black dots.' I begin to feel the old agitation as I speak of it. 'They put wires on my head. But there was nothing wrong, technically. The symptoms persisted though if I tried to look . . . It was odd, troubling. I mean, looking was part of what I did. Maybe it was my way of leaving it. So then I got married.'

'You better now?'

'Oh yes – I can look at art in books, on TV, with a screen. Not for long. But I hardly go into a gallery or a studio –' I stop myself telling her that the other day, in the gallery, it began again.

She throws me a sharp look, nostrils flaring suspiciously at my sudden silence. 'What were you scared of seeing?'

'I don't know. Nothing . . .' (Strange to think how I've never asked myself that very simple question. She is noting my reaction as if she has a master key to me; I stare her out, smiling calmly.) 'Yes, that's it, probably – nothing. Blankness. Anyhow, I'll have to do something soon, a thesis, writing. Not back to the gallery. Even if I'm cured, going back is impossible now; as Heraclitus said, no one ever steps into the same river twice.' Not for the first time, I shudder a little at lapsing into this tone with her, all glib, arrogant erudition like some philandering male 'expert'; like my father.

'But you can piss in it – the river,' she says, getting up. She is wiping her forehead. 'I can see black dots too. It must be this.' She points down at the joint. But as I watch her, I am disturbed by some half-thought tugging at my consciousness. The hair falling from the wobbly middle parting, the probing knowingness; of course, she reminds me of Lucia.

Having taken charge of the music, she moves quickly to the small wedding photograph by the window, hips swaying to the shuffling beat as she peers at it. 'You don't look like you. At all.' Her green eyes glint wickedly as she listens to my account of my wedding day, Jake's tipsy mother stalking my horrified father. She has a talent for improvised mimicry. Under the spell of the grass, we do voices, embellish on comic sketches. Our minds fire on the same absurdities. And as if guessing my observation of her chameleon nature, she takes to repeating some of my phrases. 'God, no! See, practising to be you!'

Her outlines are liquefying, now solidifying. I'm enveloped by the leathery touch of the sofa, reduced to the tips of the floating notes at the end of the pull of strings. She's leaning in, blinding me with successive circles of gold. I fall back, consciousness retreating in a fast, speckled streamer.

Outside, two, three, four booms. And voices. 'Fuck off out of here.' 'Yeah, Grandad, dis my yard.' I lurch up in panic; a car outside with stereo at top whack, with one continuous bleat of its horn. I squint hard at a flickering green spot. The time on the DVD player. 'Ten past two. Late. Bed.' The car outside screeches away.

'Shit, shit. Charlotte will kill me. I've got no keys.' Tina is now sitting forward, elbows on her knees, head in her hands.

'No keys, story of your life. Stay here. Just follow me.' I direct her hazily upstairs to the only other habitable bedroom, next to mine.

It is later, much later. I become silently aware of a figure sitting on the bed, writing something on my brow with a thumb. 'Only me. Can't sleep.' That voice, close, as if from my own inner ear. The torch-search of those eyes, scanning my face. I turn my head to the side, silently, pretending to fall back asleep. A knowing, throaty laugh. She leaves.

Her presence next door fills me with a fretful dread as if I'd left the front door open.

In the morning, the dread has waited up, hovering in the stale, night-before cloud. I also have a thudding ache behind my eyes. The door to the next-door room is open; the bed, to my surprise, neatly made. Downstairs, I find a note on the kitchen table, next to a full glass of water and two Advil pills. 'Hey, Belle, you'll need these.'

I laugh aloud. I've grown unused to people, to proximity. I shower, dress, and full of manic frenzy, begin unpacking boxes in the dining room, discarding with rapid efficiency, throwing away more and more into bin bags – holiday snaps, letters, old vinyl records, postcards. I stop, with gleeful satisfaction. Three more boxes remain for another day. I pick out four useful books for Tina: a Gombrich, a general history, a Francesca Woodman catalogue, and a monograph on Munch. The phone rings. It's Tina, launching straight in, as she does. 'You know that old film by that director, whassisname, Lynch, we agreed to go and see it, yeah?' I've no recollection of discussing it with her. Friday, 6 p.m. I'm due to be having lunch with my father earlier that day. I agree, half-suspecting she has made the arrangement up. She has a way with entering and breaking people.

The place has the urbane hush of the older art establishment, men and women who sit on committees, in genderless navy. A few heads turn almost peevishly towards my skinny jeans. He sits on the banquette, his head, rather fittingly, just beneath the right side of the frame, below the stony nude shanks. He pecks me quickly on the cheek, squeezes my upper arm hard.

'You look radiant.'

'And you still don't look a day over thirty-five,' I say to him. Recent over-indulgence shows in a faint blush on his lean face, but his hair is its usual luxuriant silvery grey, that boyish forelock edging impishly forward. Still wirily solid, drawing out a defiantly vigorous middle age into his late sixties.

A perfunctory smile is thrown at someone on the other side of the room, followed by a theatrical aside. 'Hope he doesn't come over. Little shit.' A quick half-titter, the sweep of napkin, the quick rubbing of hands, leg jiggling under the table. 'Now then. Let's order.'

Voice thickening with pre-prandial purr, he takes out his spectacles from their case, adjusts them, arches his straight salt-and-pepper eyebrows. I know better than to interrupt during the Perusal of the Menu, and the low, musical hum by way of accompaniment. We finally decide. Or he decides since

46

I enjoy indulging him by asking him to recommend. Meat. It is winter, after all. Duck confit for both of us.

Christmas in Scotland has furnished him with a new stock of comic anecdotes to perfect and polish. As usual, there is no mention of his latest woman friend.

'So, how's married life in the inner suburbs? You're glowing. Not pregnant by any chance?'

'Not yet. You know how I was never much good at biology. Anyhow, hardly the suburbs.' As always, I adopt the expected nonchalance of tone, words tossed out like cherry stones on an afternoon lawn.

It has the required effect: he titters indulgently. 'You could never be bothered to be much good at anything until I finally put my foot down. No more ideas about work? I'm sure that had everything to do with your illness, the blackouts. You needed proper intellectual focus, not gallery shenanigans. I mean, Paddy's perfectly charming. But he's rudderless; too idealistic to be a dealer, not rigorous enough for . . .'

'Well, he's going bankrupt anyway. As for me, I'm supposed to be doing up the house.'

He utters a hammy groan. 'Jimmy and Fiona are always at it. Refurbishing this and that. Your brother has evolved into a petit bourgeois DIY activist. Only the other day, I heard one of the fine art publishers, I forget which, is planning a house design series!' He concludes with his trademark snort at Universal Folly.

'Yes, I see. How to get expressionist angst in your bathroom! So how is Jimmy? Haven't seen them for over a year. I don't think he approves of me.'

'Oh no, it's sheer terror.'

I respond with a schoolgirl scowl. 'The little weed.'

'Anyhow, saw him briefly before Christmas. But I'm taking Holly and Bertie out next week. Half term. Holly has a very sharp little brain – and eye – already at six. Young Bertie looks uncannily like your mother – straight off some Viking longboat. As for Jimmy, I gather he's now flogging yoga mats and candles to fellow NA members. Thank God for the dreadful Fiona, cracking the whip in the City.' He passes me a book from a carrier bag beneath the table. I hand him one almost simultaneously, provoking mutual mirth.

'Ah now, superb. Thank you, darling. Panofsky.' He brings out his spectacles again, thumbs the book with expert delicacy.

'First edition. Don't you remember, you gave me your copy, as a reward for my good "A"'s in the crammer?'

He continues his leisurely stroll through the pages. 'Did I? Oh yes, yes, so I did . . . ah yes, Pandora.' The lilting enunciation, as if he had enjoyed Pandora on a sumptuous weekend at the Crillon. 'Rosso got it right; made all those silly puffs of smoke and fairy demons into proper, life-size vices. Strange to be punished for one's curiosity. Ignorance is a greater sin by far but I suppose curiosity is a form of envy. We'd be inhuman without it, but as we all know, it killed the cat.'

He surveys the room with a roguish chuckle. I continue, in a ridiculous panic, to hold his gaze. 'I think it was St Augustine who called it the "lust of the eye".'

But his eyes stray towards an approaching figure. 'Ah. Excellent, Fernando. Now, we must have some Burgundy, darling, with the duck. Unless your husband's finally managed to make a teetotaller of you.'

I feel a stab of protectiveness towards Jake and a second, sourer stab, of resentment, that he thinks I would alter to please a man. I turn to leaf listlessly through my gift, a new monograph on Bronzino, while he exchanges gossip and racing tips with Fernando. The wine tastes metallic to me. Finally, he turns, forefinger pointing at the book in my hands. 'It had a vivid effect on you. You can't have been more than eleven. No, twelve. You adored all the others but *The Allegory* . . . you had a violent reaction to it at the National . . .'

'I don't remember that. Why?' I am childishly desperate to know.

The duck arrives; his eyes twinkle. He moans. 'Mmmm, delicious, though you know I can barely eat more than one course these days. Pity. Even one's appetite begins to flag.'

He takes a mouthful with fast aplomb. 'Excellent.' A long sniff, a sigh. 'You don't seem very hungry.' He wipes his mouth. A sip. 'Oh, now it comes back. You were horrified by the figure of deceit, the monster, half blonde girl, half reptile. Jimmy did his usual when he thought you were scared – terrible row, you stormed off. Had one of your fits.'

He looks over at the book in my hands. 'Such a glacial, glittering fascination, the pitiless gaze . . . a polished deadness, ultimately. But then, that's your thing.'

He can slay me in a second. My senses are in revolt; the table, the meat, the glasses recede. I see him as if through several layers of glass. I refocus. 'Not exclusively,' I want to point out – I want to point out many things but no words come out.

'Oh yes. Your thing. De Chirico, Van der Heyden, oh yes,' he says with finality, savouring the wine, the deep plum colour drawing out the green of his tweed check. Behind his silvery lustre the paint fades into its muted earth colours. What of your work on Dutch Still Life, I want to say . . . or on the Emblematics of Mortality? . . . But it's absurd, our shielded dialogue, our courtly ritual, in pictures and painters, the arch gossip. Once I used to yearn to dispense with it; to hear him stray into the warm banalities of other fathers with their daughters, to talk girlish prattle.

He sighs. 'Anyhow, let me know whether it's any good. One of these deconstructive young academics who thinks he's revitalizing the Mannerists all by himself.' He cuts lustily into the last of his duck. 'How is that Paddy coping by the way? I remember when he tried to tell me that a quarter of the Rembrandts I mentioned in my monograph were fakes.' A half-bark of laughter. I've heard the anecdote many times before. He concludes with his customary exquisite brutality. 'I thought you'd end up marrying him. But then, well, he's not entirely plausible.'

He elongates the last word with relish. For all his Garrick Club chums, he's a woman's man. Men like him, his peers, must divide in the end into admired intellectual eunuchs or priapic oafs. I make an effort to rouse myself, steer the conversation along the witty, spirited discussions he savours: I taking the role of offering up one, then another example of a famous contemporary British artist, each one to be then submitted to the silky guillotine of his sarcasm. 'What I can't bear is all this vulgar allusion, all nudge-nudge wink-wink!' he almost roars, collapsing into a slow cackle which gratifies my lifelong pathetic urge to entertain him, though, as always, I fail since he is the architect of his own amusement, I the willing audience. He punctuates the argument with a brief, contented sigh. An old alarm sounds through me in an involuntary spasm. It was always the sigh that meant time to go, the end. Enough of you.

Afterwards, outside, overlooking the river, a spiteful wind lifts my hair and throws it across my face as he pecks me on the cheek. 'Dad.'

'Yes?' He turns a little distractedly. The hailed taxi purrs obediently at his side. His black cashmere coat flaps impatiently around his legs as he holds up his hand, sweeps back his hair. I am quickened by pride. People glance at him; he radiates an easy eminence.

'I forgot. I saw Adam Hoffman at Paddy's recently.'

'Ah, Adam. Had a terrible thing for your mother when he was in my department. Never got anywhere, mind. Are you taking this?'

'No. You have it.'

'Take a look at the Past and Present Sublime. It's surprisingly good.' (I would if I didn't black out, Daddy dear, re-member . . . ?) He closes the door with an economical regal wave, then settles back into the interior, gathering his coat, his face and thoughts removed, his own.

The fretful skin of the river puts me in a maudlin mood. I decide to get a cab home and try to stop myself from reliving the lunch in my mind, over-alert to his slights. I am used to him by now, or rather, used to myself around him. Shifting my gaze to the bridge and the dawdling, rucksacked figures across the embankment, I succeed in blanking out.

I notice that the board has come off the side window of the shuttered house opposite mine, on the other corner. An empty packet of Gauloises, a beer can and used matches lie just inside on the floor. Kids probably. Or a tramp.

I make out veins of cables inside, jutting suddenly out of walls. I've retained a childlike fascination with neglected houses, always half-expecting some sleeping presence to wake and shuffle across the floor moaning in her straitjacket. Out of the darkness comes the anxious burbling of roosting pigeons. I can still hear them, as if in my attic, as I take a nap to sleep off the wine. I wake with the disembodied voice of my mother in my head, that throwaway wit she used with my father: *That's what you do, look at dead stuff for a living – dead Dutch stuff at that.'* She bleaches out before I can picture her. I can hear the voice, the voice that made me think of warm, liquid toffee, so I could even smell it. And yet in the end, it began to dilute, with a vagueness born of disappointment. It begins to surge up my gut, the column of hot dread. I get up.

At the dressing table, applying makeup, the transformation surprises me. My father was right. My eyes have a dark lustre, the whites very pure, the pupils a brilliant black. Cheekbones stand out through glistening skin.

She turns up at the door, long woollen legs in a black denim mini-skirt, thick tights, suede boots and a striped beanie hat. Her eyes are heavy with mascara, giving her a doll-like air against the freckled glaze of her cheeks.

In the car, she turns to me as I'm revving the engine. 'Mercedes?'

'Jake bought it for my birthday last year. It's a bit flash but it's grown on me. At least it's a classic one. You fell on it, that night. Your boyfriend dented my door. Remember?'

She responds by fidgeting through the CDs. 'Men like to spoil you. Bit like royalty, aren't you?'

I turn to her, half-indignant. Noting her provocative grin, I uncoil, stretching out my hands on the wheel. 'Do you drive?'

'No. Carl says I'd be lethal on the roads.' Her mobile rings; she inspects it and switches it off, exchanging a complicit smile with me. We grow suddenly self-conscious in the enforced closeness of the car.

In the cinema, she tilts forward as if afraid of missing anything, absorbing the words and images like magical commands. The film is a preposterous but riveting nightmare. A man, a saxophonist, metamorphoses after jealously murdering his wife. In his new identity, he is the young, adulterous lover of a woman played by the same actress, only she is now a blonde, a gangster's moll. It's the gangster's turn to play the suspicious cuckold, but the young lover is also driven to murder, after watching her in a porn film.

The screen's rays rake over both of us and I feel as weightless as the particles of light obscuring and conjuring up the young woman next to me. The film ends as the young man metamorphoses into the first man again, who then murders the gangster sleeping with his wife. The final credits run over a heart-pumping drive along a dark road.

Back outside, my eyes blink in the velvet and neon glare of the urban night. I look back smiling over the throng coming out of the cinema. She is looking out for me – her golden head and curve of shoulders in sharp focus against the faceless faces. My mind already carries the impress of those shoulders as if they were my own. I wait for her. We crackle with life, rush at words and impressions, greedily turning the film around like a precious gem. She repeats dialogue as if inventing it. 'A corpse can tell you plenty, Joyce,' she quotes, echoing the film's quirky black menace. Our laughter skids against each other's, and in the silence that follows, I have the sensation of having recovered something – some minute memento glittering up from the rubbish-strewn pavement.

I take her into Club Riiad's neo-Moroccan bar with Moz-arabian mirrors set into the pattern of the opulent red walls. Cigarette pointed outwards, Tina affects a Mata Hari stare before sitting. 'Mahvellous, dahlink.' She wrinkles her nose, which is very wide at the bridge, giving copious space to the otherworldly strobe of those liquid-pale eyes. 'I never come anywhere like this.'

'I think you're lying,' I say, not without humour.

'Why would I want to do that?' She exudes an air of planned spontaneity. Both hands under her chin, her pointy, awkward elbows on the table, she seems to be posing for a studio photograph. I note long arms, like those of an adolescent boy.

'No idea. Just to keep in practice perhaps, it's a habit with some people.' I study the drinks list. It starts something, this sparring; we seem born to it, circling each other with relish, a disarming, toying flattery. As she quips or jokes, her head moves fractionally from side to side as if in tune to some private music.

'There's a fresco I once saw,' I tell her, 'Ghirlandaio, I think. All the figures, the women, seemed dull, schematic. Except for one. A young woman entering with a basket on her head. I think it's a birth, the Birth of St John, but it's that girl, the servant, who really signals the arrival of three-dimensional sensuality. That's you.'

'A servant, hey?' she says ruefully, yet inwardly snared, complimented. A thought lands on her face. 'Why didn't you want to mention the cardigan in the restaurant?'

'Jake gave it to me. And I'm on anti-depressants and sleeping pills, so he'd probably think I was going mad asking strangers in at night – giving them his presents –'

'I'm no stranger. What you depressed about?'

'Oh, nothing. They just gave them to me in despair after my blackouts a few years ago and I carried on. For luck. Which means I'm happily devoid of emotional nerve-ends.'

She grows suddenly fretful, one palm massaging the table compulsively. 'Just chuck that shit, those pills, out, it's all shit, doctor's shit.'

'I can't. I'm a near-extinct species – a superfluous, pill-addicted housewife. It's in the blood. It killed my mother in the end – she had a car accident.'

The response is a stunned stare. 'My mother's dead too. That's all they did – give her pills, dexies, valium. They were trying to kill her. That's how they get rid of people, anybody different. It's a trick . . . she started to look right through me.' Tearing her paper napkin into shreds, words flow from her in a soft, accelerating shower of arrows as she fixes a fervent eye on me. 'I knew we had stuff like that, we're the same. Even before, when you didn't know me, I saw you, in the restaurant, I knew we'd –' She's stalled by her own feverishness.

'We'd what, Tina?'

'Well . . . be . . . that's why I didn't bring the cardigan back. I waited for you to come –' The pupils flicker and dilate in her slanted eyes.

'So what's the real story with Carl? I'm curious, what were you arguing about that night?'

I'm thrown a calculating squint as she takes time to fashion her story.

'Carl was trying to get me to do stuff with this guy in the

car, he gets weird sometimes. Then when that didn't work he started hassling me for money for the drugs we bought; so he took my leather coat.' She glances sideways in dismissal, puckering her mouth. A shrug. 'But I expect you wanna know about the sex. Threesomes, butt-fucking.' The tone is mischievously deadpan. I lean away, resume a glacial calm, watching as she simmers against the blood-red tiles, caught in the mesh of my silent observation. Behind me, voices rise, the bar is filling. I add, 'Oh please. You're not shocking me, you know. I did all that stuff in my day, when we were all playful puppies.'

'I wasn't trying to.' A note of indignation.

'So is it something you offer as part of the evening's entertainment?'

She grants me a tight smile. She has downed her second drink almost in one, signals to the waiter for more drinks.

Some clutch in me snaps shut. 'Not for me. I'll get the bill. I expect you have some reductive little theory about me – bored rich housewife seeks bi-try.'

'I don't think that –' She is beseeching, upset, slams a flat hand on the table.

'You're drunk,' I say. The waiter looks down at her, then gives me a camp, sympathetic sigh.

'What you looking at?' she hisses at him. He stands in silent shock.

I hand over my card. 'I'm sorry about this.' He leaves us with a quick, indignant swoosh of apron.

'Poofy little twat, chi-chi man,' says Tina. 'Here.' She throws a ten-pound note down on a small puddle on the table where she spilled her champagne.

'Ah, the rest of the money you owe me. How charming. Do keep it, save it for a rainy day.' I leave the note there and stand up. She picks it up, blowing at it, shoulders hunched defiantly.

The road is frosting over with a fine white film, the night is chilly-clear with pinpricks of tight, cold stars, its freshness like a tender slap. 'Look. Stars,' she says, pointing up, swaying, the husky voice slurring, congealing, so that I want to get away. In the car, there is a long, awkward silence during which she sits unmoving, frowning down at her lap. Finally she says, 'You see, I know, I can see you –'

'Oh, Jesus . . . you're drunk and deluded.' I grow suddenly furious. 'You don't see me at all –' I've gone over a hump in the road far too fast. The steering wheel begins to move on its own, leading me sleekly into its own wayward glide.

We come to a shocked, muffled stop in the rear wing of a parked car. Now everything feels ordinary, flat, the car engine hoarse and straining. I switch it off, pull on the handbrake. A street lamp rakes the other car. Its alarm bleats and bleats.

'You okay, Belle?' She is smoothing back my hair, breathing alcoholic fumes. 'Better move before they come.' She nods at the other car. 'You've done it some damage. You'll get done, Belle.'

I drop her outside Charlotte's, a dingy 1930s three-storey council building, with rusting metal windows. My heartbeat is still racing. 'Goodnight.' I hear my own voice, cold yet very close, as in mist. As I park opposite my house, I notice a man sitting in an estate car round the corner by the shuttered house. There's something in the feral arching of his neck . . . even in the darkness, I recognize Carl.

The phone goes, several times. A bit late for Jake. It's Tina. I ignore it. It rings twice again. Finally I pick it up.

'The money, the tenner, I short-changed you on purpose, cos you wouldn't open the door, that time I came round with it. You were in. I saw you on the stairs. And I knew, if I gave you less you'd want to see me . . .' I put the phone down, saying, 'Goodnight.'

*

I haven't passed these streets for years. I glimpse the corner of our old family house through the cab window. The night before he left, the argument at dinner. Mother hissing at him, her eyes taking on a supernatural gleam; his eyes narrowing, as they always do in anger, turning, I thought, into scorpions that would fly out. I always watched their eyes. He grabbed her neck and quickly let go, and they looked, shocked, at the glass shards on the table. Jimmy, me, trembling like reeds. And later, waking to voices in their bedroom, long, startled, irate sighs. They must have been saying goodbye. Rigid with not knowing and those alien sounds, a red-hot dread sat on my chest. I closed my eyes, opened them. But it was the same. Half-lit, half-human shapes, opening and collapsing into whorls of darkness.

The cab draws up. It takes ages to find Suzy in the party's throng. The colours, the faces are all primary and garish. Sense, propriety have deserted me. I'm over-euphoric, brash. As I speak to people, I'm impatient, cutting, using charm first to flatter, then disarm. 'Don't be a jerk,' I say contemptuously to one magazine journalist with a supercilious goatee to match his opinions on 'feminist' art. Zara Marshall speaks to me about her imminent separation from her husband. 'It's probably just as well,' I laugh. 'Not a marriage made in heaven.' She looks startled, yet I am powerless to apologize, move on blithely. I look around and see only mouths bleating, the purple and red fusing. And one pair of huge blue eyes, watching, as if judging me. Who is she? Suzy is busy gabbling. A waitress comes up to me with a tray of canapés. They are worms in pastry. I gather up strength from somewhere, walk out quickly and jump into a cab, full of stormy, blind purpose.

Dark wood, trance music, raucous laughter, the Old Master tavern lighting. That is the setting for her as she sits in a corner, soaking up the dull yellow light, surrounded by young men leering with brutish merriment, all held in the thick brown pall of smoke and noise; all except Carl, who has betrayed awareness of my arrival through that feral angle of his head.

Unable to go up, to reach her, I turn away. A hand on my shoulder, the gold glare of the face. 'I saw you, looking for me.' She puts her arm around me as we talk with gauche, whispered urgency. 'Let's go into the restaurant. Here.' She leads me next door, muttering something to the waitress. I am undone, small. We move to an empty table by the window. She passes me the glass of wine in her hand to drink. I grow intolerably hot, I take off my coat.

'I'm a bit drunk. I've just been to a horrible party. They're recycling bijou boutiques. There was a woman there, looking daggers at me. But I didn't know her. I was talking like someone else . . . I hate them, parties.'

Tina strokes my bare arm, her eyes moist. 'You don't need to go.'

'I saw our old house today. When she died, Dad stopped the car in a lane and broke down crying. I was murderously furious with him. I couldn't cry. But he left her. She wasn't good at being left; her voice went thin. He said it was best not to see her, best not to look . . . but if I'd seen her maybe I could see her now . . .' I come out flatly from my reverie, aware of having given off a tragic appeal, true and staged at the same time. Tina lifts her hand from my bare arm to light a cigarette. I feel the cold seeping back where she was touching. She exhales, offers me a smoke.

Here comes her move, the answer. Call and answer. 'Carl's getting weirder, winding Charlotte up. Asking her what I'm up to, telling her, people here, shit, stuff, lies about me. He's next door, now.'

She moves her head to signal the pub room. We are hunched forward, our knees almost touching, the wall flanking us, hiding us on one side, one glass of deep scarlet wine between us, as if at a rite. Even now, I can't make it out, this preordained formality, a strict tempo, ticking away. My move, my call. 'You need to get away. He's obsessed,' I say to her.

'He's a fucking bully. He just wants me to suffer.' Something is scrabbling at my walls, crawling out from within. I hear myself say, 'So why don't you move into mine for a while? Jake's away, I'm rattling around in there. We can rescue each other. Well . . . you can rescue me.'

She is solemn, quietly final. 'Yeah, I will.'

It is agreed. I will pick her up the next day. As I pass the tables in the pub, the murmuring from all the conversations overlaps and separates, clear and crackling all at once. She takes me to the door, to see me out. We smile shyly at each other. Out of the corner of my eye, I see Carl's pebbly gaze striking us as he sniggers soundlessly at his friend's joke, head held back to watch us better.

5

Tina is puffing impatiently on a fag at the edge of the pavement. Beside her lie two large tote bags. Luminous against
the sooty council block and the smeared air, she brings to
mind Suzy's old predilection for 'ghetto glam'; fashion shots
with glittering beauties shamelessly posed in squalid alleyways
and the like. I'm still parking as her keyed-up face appears at
the passenger window. I let the window down.

'I need to go back in – you wait here,' she says.

'Relax. I'll come with you.' She looks uncomfortable at my
suggestion, but this simply fuels my already morbid curiosity.
We climb stained concrete steps up to the first floor.

Once inside the flat, I'm immediately hit by the stench:
cough tincture, the rankness of wet fur. On a faded sofa
covered by a plum Moroccan rug sits a woman all in black. I
recognize her by the faint slivers of naked white skull showing
through her thin, hennaed black hair – it's the woman with
the pit bull from the street.

A low growling comes from somewhere in the interior of
the flat. In response, her long jaw moves anxiously sideways,
rubbery mouth lagging seconds behind. A newspaper trembles
in the grip of one knobbly hand, which, like the rest of her
skin, has the dull pallor of skimmed milk. I take in rheumy
windows, rusty sills, arthritic shelves filled with books, stacked
vertically and horizontally, well-thumbed paperbacks with the
pale spines I recall from my university days. The floor, too, is
a hilly landscape of long-hoarded yellowing papers, settle-
ments of puffy dust-balls in the narrow alleyways between the
piles. In the middle of the room, a dining table operates as

half-way house for assorted bottles of various sizes, small buddhas, half-burned candles, stuffed envelopes, deckle-edged cuttings, an overflowing hairbrush. One surprisingly beautiful chair, a Hepplewhite, is tucked beneath. The growling breaks out into a cantankerous barking.

Tina is busying herself looking for something. Charlotte's hands tremble in confusion as she rises.

I break in through the barking. 'Are you not going to introduce us?'

'Oh. Yeah. Christabel, this is Charlotte.' Tina's cheeks are bright with shame – she can barely meet my eye. As if she'd only just heard some far-off call.

Charlotte straightens her back, extends a hand in gracious greeting. A long hand – and long teeth the colour of bone. 'Heh-heh-hello, sorry about the noise. I'd better let him in. D'you mind? He hates being locked up in the bedroom.' The eyes, fine, porcelain-blue pools, crease with pained concentration as she heads off and disappears through a corridor.

A furious padding noise precedes the roared charge of the pit bull terrier into the middle of the room where he stops imperiously, absurd short legs gripping the carpet. Luxuriant growls, snappish bark, much baring of fang and saliva-glistened purple jowl.

'Boris.' Charlotte's voice betrays a fluted despair. Tina is silent, looking down at the dog with venom. He moves closer in.

'Boris. Oh dear.' Charlotte's long hands wobble up in gawky supplication. At this plea, the growling ascends and descends as if on spiteful whim. He has decided to practise his repertoire. Tremolo, vibrato, basso profundo.

'Now, Boris,' I say, cold and firm. The dog stops and blinks before me with a conciliatory yelp. 'Good boy.' I click my fingers. 'Here.' He smacks his chops and pads over to permit me to stroke his neck, psychopathic darting eyes attempting a 360-degree turn around the room. As I pat him, I notice a dark, glutinous oil painting above the table; an impastoed mulch, a face perhaps, behind meshing. I am careful not to look at it further. Just in case. I wouldn't like to pass out in this little grotto. Still stroking Boris, I turn to her. 'I hear you used to paint.' Out of politeness, I daren't ask her if the rectangular growth on the wall is hers.

Charlotte brings her hand up to stroke the crown of her head as she casts her eyes downward with self-deprecation. It's a gesture I've seen Tina make. 'Oh, Lord, I gave up ages ago. Just a few group shows. You know.' There follows a nervy, clockwork 'Heh-heh-he'.

We chat about this and that and I become aware of addressing her over-jauntily, as if she were some deaf spinster aunt. Those porcelain eyes wrinkle with censure. She brings to mind the disapproving, lankily decent types at school, horse-featured, big feet, a perverse attachment to honesty. My badness is being quantified.

'Tina's told me a lot about you. Since she met you she's been devouring all my art books. I'm terribly impressed.' A fleck of irony. 'You work in the art world, in The Big Room, don't you?

'No longer.'

'Yes, I-I-I . . .' the stutter continues for a painful length of time. 'I, umm, you had friends at St Martin's, didn't you?' Her tone is altered, knowing.

'Light years away.' Stunned by finding this link with the past through Tina, I will myself into an easy glibness. 'I rather OD'd on conceptual art.' Immediately, I flinch at my own allusion, the perverse use of the verb.

'Mmmm, yes, I remember . . . you look like your father, of course. And you sound like him. Has he written anything recently?'

'No, no books. He only lectures occasionally. He writes

lengthy reviews; sits on committees, grouches about the new philistines.'

'Oh really? What's his beef?'

'Well, to him a lot of so-called postmodern art is just "an appallingly told bad joke".' I exaggerate his voice.

'He used to be on TV, didn't he? Didn't suffer fools gladly. And you, I remember you well . . .'

I have an urge to thwack at Charlotte as if she were some irksome, dying bluebottle. But I must stay, conquer the panic. I turn my attention to Boris, who, scenting hostile fumes, is diligently following my every move. Charlotte is watching this. 'It's extraordinary, he rather likes you.'

I mock-growl at him, ignoring the sting in her comment. 'A grumpy soul but he's okay, aren't you?'

Her mournful face opens out like a fan in contemplation of the dog. Deep colour wells in her eyes. 'I found him in a rather mangy state. Or rather, he found me,' she says.

'They have an unerring instinct for the soft spot – for the soft touch.'

'Oh yes, I am a bit of a soft touch with him, aren't I, Boris?' I recognize a touch of Thomas Lawrence in her physiognomy, the faintly ostrich-necked Princess Lieven, even her namesake, Queen Charlotte. One turn of the screw less and she would have been selling watercolours at chummy private shows in Chelsea before returning to a sprawling country farmhouse, braying children and a less barking version of Boris.

I try to keep her to the canine subject. 'They sense who needs to rescue them. I used to have a hopeless Jack Russell –' Impatient shuffling and clicks sound from the direction of the front door. A departing Tina butts in with callow briskness, 'Okay, Charlie, gotta go.' She is gripping the doorknob, a carrier bag in the other hand, looking at the floor, seemingly as desperate to leg it as myself.

'Yes, yes, of course, you'd better get going.' Charlotte's hand begins its old agitation as she looks round for Boris.

I turn. 'Bye bye, Boris.' He blinks, sits, gets up, circling, in the manner of mad dogs everywhere. Tina is already out on the stairwell, calling back rapidly, 'Call you tomorrow, Charlie.'

'Yes, yes. Good luck.' Charlotte turns to me at the door. 'Goodbye, Christabel. At last I've met you.' She hesitates, thinks better of holding out her hand, looking me in the eye with flinching challenge. Of course, I remember them now, those accusing blue pods, in Richie's studio one afternoon. They were there, all three of them, huddled in their circle, their triumvirate of smack-taking, Lucia enjoying my discomfort, my exclusion, as she always did. She had grabbed him, Richie, from under my nose, but it wasn't enough for her, a petty triumph. Lucia, who had the knack for it, ever since childhood, the knack of unpicking me with her cadences. 'Look who's here,' she drawled languidly, those pinned eyes alighting on me; the sly allusion to my cringing return to their company. Then, the typically sudden volte-face; the giddy, passionate embrace, the powerful suction of her moist, magnetic gaze as she said, 'I've *missed* you.' The brazen confidence in her own powers of seduction. Fury dims my vision: I throw Charlotte a devastating 100-watt smile. 'I'd better hurry before Boris gets out,' I say. Once more, the ferocious barking, this time behind the closed front door. I'm careful to trot quickly down behind Tina, to hide my face.

Tina's own face puckers with shame as she lifts a tote bag into the boot. I bring the boot down hard, shutting out my unease at the unwelcome invasion from the past. She looks up, startled. I pretend to be looking at the sky which is now busy with huge cloud convulsions of grey and blue as if a missile had launched in its midst. Finally I say airily, 'I thought you said she was off the gear, her hands . . .'

'She is, it's the fucking pills . . .' She shoots me a devious glance from her seat. 'Fancy her knowing you. I thought you were younger than her.'

'Oh, I doubt she does know me, she's just bonkers.' Tina has picked up the wrong scent. As if responding to my veiled enquiry, she begins, 'She came into The Castle, last year. Not supposed to allow dogs, but it was in the afternoon so I let her sit in a corner with Boris and we got talking. A bit ragga, but quirky, kind. Just came out with everything – she'd just been put on some medication – I could tell she'd just had some sort of fix. Told me how she'd married young and one day she found her husband in bed with her best friend. They were all on the scag, but the lovebirds came off it, fucked off all cosy to the country and left poor old Charlie behind. I mean, I'd have fucking slaughtered him.'

'God, all this devastation with love. What gets into people?' Through the rear-view mirror I see the cars halting and gathering like a pack of badly shuffled cards, the familiar playground wail growing louder. I stop, moving to the side, my heart jumping irregularly to the wail. The police car finally passes. Tina continues, equally oblivious to traffic, bombs, hurricanes.

'Stopped painting, got over to Africa to come off the gear, did some teaching there, came back and worked for some animal charity, but she started usin' again. Sold her flat to pay off the debts and carry on with the brown and her family have had it now . . .' She looks out blankly at the encroaching park, sighing. 'I tell her to keep on the NA gig, see people. But after that Albanian loved her and left her –'

'Don't tell me. She worries about leaving Boris.' Our loud hilarity subsides into an embarrassed hush as Tina begins squirming in her seat and rubbing at her arm with guilt. 'It's not the dog, Tina. She's lost it.'

'She can surprise you.' She leans forward, as if looking for herself intently in the wing mirror. 'I forgot to say thanks, she's been a good mate. She never wanted anything from me. She's kind.'

'Rubbish.' My harshness is hardly unbiased. Charlotte's threadbare integrity dares to judge, know. But she knows nothing. I fortify myself. She's simply a ghost, a minor ghost at that, one I've unwarily summoned by inviting Tina, herself a faint echo of Lucia. 'Everyone wants company,' I continue, interrupting my own thoughts.

'Maybe, just company. She's alone.'

'Buy Boris a present – a collar.'

'Yeah – a diamond one, like yours, Belle. Boris really fancied you.'

'Hell, I don't mind a bit of rough . . . so, here we are.' Tina has turned very pale, her chin all a-tremble. 'God, don't look so glum.'

'No.' She turns to me, eyes brimming with momentousness. 'This is it. I'm here.'

'You're daft.'

I give her the bedroom next to mine, a sweetly old-fashioned room with a large window overlooking the apple tree, still with its old original fleur-de-lys wallpaper and a small white grate. She sets up her iPod and speakers first, sings in a melodious voice, as she unpacks, along to that song which begins with a woman singing about the morning rain clouding up her window before breaking into the rapper's menacing rant.

I look into her room after she leaves hastily for her shift in The Castle. The window is open. The sun is out now and even from here there's a heady scent of narcissi outside. Clothes, CDs, makeup, hairdryer are all in a huge pile on the floor, the soft afternoon spring sun holding them in an enamelled yellow stillness. Unthinkingly, I lift a woollen striped tank-top from the bed. Coconut, fags, singed plastic, and a more alien, tarry sweat. A man's perhaps. The phone rings.

'You sound cheerful.' Jake's jokiness always sounds a disturbed, interrogative note these days.

'It's a lovely afternoon,' I say.

'It's going to be scorching here today. Mmm.' The nervous tactful catch in the throat. A loud whirr sounds from his side; it's nine or something in the morning over there. He must be in the clinic.

'You'd better answer that,' I say. I hear him speaking with soft authority through an intercom: 'I do know who he is but he'll have to wait like everyone else if he has no appointment. Tell him it won't be longer than half an hour. Offer him something to play with.' A few seconds later, he is back on the phone.

'Who's the big child star?' I ask.

'It's no child, just a brattish star. Oh no, can't say. Strictly LA confidential.'

'It's not the fact that you're so discreet that annoys me but that you actually enjoy depriving me of information.' Now I have set him chuckling, I say, 'Oh, I nearly forgot, we have a house guest. Tina, she works round the corner in The Castle. She's staying just for a bit – while she finds a place. She won't bother us.'

'Oh.' That flat, anguished, soft 'Oh'. I envisage his mouth slackening with alarm. While calm in the face of disease or colossal bank loans, microscopic alterations to his rituals, to his immediate eco-climate, to a train schedule, instil in him a brooding tumult. 'The tall, fair one?'

So he did notice her. 'Well, it's good for me to have the company.' A nifty reproach, here, at his absence. Totally fake, of course, but it will have the required effect – inspire guilt. 'She's great.'

An asperity to his voice betrays that he is still reeling at the prospect of domestic Armageddon. 'Mmmm. Well, try not to play Lady Bountiful and lend her the car so she can go joy-riding – at least not in the first week. Anyhow, we've come up against problems. I may not be able to get over for three weeks. Don't expect I'll meet her.'

'Oh, she might be around for a bit longer than that,' I say with some enjoyment. As I take my leave, replacing the receiver, I can still hear the metallic echo of my over-bright tone.

She usually works three evening and two day shifts a week. Over the next few days, I get to sleep later and later, watching the television, drinking wine with her when she clatters in, full of salty bar-room tales, acting out drunken exchanges, offering grass or occasionally coke.

The house feels light and reckless, as if the space had receded, become an indulgent audience. The creaks and gongs have lost their crankiness, transformed to melodious hums and trickles. Alluring sizzles escape from the kitchen. Wafts of olive oil, ginger and garlic perfume the corridors. I begin to eat well, for me. Tina has turned out to be an accomplished cook. I've never had much sense of taste and touch, but all Tina's senses seem to come with a full-blown guiltless eroticism. When she eats she actually moans with pleasure.

In an ironic reversal of our different ages, she is clucky at my paltry diet, chides me like a teenager. 'You need feeding up. It's me that has to worry. If I wasn't in that restaurant traipsing up and down I'd be a fucking whale.' True, there's a hint of future heaviness in the lumpy roll of her walk.

I suggest I pay for the food because she cooks. She insists on doing the shop by way of exchange. In fact, she blissfully insists on doing most chores in the kitchen – in the whole house. She veers from sulky morning indolence to manic afternoon activity when she bounds around with urgent-browed efficiency as if by her actions she is saving us from some imminent catastrophe. She fetches and carries for me with alacrity – everything except going up and down stairs, to which she has a stubborn aversion, often postponing these transits until it is absolutely vital, and then it is always done quickly, as if pursued by a pack of wolves. Her mind is a nest of worming fears. She is forever opening and closing windows, fearful of infestations, full of statistics on a breed of super bedbug that cannot be eliminated.

I've known much fake weirdness in my time – types who affect eccentricity, call their mopeds by pet names like Tantalus. But Tina is the real thing. Not simply a real fake, but a real weirdo. Doors are on a mission to shut her out, hoovers talk back, lost keys 'look right through' her, wine stains speak their own voodoo, strange texts on her mobile are conspiracies in the making. The dining room gives her 'the creeps'; she hears voices in there. In vain do I tell her that it's the people passing outside the wall. Once, a little irritated at her rant about the dust from there 'infiltrating' the house, I wondered aloud how she could have existed at Charlotte's. She adopted one of her trademark mammoth sulks, all glassy, slant-eyed pique. But then I realize by little slips she has made that she's hardly stayed at Charlotte's. It explains why she didn't want me to meet her – her sulks can be convenient cover-ups.

What with the company, the wine, the fat joints, I begin to sleep soundly, sticking only to the day pills, often forgetting to take the diazepam at night. In the mornings, I wake very late but with urgency, a spinning body in a spinning world. Instead of resenting her unspoilt face, I enjoy its contours, the alterations in colour, from rose to creamy to gold, the planes full of slanting, near-Slavic drama as her cheekbones catch the light.

We never go to The Castle. That's Carl's domain. She's now down to three shifts and claims to have stopped drinking there. 'He's always in,' she claims. I don't tell her I've caught glimpses of him on our street corner a few times. Perhaps he's using Ali's to shop as an excuse to hang out, keep an eye on her.

The other day she refused point-blank to shop in Main Road. 'It's bad enough having to work there. Eyes all over the place. Wanting to know your business.' The weather had the devil's smile: wind, showers and sun rapidly alternating. And suddenly, a perfect spring afternoon, softly veiled sun, delicate breeze. We decided on a walk. Not in the Park. So we headed the other way, to the Broadway with its ragged line of tall buildings juxtaposed beside low ones, like crooked teeth. Signs everywhere, jutting out unevenly from buildings, signs for first-floor chiropodists, for obscure firms of immigration lawyers in cramped fourth-floor offices; signs for pawnbrokers and travel agents which double as international phoning centres. Cheap clothing stalls, fake sunglasses stalls, pigeons pecking around overstuffed bins. A drunken brawl erupted from a newly refurbished pub. In its dark depths, the new brass looked gaudy. Old men with concave chests sat worshipping huge screens amidst fake Victorian interiors.

On the pavement past the pub, a pubescent boy in a hoodie using a phone box winked at us as we passed. He turned to the receiver again. 'Yeah, right. That's ten CDs, yeah?' I noticed he had a mobile phone sticking out of his back jeans pocket and pointed this out to Tina.

'Drugs. Only drug dealers and au pairs use phone boxes any more. God, let's leg it. Fuckin' sad low life,' she said, loud enough so the boy could hear.

According to Tina, everyone's 'bang at it' – the drugs, the Charlie Chan. In her knowledgeable opinion, it forms the nexus for the local economy, high and low. She therefore decides there and then to take coke only at weekends, to resist all temptations in The Castle. The grass, or rather skunk, can continue apace.

*

As we moved out of range of the phone box, my mobile began ringing. I heard a man whispering, 'I wanna eat you out.' He said this several times. I held it to her ear, and Tina said it was the DVD shop manager. 'He's a perv. He gets high and calls women saying dirty stuff. He's probably heard something about us, in the pub, from Carl.'

We made our way to the shop. 'He's there, come on,' she said. We entered together, smiling pleasantly at the small man behind the counter. He wore a black baseball cap and a black grunge rock t-shirt. Small, dark, with straggly hair, and a soft, hanging lower lip, he looked like the kind of geek who'd murder his rock idol.

'Good afternoon,' said Tina, leaning forward at the counter. 'Do you have any films to recommend?'

'Er, what sort?' A slick of dirty sweat had settled on his pasty face. His eyes swivelled sideways.

'Well, you know . . . what's that one where she takes a scalpel to his eyes, Belle?' Tina's voice was breezily matter-of-fact. 'Or that other one, *Repulsion*, where she knifes them all for looking and lusting after her. In that apartment, one by one. Makes a right old mess in there.' Tina leaned further forward on the counter, chummy and confiding.

'We don't stock much of that in here, I'm afraid.' His voice was reedy with disquiet.

'Oh, shame.' Tina's luminous eyes scorched down the racks, suddenly flaring up. '*Peeping Tom*.' She took it up to him, crossing her arms on the counter as she said, 'We'll have this one, thanks.' He handed over the DVD, took my card. Tina turned to me. 'You know, my friend keeps getting emails from some saddo: "Shove your walloping cock in her cherry pie."'

'Mmm,' I said, eyes stabbing at the sweating wreck. 'I got Savage Cock Shearers the other day.'

'Oh yes, that's what's needed.'

The door clinked loudly behind us. As we rounded the corner, we exploded into peals of laughter, clutching at each other for support. Tina leaned against a wall, arms gathered before her, hair trailing, her laughter skidding, growing more abandoned, just as Lucia had done all those years ago. Her skin took on the moss-green stone of her surroundings. The action caught in the loop of the past. Richie had jumped on us as we'd walked out of the shop, uncontrolled, like an overwrought boy, excluded from the female laughter, taking the game too far. The stoned feverishness in his eyes had made me say sternly, 'Calm down.' And I saw a movement in Lucia's face, a decisive tightening, as she intercepted Richie's furious glance at me, ensnaring it with her half-smile. The fun was over. We had all walked back to her flat in silence. He went straight to her bedroom, and she looked right through me and stood up, tin foil and smack in hand, going in to console him. I listened in the long silence, then, to their whispers and stifled groans. I thought of the letters she'd sent me from New York as a twelve-year-old, the desperate letters which all went unanswered because I knew her by then, she'd betrayed me. I knew her love was really envy, and I should never have let her in again. Strange, how envy engenders itself through infection; that was her great victory, that I became infected – began to envy her back. She couldn't bear to envy all on her own. It hardly touches me now.

I turned my head quickly, my hand rising to focus on the end of the street. At the far end, by the Park, stood two men, their heads turned our way in repose. They were still, like carved, gesturing figures, the tops of the trees rising above them, the sky perfectly blue and still. The fair one's head began to move. Carl. A train whistled by somewhere to the right.

'What is it, Belle?' She was scrutinizing my discomfort. I blamed Carl for my lack of composure.

'I think I just saw Carl up there. Do you think he's following us?' I said, hurrying my pace.

She turned to search behind her but she only frowned a little myopically, unconcerned. 'Oh, there. He's got a friend, some student who's working as a gardener in the Park.'

'Oh good, so he's just an accidental stalker then,' I said. 'What does he do?

'He's a builder, decorator, deals a bit in furniture and some antiques on the side. Fancies himself as a future empresario' – I didn't correct her – 'obsessive about money, about everything.'

'Especially you.' I put my arm through hers; as much for his benefit – provocation fortifying me. Tina turned, her face very close to mine. 'The fool. Ha, ha, ha. Ha!' Even her cod Gothic laugh was like Lucia's. But she isn't Lucia: she has a heart. Drizzle began to fall, like a fresh reprieve. We decided to celebrate our glorious victory with champagne and coke, even though it wasn't, strictly speaking, the weekend. We picked up cigarettes at Ali's. This dampened my mood a little. He has ceased being quite so friendly, always greeting me too correctly. With Tina he is almost, for Ali, impolite. I realized why as she paid for her cigarettes; she thrust herself forward, fingering the letters on Reza's t-shirt. 'What's this rubbish then, Reza?' The boy stood there, hands in pockets, and I actually saw a shift in his crotch. Ali emerged from the back of the shop. As he reached the counter, he broke out scatter-gun into his own language. Reza hurried off inside. It was as much as I could do to get Ali to look at me as I paid.

'Tina, you must be careful with Reza,' I said when we came out.

'What you on about?' she whined.

'He's young. And well, their religion – they have a different thing about sex.'

'Oh yeah.' She regarded me coolly. 'Since when did madam

get so pure and holy?' And it struck me that the enjoyment for her had nothing to do with Reza, and everything to do with angering or even taunting the father.

She scored the coke with lightning speed. As soon as we'd had a line, a big one, we drove off to my favourite boutique.

I chose things carefully, with more care than for myself. We shut ourselves into the changing room to take another line. I watched as she tried on one thing after another, sensing the power men must feel, dressing a fantasy. But I revelled in it because the sales assistant was all sloe-eyed wonder, piqued even, by our display, by how to read us. I exaggerated a proprietorial air. Tina caught on beautifully, playing up, all churlish sexual ambiguity and sly glances. She stared at herself, beguiled by her transformation in sparkling mini-dress and slingbacks. I bought a tight off-white trouser suit for myself – all wide lapels and vintage seventies YSL chic. Though it's spring, I couldn't resist the boots (long, slinky black ones with buckles at the top). I bought us both a pair. And also, two pale silk kaftans.

'We'll wear these in Morocco, my favourite place on earth,' I told her.

We walked through a small Victorian cemetery towards the car. The air around me like a heady tonic, the world taking on distinctness, discreetness. Trees were filling with fresh acid greens. Beside me Tina seemed to quiver with the same life as the leaves. The blossom was out, pink cherry and white. It's miraculous, so overnight, we said, unused to being out of our bower-for-two. I came to a sudden stop before an arch-angel whose brow and eyes had been sprayed with a line of red paint. It shocked me as if it were human, alive. I talked to her, to steady myself.

'In the Spanish Civil War, the film director Buñuel said he saw a vanload of Republicans descending to fire at a statue of

Christ in the street. All through history, statues have been attacked, mutilated, smashed.'

'Because they look right through you,' said Tina, eyes fixed on the blinded angel.

And I felt a pinch, a rare protective ache, because I realized all these words were a poor way of compensating her. As she gives me life – albeit a bizarre, distorting vivacity – I sour her with the dregs of words, of experience. And I was suddenly frantic, eager to atone for myself. The sun was out again. We put on our new Gucci sunglasses. I accelerated off, back to the house.

I have an occupation, my role as tutor to prepare Tina for her autumn Access course. I've taken to it with alacrity, babbling away on anything and everything – the postmodern found object, Freud on Leonardo's narcissism, apotropaic theories, Dali's onanism – she has taken to ceaselessly repeating his quote, 'Her eye resembling her anus'. She gobbles it all up, but clever though she is, her knowledge is spasmodic, barely existent.

She has gleaned a few images of bloodied heads and pickled sharks. With tedious predictability, Charlotte had introduced her to German expressionism and Frida Kahlo. So I insist on some structure. I push Gombrich on her, suggest she take regular trips to the National and pay unfashionable heed to tradition. We begin by shining the torchlight on one work at a time as a way of learning to look, to read closely. Since she will inevitably be swamped with 'issues' of gender and the body at college I begin her on the *Rokeby Venus*, followed by one of Francesca Woodman's photographs, something she will easily respond to.

She makes notes and scribbles away in her special 'red' art notebooks with the Mont Blanc I've bought her (she was forever borrowing mine). The results are, if not rigorous, a little unnerving. To my amazement she adopts a nimble, ludic tone with ease.

Nothing can quite prepare the viewer for the whirlwind of Woodman's imagination. At first glance, *House #4* shows the artist, reminiscent of a teenage Alice in Wonderland, crouched on the floor behind a loose fireplace surround, legs either side of one column, as if trying to wedge herself into the fireplace itself. What we see of the surrounding house – bare floorboards, rubble, peeling wallpaper – suggests an empty, derelict, near-Gothic landscape of fantasy. On either side of the fireplace are the corners of two tall windows, bringing in a strange dazzling light from the outside – from which the figure seems keen to escape. Her blurred head, long ghostly fair hair tangled as if made of cotton wool, lend a feel both playful and sinister, a sense of a scene suspended between memory and present, darkness and light. Her borders are dissolving into the darkness of the fireplace. One has to ask what to make of this blurring, this move into the dark interior of the fireplace.

I tell her, a little astounded, about Woodman's death wish – her suicide. She appears genuinely surprised, even quietly spooked.

At first I wonder if she has copied this but I realize with time that she doesn't plagiarize, she mimics. Having acquired the tone, the voice, by osmosis, she can improvise like an actress. Her memory is as extraordinary as her talent for mimicry. After a while, I devise a game in which I pick out various images (some by artists whose other works we have looked at; others by very similar artists, all mixed in, untitled). I ask her to guess the artist. She is invariably correct on those she has studied. It's an unsettling talent, to absorb, so exactly, a style, voice or eye.

She does not pore over books but into them, as if opening a secret casket. Her hunger for knowledge seems on a par with her avidity for the minutiae of my own history and my being. The other afternoon, she didn't hear me come into the sitting room; a gentle breeze was coming in through the window, the blind's edge nibbled fitfully at the frame. She lay on the sofa, wine glass in one hand, totally focused on the page before her.

'What are you reading?' I asked. She turned, hand over her brow, showing me the cover. 'Ah, Panofsky. *Pandora's Box*. A gem of iconography,' I said.

She read out the inscription on the title page with the stilted solemnity of a child. 'To my darling Belle. Well done. Leo.' Her fingertips caressed the surface of the script. I took the book from her, straightened the glass in her hand. 'Who's Leo?' she asked.

'My dad. He liked us to call him by his name. Not that I did.' Replacing the book on the shelf. 'And if you spill wine on it I'll never forgive you.'

Since then I've sometimes come across her in the sitting room, and she gets up, replacing the book in one sleek move, as if caught accessing forbidden material. I am sure it is the same book, but I pretend not to notice. I wonder if she envies me the gift, the dedication from my father, the memoir from the past, for she appears to own none or carry none herself. Not even a photograph.

It somehow follows that her favourite films feature horrific invasion, in the shape of monsters, grotesque diseases or psychic intrusion. She will insist on watching a film several times, and is able to recite long chunks of dialogue in character. For days I hear her in the corridor perfecting the clipped Scottish-American tones: 'Tonight, Marnie, the door stays open.' She has the instinct of the oddball collector, returning with bizarre acquisitions: old country singles, a collection of anonymous photographs found in a junk shop of a seventies family in an alpine setting, around which we fashion a comic soap opera for one night, high on some powerful skunk she scores from Tania or Dylan in the pub. She has bought the menologium I was reading that afternoon she found me in the junk shop and has become zealously attached to the legend of St Christina. Deeming our Christian names to be effectively the same (itself a source of great mystic import to her), she reads much into the biography of our patron saint.

'I hope we have as many lives. She's like something out of *Cape Fear*, Belle.' Gawping at the book, she flaps her hand. 'Listen. She took her father's gold and silver idols and broke them and gave them to the poor. He had her whipped and thrown in jail and then tied a millstone round her neck and threw her in the river. But she miraculously floated . . .'

'But they got her in the end.'

This evening she comes in later than usual from her day-shift.

'Where have you been, St Christina?' I ask her.

'Getting a bag from Charlotte's.'

But I can't see a bag, unless she's put it in the hall. Registering my suspicion, she says, 'Carl's been sniffing around. She didn't tell him where I was.' But she knows full well that he knows; that there have been several phone calls, cut short when I answer. It smacks of another of her smokescreens.

She is in the kitchen filleting a sea bass. Dagger-like shadows from the sun fall on her back. More and more I see us in those Dutch interiors depicting a dark-garbed mistress and an earthy maid, grabbing for some hanging fowl, surrounded by dead rabbits, game, vegetables, sleeves rolled up for the fecund business of life and death, killing and eating. Tina slices off the head and slides the knife blade expertly into the side of the fish without looking up. Her tone is light. 'Charlotte was mates with an old boyfriend of yours – Richie.'

I retain my pose. 'How curious.'

'And,' she turns to me, knife-hand upraised, 'she knew Lucia, his girlfriend, and then you, you fell out, you took – you went out with him, and . . .' She has uncovered the packed white flesh.

I affect a weary tone. 'And I'm sure she told you I snatched him from Lucia, tortured him and then chucked him, leading him to die of a drug overdose shortly afterwards – oh, anyhow, enough –' I pluck out a grape from a bowl. My fears were grounded; Charlotte is an unwelcome spook. She certainly looks the part.

'Is Lucia the one in the school photo, next to you, the blonde one?'

'Yes, where did you see that? Tina, I really hate people prying, touching my things –' I've knocked back a chair. I storm out of the kitchen into the hall.

She follows, grabbing my arm, her eyes so turbulent they would be disturbing, were her hands not sending up fresh harbour whiffs from the fish. 'Belle, I'm not prying, I'd do anything you asked . . . I . . .'

I smile. 'Stupid,' I say, having restored my tranquillity. I must curb the old fear, deny it any power. But for a few hours I sense her sniffing at unsettled air, as if she'd forgotten something she knew about me. It passes but she knows that it has opened a crack, rather than closed it, that I am perversely half inclined to let her poke around; that I've allotted her an obscure role. Her tactic is bold, using quick, deft strikes. My thing is to hold back, in both enjoying and repulsing the probing, and then to counter-attack.

She sits cross-legged on the floor in front of the sofa, cogitating, sucking greedily at our third joint. Something troubles her. A thought is scuttling slowly across her face.

After a while she says, 'Why did you come to Ladbroke Park, Belle?' I sense she means, why did I marry Jake.

'As my father likes to quote, "The desires of the heart are as crooked as corkscrews." We have to thwart ourselves a little, or else what would we do, how could we want?'

'I don't get it,' she says. 'Are you in love with him? Jake?'

'He's old-fashioned. He's honourable. He makes me feel safe.' The last word comes out with too much drama, like a lifejacket in a storm. I resume my customary irony. 'You'll realize the people who excite you are never usually much good for you. Like fizzy drinks.'

Tina's eyes narrow. 'Not as bad for you as people who don't excite you.'

'Perhaps the truth is that he actually puts up with me, calms me.'

'Calms you? You make him sound like your flippin' doctor.' A thick lock of hair falls angrily over her face. 'Calm you! Most of them are serial killers!'

'He's a dermatologist. It's part of his appeal. Doctor Jake. He has faith in finding a cure. I believe he has a long-term plan for my good, filed somewhere in his medical brain – to smooth my psychic blemishes, make me – human, bake him tofu pies. You see, I come from booze-soaked Bohemia while he is hyper-real, the fruit of reproduction furniture, sparkling sheeny floors, lawns and vices trimmed and clipped. His mother, Mrs Fellner, told me, "Of course, it did surprise me. He was such a shy, lanky thing. His brother was the live wire".' I turn, handing Tina the joint. 'His brother legged it to San Francisco to run a range of gay sex supermarkets . . . the truth is that Jake has superhuman patience.'

'You don't suit that name – Fellner.'

'That's Jake's surname. Mine is Rose. What's yours by the way?'

She has a way of wetting her lips with the drink before taking a proper gulp, as if considering her next move. 'Vaughn.

Mmmm. Rose – that's much prettier. Christabel Rose, sounds like a country-and-western singer.'

'Or a cheap perfume. Anyhow, it's a relief to take on a new identity.'

Her face closes down, turns bafflingly mean. She clicks, repeatedly, at her lighter, before asking, 'How'd you ever get it on then?'

I laugh. 'The first time, it was a summer evening, and I hadn't switched on the lights. I was drunk. I told him not to speak to me, to fuck me quickly from behind, to leave my clothes half on. Mind you, on our honeymoon, in Morocco, despite the opulence of the Mamounia, the sultriness, he said he hated the wailing from the mosque. He's a perfectionist; he art-directs his breakfast, his wardrobe, sex.'

'So what rocks his boat?'

'My neck, pale, arched just so. Until . . .'

'Yeuch. Like a vampire . . .'

'No, no, he doesn't bite. He likes to look, to look at my neck in particular . . . that's why he bought me the Graff diamond pendant. Cost a small fortune. He used to like me to keep that on. And as he looks at it, I imagine, he has some fantasy that he's tied to some stake, being made to watch –'

'YOU being fucked in two orifices by two faceless men – one black, one white, with SERIOUS cocks – one in your mouth, one in your arse.' She draws heavily on her joint. 'One of them comes – semen spurting all over your lovely necklace.' She hands the joint over. 'You've just got nothing on except long black boots with very sharp heels –'

'You should do porn for a living –'

Tina's skunked eyes film over, their slant dramatically low and louche. I guess, I know – she has fucked for money. Her eyes catch fire, green against the stoned redness. She comes over to sit by me.

'Let's go there. Morocco,' she says.

'I'll take you.'

'Promise? Just us.' She has turned me to grip both my arms tightly, nearly tilting us both over the sofa.

'Promise. God knows you'll drive those Arabs bonkers with that hair.'

The phone rings.

I leave it, thinking it might be Jake, not wanting him to hear my stoned voice. The answerphone clicks on. A gnashing roar, a pub noise, but no voice. We wait. Tina lies back, arms crossed behind her head. Then a savage cutting-off at the other end.

I say, 'It's Carl. Tell him to stop.'

'No, it'll make him worse.'

'I don't want it, him, in my house.'

She looks up towards the sofa with heavy-lidded knowingness. 'You asked me in . . . anyhow, how serious is it?'

'What?'

'Jake's dick.'

'Oh, normal.'

She clings to forgotten conversations from nights before. Her strategy will be to begin with questions about art ('This morbidezza . . . is it a sort of tone? How can Matisse's colour be form then?'). From these she will somehow attempt a link to a more personal domain ('Is that what Morocco's like then, colour more than form?'). I continue musing aloud, opening drawers of the self barely opened, but in our anonymous, drugged intimacy, without fear of judgement, I have the illusion of a suspended, ethereal peace in a house whose windows have no glass, no outside. It's as if her young self, bold but so precariously at the cliff-face, must find footholds to cling to in my hidden fissures.

Tonight, I returned from a spirit-sapping rare evening out

with my brother and his wife to find her asleep on my bed, the photograph of my mother from downstairs lying beside her. The ashtray on the bed overflowed with dead joints and half-extinguished fags. (It's simply a matter of time before she starts a fire or some minor explosion.) She must have been up there for some time, lolling in my white silk pyjamas, lapels strewn with ash. I recalled that first night she lay on the sofa with the arc of lamplight on her soiled, burnished gold hair. Her eyes fluttered groggily open. She picked up the photograph. Her tone was incidental, drawling, as if she had been carrying on a stoned conversation with me for the whole night. She put the photo down, turned her head to face the window, away from the glare cast by the bedside lamp. I picked up the photo and clutched it with an open hand against my stomach, rubbing the smudge off the glass to look. I tried to register her features, but as always, they began to bleach out, prickles of frustration burning my eyelids.

She said, 'She's fair. My mum was dark. When she came back from the hospital her hair wasn't shiny any more. Never.'

And this is how any of her history, or story, reveals itself, in the smoky warp and weft of her digressions. This much I've gathered: a scraping-by sort of life in the capital's far-flung northern suburbs, names I associate with the end of the tube line. Shopping mall, the bookies, huge pubs on roundabouts with psychopathic bouncers, teenage troilism in the Asda car park. The mother has been dead now for seven or eight years, of an 'overdose of her medication' – blamed on the stupidity of doctors. There was a stepfather, I gather from reluctant replies to my questions. Bob, an ex-army man turned grocer and newsagent, blanked, forgotten; a younger half-brother, 'the Mall Rat' by name, from that union, living somewhere unspecified in Scotland. Her real father had left when Tina was three. 'I don't see him now,' she said with finality. Dates, ages, places lived in, all vague and contradicted. Not a ruse, I think, but a habit of lying as a life strategy, and an acute fear of being pinned down or labelled. ('I don't want to be on any computers,' she moans, when I suggest she order something on the net.) She will often tell the truth as a deliberate tactic, as a way of making you doubt and lead you to a different conclusion. And who, after all, doesn't manipulate their story? But then, a wrong epithet or teasing assessment of her will send her off into injured hauteur for hours. 'That is not me,' she hisses, the autocratic blaze of those eyes always suggesting some extraterrestrial genes.

Of recent history there's more detail. She left school at seventeen, after her mother's death, worked in pubs, waitressed, sold a bit of dope, moved in the clubbing scenes of Ibiza, the warehouse parties of East London. People were 'losing the plot – on ketamine, hallucinatin' on this and that'. Then, 'I shut the door' (she is fond of reincarnations; the cliché of the shut door: 'I had to leave it behind, Belle'). Hence the move west across the city to Ladbroke Park. Carl seems to crop up quite early on. I sense a curious reluctance to rid herself entirely of him; a taut, hostile bond, as irreversible as that between siblings or old conspirators. And then, being assiduously loved is a habit more binding than most.

Carl may be at the bottom of Tina's fitful relationship with her mobile. She has stopped her customary peering and scowling at it and has lately taken to switching it off. Just occasionally, she forgets, and a phone call will send her out to the street, where she will pace up and down, shoulders shuddering with cold, in convoluted argument, for ages. I watch her through the crack in the blind. At times, her gestures seem curiously businesslike, all swift, punctuating nods, as if arrangements were being made, times being altered.

Sometimes, I wake to the slow splatter of murmurs on the other side of the bedroom separating us. The phone calls to my landline have stopped. A couple of envelopes have come through the door for her, which she quickly stuffs into her back pocket. Whether skunk, charlie or love notes, I've no way of telling. If anything, she barely mentions Carl, and usually returns home straight after her evening shift. We drink, smoke, sniff, talk, read, watch DVDs into the late hours – gathering in on ourselves with the intensity of hideaways or the last of some excommunicated race.

Jake has delayed his arrival twice. Not that it matters. Yellow light collects in corners of the house with the arrival of May. Life unfurls itself with the ease of a pampered cat. We wake late and in the afternoons, after a few errands, I stay in the cool, north-facing sitting room, preparing notes to guide Tina's studies and occasionally, for any future research for me. But Tina's studies seem to have effortlessly taken preference.

Tina has been weeding and clearing the garden with the vague aim of loitering there on hotter days. But it's back-breaking work. I need to call in a gardener. The spare rooms remain closed, the dining room too, but when I mention calling in the builders Tina always protests. I have to say, I agree. We have both taken to switching our mobiles off most of the time.

I like the sound of her singing. Many of the lyrics are far older than her, drawn from scraps of distant memory, from other people's memories. Her current favourite is the song about the Rhinestone Cowboy. Hearing her humming and yodelling, she sounds pure and contrived all at once. Even now, I can't fathom whether her adoration is wholehearted or manipulative. Like her wardrobe, she is full of the gifts and cast-offs of others.

Tina is excited. In her hand is a seventies soft-porn sci-fi video. Helga is a forbidding nurse in a nameless clinic with a taste for inflicting gratuitous pain on vulnerable young women –

whether patients or trainee nurses remains unclear – whom she hypnotizes, seduces and then pimps to businessmen who turn out to be aliens. (That too is perhaps our own invention.) Candy, a slinky submissive waif, becomes Helga's principal sex slave and major money-earner. Much happens that is an excuse for triadic sex in various permutations (except anal; I inform her that 'anal' became the big thing from the late 1980s onwards. 'The things you know, Belle,' she says sarcastically). In the end, Helga kills Candy accidentally by electrocuting her on a strange contraption in the clinic used to pound orgasmic electric currents into her patients.

Over the next few evenings we take photographs as Helga and Candy (frequently exchanging roles) on the brand-new digital camera Jake bought for me. We surprise each other in the bath, take moody Vermeer-like profiles by the window as mournful sex captives in the clinic. We use the self-timer. Finally, we take turns on the Jacobean chair in various states of undress, wearing our black boots, tied up with rope and shreds of old curtains, in imitation of the orgasmic electro-cution. We place ourselves in front of the long bedroom mirror. We show off, out-miming and out-gasping each other. Our excitement intensifies under our unified, eager reflections. As if there were four of us in the room watching: I, she, my reflection and hers. And a fifth, a fifth presence to provoke. We both agree it's a bizarre but powerful turn-on as we click through the images on my laptop which she has comman-deered and taken into her room. We look absurdly young – even me – with the slant-eyed, sluttish disdain of tipsy school-girls in photo booths.

It was probably something to do with being Out There. Today I realized that our peace is made of fragile filaments, easily torn by exposure to third parties.

We finally made it to the gym – I wanted Tina to accompany

me; if anything, to entice me back. As she pounded heavily on the treadmill, watching MTV, wisps of hair escaping from her headphones, I watched a man's eyes on the next treadmill compulsively drawn to the flesh on her upper arms as they blushed rose with sweat; his sidelong glance sliding to the tips of her jumping breasts. Men's eyes burn with a sort of gnawing despair, nibbling hungrily at small, fugitive sections of her. I'm not resentful. If anything, it sends a charge through me – more so when she is wearing my clothes.

In the changing room she was her usual brazen self – no, more exaggerated, parading around naked, pert tits in the air, not dressing for ages. Her designs on me are born of habit. She can't understand not being clawed at, or groped into bed by anyone, including women. It's her currency, her mode of exchange, barter and control. But she can't pin down the exact nature of my interest. So perhaps her subsequent behaviour would have some obscure connection to this. I'm still unsure.

Once we were showered and changed, I stopped at reception. I asked the receptionist for a joining form. 'Name?' said the receptionist. I said, 'Tina . . . Vaughn.' I turned. 'Tina, you'd better fill it in.'

Her face furled in, mouth clamping. 'Another time.' She turned to go and I touched her arm.

'Come on, Tina – two minutes. My treat.' She smashed back into the wall, eyes darting with hostility, hands clutching her rucksack. I waved goodbye to the receptionist as if to say, 'Another time.' We were silent on the way to the car. She may have been angry that her brazenness failed to seduce me. (I studiedly ignored her.) Or it may have had something to do with being 'pinned down'. Perhaps she has a record of some kind, for drugs or theft, and her paranoid mind thinks it will ping up on every computer. I didn't bring up the subject and she rushed off to work earlier than usual.

*

Suzy turns up unexpectedly after an early dinner with a friend. 'I thought I'd drop in since you never go out these days. I see you haven't called the builders back.'

'It's Tina. She's a wonderfully bad influence.'

'I saw her in The Castle. I must say it's quite funny, how fast she got in.'

'It's my house; if it doesn't work out, she's cool.'

'People are never that easy to discard – not even au pairs. As you well know from . . . it's just that she clearly idolizes you –' Suzy puts her wine glass down with finality. 'I give up. I'm going to have a fag. I can't hold out any longer, not when you're at it like a revamped chimney.' Grasping one greedily from my packet, she exhales, calms down, adding breezily, 'It would just make me feel dreadful having a gorgeous young thing around.'

'Actually I enjoy watching her, it's easier on the eye than looking at myself. And I like watching men watching her, helplessly dragged by all that sexual suction.'

'This one seems to use it all right.'

'I don't much care, maybe I like her to use a little.' I savour Suzy's unease, stoke it further. 'I'm atoning for my empty existence by allowing some beautiful ragamuffin to have a slice of the pie.'

'To be led by the nose, more like. She might be after your Julien Macdonald dress *and* your husband. Both.'

The door slams shut on our ensuing laughter. Tina's head appears round the door, her hair shimmering with silvery raindrops. I am woozy with drink, but her presence sparks my edges, incites me to anarchy.

'Check out dem proper skets.' She throws off her denim jacket. 'Got the sensamilla here.' She is frowning, hiding her nervousness of Suzy's presence behind the Jafaican babble. Her eyes are zigzagging all over the place; not a few lines have been snorted.

'You roll it, I'm shit. Come and sit over here. Look at that sparkling hair.'

Suzy is acknowledged with a quick nod. 'All right?'

'Yes,' replies Suzy's mechanically smiling mouth. 'How are you?'

Tina responds by bending over and scraping my hair. 'You eat dat dere salad I made?' she asks. But she seems trapped, cornered, breathing in strange rhythms. I think of this afternoon in the gym. She rises to fetch more wine.

Suzy makes a point of waiting for Tina's return before asking, 'So, what will YOU be wearing for the wedding? Jonty still has a soft spot for you. God, he still bangs on about how alluring and mysterious you are and so forth.'

'Like some dark chocolate ad,' I say, yawning.

'By the way, he invited us to his party at the Medusa Club.'

I flop back on the sofa, roll my eyes childishly. 'No bloody way. Rather sniff glue for a hobby, thank you, than hang out with Brideshead Regurgitated.'

'Actually, he has all kinds of friends . . . well, you don't have to come.' Suzy looks as if she has been whipped by an impertinent child. 'I think Paddy is going.'

'Paddy? I can see him any time I like.' I sit up, surprised. Seated at the floor, rolling a joint at the coffee table, Tina catches on to the move.

'Yes. But perhaps it's just as well you don't see each other.' Suzy's tone is full of dark underlining. We are all three seated in a triangular formation around the table, lit dimly by a lamp behind the sofa which condenses the friction. Bubble, bubble, toil and trouble.

'Actually,' I say, 'I saw him quite recently – you were there – at the gallery.'

'Oh yeah, mon, Paddy mon, he call,' says Tina.

'There is a pad beside the phone, Teeeena dahlink. Can we have a bit of a break from the patois?'

Suzy cuts in. 'I thought about asking him to Nick's fortieth; but perhaps not.'

Tina suddenly lies full-length on the floor as if to blank us out. I reel her back in, aware of a distortion in her face. 'What Suzy wants to suggest, Tina, is that Paddy and I have a History . . .'

'If I do a surprise party, though, I must say the thought of all his Old Harrovian chums is a bit oppressing,' continues Suzy.

'Oppressive?' suggests Tina, standing and stretching herself on my sofa so her head is close to my lap as she smokes. I stroke her hair as I take the spliff from her.

'Oh yes, perhaps.' Suzy's eyes wobble furiously in their sockets. 'I couldn't wait to get away from my school. Two baths a week, ugly old dykey form mistresses. Where did you go to school, Tina?'

'Young Offenders' Institution . . .'

I begin coughing up the huge toke.

Suzy says, 'Which reminds me, I need a new babysitter. Tina, do you know anyone?'

'No, 'fraid I don't.' Her mood has curdled again. She pounces, as if to leave.

I reach out my arm to hold hers, still cackling at Suzy's comical links. 'Don't go. Oh, do J'Lo. She's a brilliant mimic, Suzy.'

'You should go on *Stars in Their Eyes*,' says Suzy, casting a full eye over Tina's upright figure. 'They're pretty boots, Tina.'

Tina flashes her row of tiny opalescent teeth. 'Don't you recognize them? They're Belle's. Sick, innit?'

We both watch her leave. I relieve Suzy of her confusion. '"Sick" means fabulous.'

Suzy's bracelets jiggle into life. 'I can't keep up. I take it Jake will be around for this wedding? Does he know about Tina?'

'Know? Know? Of course!' I almost splutter. 'Though there's

nothing to "know" about. And no, he doesn't actually "know" her as in breaking bread at The Ivy sort of knowing. Not been back since she's been here, actually.'

But I am flattened, irritable without Tina in the room. Suzy begins gathering her bag abruptly. 'I'd better go. I'll see myself out.' Her censorious scuttle provokes in me a helpless mirth. I hear her close the door behind her.

Tina's room is dark though I hear her quietly muttering. I go straight in, still laughing. Lying naked in the tepid darkness, one arm bent over her face, she is all glazed, dark statuary, the ripple of hair a carved outline. I quicken at the sight, not at her nakedness, but at the stillness. Yet as I come close up, her entire body pulsates, lit by some fitful flame. Then Suzy's voice comes out at me from the darkness. 'Where did you go to school, Tina? Dissin' old cow, always some message in there – yeah, and you play up to it, don't you, Belle? I'm not a performing monkey.'

'Well, don't act like one. Oh, come on. She's envious.' Her face is in shadow. She smells a little of custard.

'Oh yeah, what of?' she asks, raising herself on one elbow suspiciously.

'Your youthful beauty. God knows. As she sips her peppermint tea, she lusts for bloodfests, lunatic copulation, ripe young flesh – like all us elderly people from Ladbroke Park. Anyhow, she happens to be my friend.'

Breaking out into a mocking cackle, Tina rises. Both arms stretched out like a go-go dancer's, she lets out a funky bass yelp. She begins to dance, palms up, singing of burning disco infernos. I leave her to it.

Holding myself against the basin, clumsily guiding the electric toothbrush, my face refuses to focus on itself, lines fade and reshape. Bumping against every solid object in my bedroom as I try to remove my clothes, I suddenly recall not having locked up. Back out on the landing, Tina stands in the gloom, her back against the wall as if trying to recede into it, head stretched sideways, eyes averted from the corridor, the floor. As I reach out, she starts, swallows. In the shadows, her face – eyes tightly closed, her hair sticking flat to her head with sweat – it is the face of a corpse underwater. For an instant, I am sucked into a swirling fear with her. I blink, fumble for the hall light behind me. 'What is it?' In the sharp light, she droops, a deflated doll, her eyes flat, avoiding the landing around her, turning into themselves. 'Felt weird, had a whitey for a minute.' I flinch from a slack, beseeching need in her. She tenses at my mood, mumbling, 'Zac had some ketamine at work. Makes me get vertigo with the skunk.'

But why does it occur to my befuddled mind that she's been candid, as always, to throw sand in my eyes? That it's nothing to do with the drugs.

6

I'm pacing my bedroom, half-dressed, smoking. I pick up the empty champagne glass on my dressing table. 'Time for a top-up. Go on, go fetch.' I smack her bottom with the back of my hand. She stands glowering at me. I say, 'Here, look. If you go and get it for me, you can have a pair of knickers.' I open the drawer for her, running my hand over the surface of the textures. 'Choose. Many-hued, a silken treasure trove of knickers and bras from Argentovivo, La Perla, Moschino . . .'

She glances down, opens the drawer and says, 'Gee, thanks!' She fingers the underwear, picks up a garment here and there, letting it drop back in contemptuously. 'Spoilt bitch.' Her finger brushes along the velvet jewellery box. I open it and pick up the diamond pendant, holding it up to her neck.

We're both standing in front of the dressing-table mirror, looking at ourselves, me behind her, my hand holding the pendant round her neck. My hair seems to have grown, nearly reaching my shoulders. The perfume bottles, diamond, candle are all darkly vibrant, rippling under my coked-up gaze. Tina also is brilliant, enamelled. I am underexposed, tarnished. Behind us, the bed linen falls in crumpled thick grey cascades. (I never seem to bother making it any more.) In the mirror, she shoots me a look of wary tension, as if reading my mind. I'm unsure whether to mention Jake's imminent arrival at the last moment, or now, earlier in the night.

Ideally, I would like her out of the house. I don't want them to meet: not only does she resent people who have some claim on me but I can't rely on her discretion in front of Jake. She will deliberately make references to charlie and skunk, say too much, be too much. The truth is I don't trust her, or at least, not her unpredictability. She moves over to his dressing table, which is less crowded, to chop up the coke on a CD cover she is holding. 'No more,' I say, 'in case Jake notices. He's back tomorrow evening. Now we're not even hungry enough for dinner.'

She ignores me, snuffles up her line. 'Don't worry. I'll be staying with Tania from The Castle while he's around.' And I suddenly feel bereft, irate, as if Jake were a tyrant, the intruder. 'I wish,' I say, and stop. I don't want to say that I wish he'd stay away longer. She has a knack of reading my thoughts. She tries on her kaftan for the umpteenth time. Then mine. For Morocco, she says, stroking it.

At the same time, over on the plasma, the Prime Minister is giving a speech about the latest foiled bombing attempt. Apparently, they caught them yesterday. I haven't watched television or bought a paper for days. 'He looks like a cornered rabbit,' says Tina, as we share the last line. 'Let's get out of this grotty hole, Belle – go and live in Morocco. We could do it, Belle. Dylan told me it's dirt cheap.' Morocco has become both a mantra and a storybook destination. The mere mention of the word inspires her with the zealous fire of angels. In her considered opinion, Jake will hardly notice us gone.

I am at the bedroom door watching Jake sift tentatively through his things. Usually, he returns and folds things away neatly, in their proper place, before anything else. But this evening he's not simply unpacking and folding but methodically emptying out the drawers, one by one, on the bed and redoing them.

When he finishes this, he turns to the top of the chest. (I wince, watching him rub at the surface with his finger, in case he picks up on any coke crumbs which may have fallen off the surface of the CD.) He stands, inspecting the view in puzzlement for a while, before moving on to rearrange his cufflinks in their small wooden box. Now it's the turn of his brush and comb, his aftershave. Time for the wardrobe. He opens the door, hangs up his jeans and trousers, his shirts from his tote bag, but as he does so, he automatically lifts every hanger in there and replaces it. All this he does quickly, efficiently, but with shoulders tautly raised, alert to the minute changes in the air, the tinny echo of hanger on bar. Though Tina is out, working, I am in the febrile morning-after state, keen to get out of the house as if it were strewn with forensic evidence. I go downstairs, unable to bear it any longer in the bedroom. 'I'm tired,' he says when he comes down. 'Can we stay in, have a Japanese takeaway?'

I steer him to the sitting room. (It's darker in there.) Jake has some news. The funding for the three extra clinics is about to be given the green light. He is chirpy, hyper for him. But I tense up as he halts in mid-sentence and begins a careful scrutiny of my face, hoping his medical eye won't notice some stray white coke grain working its way down my nostril. Or something else, some alteration.

'Are you growing your hair on purpose?' he asks.

'No, a little . . .' I touch the ends of the hair round my neck.

'You've had the same style since I've known you.' His pale mouth attempts a smile but his brow reveals a puzzled mind, ruminating on the issue long after his reason has dispensed with it.

'So don't you like it?' I say, handing him the tray of sushi.

He ignores the food and looks again carefully up and down my hair. I make an effort – with a ridiculous rictus grin. Finally he says softly, persuasively, 'It's fine, but at the bottom, it used to hit your neck in this feathery way. She cut it perfectly.' He speaks strategically, elusively.

I remember – of course, he likes to see my neck. 'That's

because I haven't been to get it trimmed for ages. You've just reminded me.'

He drops his gaze, brow smoothed, working on the chopsticks as if he were holding precision instruments. Night is drawing in. We have grown silent. Somewhere in the house, a door slams. He jumps a little. 'That reminds me. Shouldn't we be seeing about getting a burglar alarm?'

'Yes, yes, but since we need builders around soon . . .'

'I think it would be a good idea. With people coming in and out.'

'Oh, I wouldn't worry. She's hardly ever here. And I'll keep forgetting to turn it on.'

'I'll see to it while I'm here,' he says gently, firmly.

I wake to hear the front door closing and an unusual pattern of treads on the stairs, the swish of her door, a stealthy click. I hear soft hissings. A cough, not Tina's, a muffled laugh. She's not alone. The sharp click of a lighter. Piqued into angry alertness, I listen, compelled. Rustle of clothing, joints banging, escaped moans. A fast, suffocated sigh. This continues for an interminable time, until I fancy I hear a final exhaled moan. After a click, a soft padding down the corridor (whoever it is going downstairs has no shoes on), the front door closes very gently. I listen out but cannot hear a car. She is doing this on purpose, because of Jake. Is he pretending to be asleep? I feel a fast, steady beat in my cunt. Anger grinds circularly for hours around my head and eventually I fall asleep at dawn.

The morning has too much of that blinding, sunless, silver-yellow glare as I enter the kitchen in my dressing gown and put on the coffee. Jake sits at the table, cutting his toast in four, scraping the marmalade off the edges. I open the French doors. 'It's like a furnace in here.'

'Garden still a mess I see,' he says, nodding his head towards the doors. As usual with Jake, he corrects any implied criticism, leavens it with humour, as a form of further underlining it. 'Frankly, after LA it makes a refreshing change to be in the Congo.'

'I thought I might leave it to you, darling.'

'Am I never going to meet our house guest? Where is she?' He is toying with me, aware that his curiosity is unwelcome. 'Perhaps you've made it up. Perhaps it's really a man staying here,' he banters, taking a bite of his toast.

I begin unloading the dishwasher, just to make a noise. 'How *did* you guess, darling? Oh, she's off doing young things with her young friends, I expect.' I have already noticed her door open. She must have left last night. It was a wind-up, deliberate. I was right about her unpredictability, her vein of spite.

'Why, do you fancy her?' I ask him.

'Blondes aren't my thing.' He is standing behind me now. The teacup I am holding slips from my hands, drops, rolling on the work surface.

'Losing your grip,' says Jake, keeping his gaze on me as his hand reaches out to stop it as it rings and pings but doesn't, finally, break.

Of course, I was never, I realize, going to ring Jonty about bringing Tina. It's a predictably swanky affair at Medusa's, the members' club. At a long bar lit by a row of orange bulbs, a whole line of barmen pour pink drinks. The throng clots and unclots on to the numerous floors, mezzanines and private rooms where small groups take coke in ostentatious privacy. Minor rock stars mingle with minor aristocrats and minor celebrities. There are many people I haven't seen for quite a few years. Hair thins, skin grows gradually suety in the heat. I need a drink. I'm wearing a black vintage Balenciaga dress Jake bought me in LA: a look that I can wear like armoury – and the diamond pendant. Jake looks pleased, though I've yet to get my hair cut. He's already being accosted by women. They idealize him as the noble, sagacious doctor-husband, in stark contrast to their boy-men. Nappy rash, candidiasis, there is nothing they won't ask about as a decoy, a preamble to more hushed queries about facelifts or liposuction. (He is always ineffably polite, pointing out that cosmetic surgery is not his field, but that never puts them off.) I'm in the mood for riotous types like Paddy, but I can't find him. Suzy catches up with me, tottering in diamanté heels, cocktail in hand. 'Olivia just said you're looking divine. She wants to know the secret.'

'She's probably implying that Jake's pumping me full of free collagen.'

We climb some rickety back stairs up to a small, dimly lit room with velvet curtains and a large, round dining table in the middle with a white cotton tablecloth, littered with half-drunk champagne flutes, a vase of tall, spiky flowers, a tray of glazed prawns. At one end of the table sits a young woman, her long brown hair falling in a curtain from her back-arched head, her retroussé nose twitching like a pretty little rodent's. She's just done a line from the bare table surface. And there is Carl, next to her, sitting astride a chair, his insolent pebble-eyes stopping on me. His stare has a mask-like rigidity, no hint of self-questioning. A sense, not quite a recollection, of vaulting coldness, travels through me.

'Ah, Carl darling, sorry, I'm back now. Christabel, this is Carl, Tina's –'

'I know who he is. Hello.'

'I know who you are as well,' he says quietly. He gets up, turns the gold chair round to sit on it properly, his block-body leaning back so it screeches thinly beneath him. He turns to the girl, who is still busy with her nose, holding a finger up to close one nostril to ensure a clearer nasal passage. He continues, in a surprisingly persuasive, soft voice, on the topic of

Dark Matter. He's taking his time about not producing the coke for Suzy, relying on the politeness of his audience. 'It's got a mass nine times bigger than the mass of our whole universe but it's not accessible to us, see.'

'I saw that programme,' I say, seating myself next to Suzy, opposite him.

'What programme? I never saw no programme.' I receive a fast flick of contempt from his drug-hoppy eyes, all the harsher against the sandstone blondness of his colouring. He goes on in his caressing lilt, 'But you see, it's not the same as black holes . . .' The girl's face is on him but her mind is a feather floating elsewhere, wafting on a breeze of serotonin. Her strappy orange dress accentuates that wan frailness Jake fancies. Only her eyes are alive, coke-wild. She gets up slowly, touching his shoulder, mumbling beneath her veil of hair. 'Better go. Been here far too long. Thanks for that. Name's Camilla.' She is hesitating, one foot out of her shoe scratching at her leg.

Fixing her solemnly, he asks, 'What you doing later? Like later, later. There's a party after my friend's gig. The Change-lings. Heard of 'em? Portobello Hotel in a suite.'

Her skinny shoulder blades open and shut by way of assent. Carl pulls a phone from the outside pocket of his shiny-denim designer jacket. It's an exact replica of Tina's. The girl gives him her number, and while he takes his time keying it in, she casts a vapid half-smile at us, as if registering us for the first time.

'See ya.' She lopes off. I have the sensation of having been the audience to a demonstration on his part – for Tina's ears, perhaps.

He turns to face Suzy, sitting opposite him. I'm perched to her right. He reaches slowly into his inside pocket for a small square plastic bag and hands it to her with needless furtive ceremony. Several wraps are inside. So it must be Carl who supplies Tina. His hand lingers briefly on Suzy's. 'Two in there. Good rocky stuff.'

'Carl, thank you. The money – I'll find Nick.' He presses his hand tighter on Suzy's, looking her intently in the eye. 'Don't worry. Sort me out Monday, yeah? At yours.' He's now taking a small wrap out of his pocket. 'Line?'

Suzy wiggles her shoulders, giggling. 'Gaggin' for it.' He finally pauses to look at me and I realize why his eyes are so hard: they don't seem to reflect light. They are eyes that give you back no shade, no reflection of yourself; only his view. 'One for you?'

'No, thank you,' I say crisply.

He raises his blond brows. 'No? You sure? On our best behaviour tonight, are we?' He points his head at my diamond pendant. 'Got the tiara to go with that?'

Suzy titters. 'She's very regal, our Chrissy.'

He looks over my neck, down to my arm holding the champagne, and intones, like a cracked preacher, very softly, 'And decked with gold and precious stones and pearls, having a golden cup in her hand full of abominations . . .' His is a private, mirthless snigger of a laugh. Despite being work-roughened by physical labour, he has long, deft fingers. He looks at the table. 'No room here,' and with one arm flat on the table, swipes back, scrunching the tablecloth away towards one end. The vase nearly spills over, its long flowers, birds of paradise, falling beady-eyed in shock. Glasses clink against one another, the tray of prawns tilts precariously on the edge. He works with taunting slowness, swishing his card up and down on top of a note, then forming very strange thick lines, pointed at the end.

'So talking of hoes, how's Ms Devlin – I meant Ms Vaughn.'

'She's working, I think.'

He shakes his head. 'Oh no. Tonight she all trash 'n' ready, she think she going to wedding partee, but your mon, he cum back to da crib.' He resumes his normal voice. 'Since you're in close touch, maybe you could mention my two John Smedley jumpers, oh, and the Diesel leather jacket.' He arches a brow at Suzy. 'And three hundred and fifty quid.'

'Wouldn't do for me to get involved.'

His face forms a mask of pantomime incredulity.

'Something seems to bother you,' I say, lighting up calmly with his lighter.

He makes a point of taking the lighter back. 'Oh no, I think it's mahhhvellous, you taking her in hand like that. Such a bright, pretty little thing, isn't she?' He turns to Suzy, as if to bat me away. 'D'you know this place has had a fire twice in its history? Used to be a brothel, then summat else, then, when it was a brothel again, another fire. But get this . . .' He is making a meal of offering her one of the lines, dangling the moment, subtly reducing her to the status of a waiting dog. 'Exactly a hundred and twenty years apart, same day.'

'No!' exclaims Suzy, as if he'd just revealed the whereabouts of God, as she dives down for the offering.

'Yeah. But don't worry,' he chortles blackly, 'tonight you're in luck. You've still got two years, one month to go.' He sniffs up his own in one efficient scoop, his face coming up hard and smug as if triumphant from a ruckus. He folds the wrap, puts it away, and stands rubbing his stomach beneath his t-shirt to expose his toned, hairless belly. I catch a whiff of flint and tar beneath the light cologne. 'Well, be'ter tings to do,' he says, getting up (it's one of Tina's valedictions). 'It's their comeback gig.' At the door, his smile radiates angelic irony. His is the kind of cool that rarely permits itself a true smile. 'Hasta la vista.'

'What's he doing here?' I ask Suzy when he's gone.

'What do you think? Delivering our charlie. Cute, huh?'

His head reappears round the door. 'Left my lighter.' He enters and picks up his Zippo from the table, stroking the surface with his thumb. 'Carry on, ladies.' He leaves a second time.

Suzy begins gabbling. 'Nick says he's great – he is – fabulous – doing the children's bathroom and the floor of the sitting room – great on detail – God, this stuff's strong or maybe I've just forgotten what it was like – sure you don't want some?'

'Not fair really. Jake doesn't take it.'

'Very noble of you,' she says doubtfully.

'He must have offered to come so he could check on Tina.'

'Why on earth would she be here? She doesn't even know Jonty!' Suzy splutters indignantly. Now she casts avidly about the room for some explanation. 'No, no, he's just being nice. Nick could put some good work his way – mind you, he does rather bang on about Tina – how she's light-fingered and unstable . . . you never know what to believe, do you?' There's much to-do with her small velvet handbag until she finally fishes out a compact and begins a pecking scrutiny of her face.

'He's jealous. He spends half his time stalking her,' I say.

'Stuff and nonsense! So why does she ring him when he's working at mine? Oh, who cares about them! Let's find Paddy. I saw him with Eva Hussein earlier – d'you know, she's actually very sweet, definitely not the monster they make her out to be in the press . . .'

Clapping the compact shut, sniffing as if at a job well done, Suzy leads the way up some rickety back stairs. We find Paddy in a small library room at the top of the club. His features are blearily swollen, his eyes clouded, his mouth shapeless with gurning. There's a spot of blood on one white cuff; the other is smeared with ash. He drawls incoherently by way of a greeting, nearly knocking me over with a prolonged embrace. Over his shoulder I spy Jake in the doorway and wink awkwardly at him. On the library table beside him, there are five lines of coke in five dusty, winding paths over a biography of Gladstone. It's bound to be Paddy's gear. People always lig off him.

When I disengage myself, Jake has disappeared. Around the table are four men I don't recognize; all dressed in the androgynous raffish chic of young artists, all bent over the coke with weaselly expectation. Standing, his hair bathed in sweat, is a half-familiar face delivering a rapid-fire monologue. 'I mean, the thing is, you know, it's like we're fucked, finished, and they know it. Whole city, right, we gotta put one thing each in a huge bin in Trafalgar Square, thing we most value . . . bin it . . . that would be the concept –'

I sneak away with relief. I haven't spoken to Paddy of his financial problems. Somehow, I can't face it now. There's Jake, standing very straight-backed like a benign guard against the bar rabble, a woman gabbling drunkenly at his side, her hat a thin silk torpedo with a feather at the top, aimed ominously at his right eye. As he introduces me, he contracts his brow at me in comic distress. I squeeze his arm, grateful for his sanity.

'Ah, I assumed you were in for the long haul with Paddy.'

'He's out of it. Let's go.' He passes his fingertips quickly over my bare arm and traces the line of my dress collar.

'Fine by me,' says Jake, taking pen and paper from the drunken woman who is having trouble matching up one with the other while simultaneously pushing up her errant dress straps.

'You're sure, now, you're sure he's better than Dr Eakin, I can't go through that again, I really can't, he's a sadist as many gynaecologists are, aren't they? Why on earth would a man want to poke about in there . . . ?' She takes breath.

'I guarantee he's the best. It's been a pleasure,' he says, shaking her hand firmly and cupping it with his other hand, as if she were a pillar of dignity.

I'm switching on the laptop downstairs in the sitting room; it's the middle of the night. It lights up with a grotesque fairground jingle in the silence. Wood croaks somewhere by way of response. My ears strain out towards the darkness in case Jake has heard. I must delete the photographs.

When he asked to borrow my laptop to check his emails he must have caught something of my panic as I ran up the stairs: 'I'll get it.' As I'd got it, I'd realized with relief that Tina had not been in all night. Good. Vaguely apprehensive as he took it into the sitting room, I made the two mint teas. I heard the relentless clicks as I approached, heard the machine's hot breath as I saw he had opened the file with our photographs. I stood behind him, humming. There we were, in smouldering or childish poses, playing Helga and Candy. I tried an offhand laugh. 'I was trying out my new camera. I think we were a bit worse for wear that evening.' He remained fixed on one where my face was facing the camera but my eyes were glancing sideways at Tina. Tina's hair escaping enticingly from her rough ponytail around her long white neck. I'd obviously just said something – there was a curl of imminent laughter on our mouths.

'You look very young.' His voice was steady, inscrutable, as if pronouncing on the progress of some radical red vein treatment.

'What, even next to Tina?' I heard the nervous appeasement in my voice. There was worse to come, I knew. The ones where we were tied up in our underwear playing dead Candy. But he stopped, turned his glinting reading glasses up to me.

'Did you use my digital?'

'No. Mine, I think.'

'Where's mine?'

'God knows. Not in LA?'

'No. That's another one. The Konica was here. In my chest of drawers.'

'You're always anxious about your gadgets.' I ruffled his hair. I was challenging him not to turn back to the laptop and continue looking. We remained as we were for a few tense minutes and I registered the familiar muscle tautening in his cheekbone. 'That's enough,' he said, pushing down the button, the computer uttering its tinny dying sigh. I'd won. He sipped his tea and said dryly, 'I didn't think you liked mint tea. You never did before.'

'I don't,' I said, realizing that I'd made one essential mistake that night – I'd been too 'good' for me, stayed sober. This more than anything had roused his suspicions. But of what exactly? He seemed unfazed by the photographs, as if he'd been looking for something else. I checked Tina's room for his camera while he was in the bathroom. Suzy's words and Carl's accusations about her sprang immediately to mind. And now, doubts about her, or something, have taken root in Jake's head. On various counts. Has Suzy suggested something to him? Or Nick? Looking at the screen, I realize that Tina has created a desktop shortcut for the photos called 'Helga and Candy'. Is it a deliberate tactic? I delete them all. I check our bank account. Nothing untoward – even if I'm spending a little more, Jake spends five times that on clothes, gadgets, ointments and his macrobiotic foods. It occurs to me to check the 'history' section. Before starting on the photos, Jake also looked at our bank account today. But then, I see, there's a perfectly obvious explanation for this: a transfer of 23,000 dollars earlier in the day. He was probably just checking on that.

It is evening; he's leaving, gathering the last of his things. Though he has showered twice, once in the morning and once, three hours later, before leaving, he seems exceptionally calm. He hands me a package – professionally wrapped. 'I bought you something.' I open it slowly but I only have to see a fragment to guess. A cashmere cardigan, Hermès, exactly like the red one – in black. He regards me piercingly as I hold it up.

'Thank you.' I smile.

'Like the red one,' he says, surprising me by nudging me

against the wall and kissing me lingeringly on the lips. So did he see it on her, in the restaurant? It strikes me that we share, Jake and I, a tactical poker heart, too apt to conceal itself in stealth, to freeze in distress.

No response to my message yesterday for her at The Castle. Today, I walk through the house listing the work to be done in a futile attempt to act like Mrs Fellner again. I recall Jake's joke, the complaint, about the overgrown garden. But as I stand in the dining room, it feels as if the house is one giant mocking eye, following the foolish buzzing of a restless fly. The eye has the advantage. I don't know from where it looks. I am trapped inside its box, its peepshow, a projection, only visible from one angle, for his amusement. Not only can I not see myself in my entirety, but around me are others I can only glimpse as flat distortions.

The phone rings several times but whoever it is hangs up. I dial 1471 but the number is 'withdrawn'. Another day. I send her a text message: 'Vere are you? Helga all helter-skelter.' Prising at the blind a few times in agitation, I notice a car parked near the corner, a black VW, and a man inside, looking out towards the end of the road, waiting for someone.

It's certainly not Carl, who would know where she was anyway. Now that I've met him, he strikes me less as a stalker than a pretender to omniscience. In the case of Tina, he must see it as a natural right, a metaphysical duty, to keep her within his sights. It is unlike Tina not to return my call. It's a form of protest at being ousted. I leaf through listings for exhibitions, make art notes for her, as if luring her back subliminally. Finally, in the evening, the door clangs with her customary noise. Her footsteps hesitate outside the door, which then swishes open.

She is a pallid reduction of herself, lilac shadows under her eyes, bones jutting out, mud-blonde hair, her usual luminosity absent. I have never seen her look more beautiful.

'So where have you been, monster?' I pat the cushion beside me. 'I've missed you.' A tightness slackens in her face.

'Out of your hair like you wanted.' She flops down, face cast down in bruised accusation before jumping up, marionette-style. There follows one of those anecdotes she conjures up to relieve her own tension or deflect the listener.

'So in comes old Charlotte,' she says, 'with her dog and her hair all weird. Well, she decided to splash out on the hairdresser cos she's in NA, not blowing it on smack. Anyway, they rip her off and make her look ten times worse, with bits of orange streaking, like a skinny Goth hen.'

Tina is bumbling around in imitation of Charlotte's gaucheness, her voice careering as it picks up manic speed. 'So Carl's sitting there and we all look round when she comes in. Poor Charlotte,' she sniffs, 'he's taken to calling her A Wig Too Far.' She chews on a nail while studying me from beneath her lashes. She has offered this information by way of a bait, to fish some of her own.

'I thought you didn't want contact with him,' I say.

'Yeah, well . . . he's there, isn't he? Just shows up.'

'According to Suzy, you phone him all the time.'

Her blush is a violent purple. She bats away at the air with one hand. 'Well, darling, you'd be bored with me if I told you the truth, now wouldn't you? There's a vast gulf between frankness and truth.' I am stunned. It's the most perfect imitation yet, not just of my voice, but of the being that speaks with that voice. She goes on in a faintly irked register, 'Matter o' fact, I stayed with Tania but Mark, yeah, her boyfriend's a total beast. Can't face it every night.' I opt not to pick up on the obvious gambit.

'I met Carl at the wedding party. He came to deliver some charlie. He's working in Suzy's house.'

She stretches her arms wide, like a swimmer, letting them drop by way of response.

'Does he do that often? Deal? Is that where you get it from?'

'Now and then – for his own use. He deals a bit in dope – does exchanges, I don't know . . .' She is picking compulsively at the fluff on the sleeve of a jumper I don't recognize and keeps her head down when she mumbles. 'What's with all the interrogation?'

Ridiculously desperate not to send her scurrying off again, I decide to apologize. 'Sorry. Sorry too I forgot to ask if you could come –'

'You didn't forget,' she says quietly. 'But he was round, wasn't he?' I take it she means Jake.

'He's got the green light on the clinic project.'

'Loads of wonga then.' She grins, rubbing her hands in glee, as if it were already falling into her lap. 'For Morocco.'

I reach down for her new books. 'Look, I bought you these. One's very useful – on iconography.' I look round. Her washed-out, messed-up colour, the slight hooding of her eyes, continue to snag me. 'You, young lady, have been partying too hard; you've lost weight in three days.'

She brings out a crinkled wrap. 'Just a couple of lines left.'

We decide not to bother to order the takeaway: the coke takes our hunger away. After all the talk, the hazy gossip drifting upwards with the smoke, we lie silently at separate ends of the large sofa, fretfully smoking, as the drums come through the speakers performing the endless, trance-like rituals Tina likes. She starts her irritating habit of getting up, dancing for a minute, changing the CD half-way through. I begin to feel twinges of chemical paranoia, over-exaggerated foreboding. Jake's recent presence has tilted our peace.

She ignores me, humming along to a new CD she has acquired, building up with the singer's staccato acceleration. *'Take, take, take it, take him, take it, take him –'* she shouts. The guitar interrupts with manic, jangling strums. Finally, drums clash into an apocalyptic, seemingly endless finale. She leans back, long eyes a deep yellow-green, mouth rising into a secretive smirk, and I'm reminded of Suzy's insinuations.

'By the way, have you seen Jake's digital camera? He's fretting –'

Sitting up, she points at her denim bag. 'In there. I borrowed it. Didn't realize.' She hands the camera out to me, her jumper heavy with pungent, alien smells. I click at the controls on the back, realize she has taken her own pictures. Grinning faces in various stages of intoxication. The last three are of male hands on a breast; a hand on an erect cock and finally, a thigh, Tina's, in the foreground, a head half-obscured, nuzzling in her crotch. 'Tina.' I slap her across the crown of her head. 'I'm deleting them. And don't put anything on the computer. Jake saw our photos.'

'Horny, aren't they?' She gets up to glance through the blind, turns round. 'Anyhow, what's he doing looking at our photos?'

'You made a very obvious folder. Don't borrow this again. He's very weird about his things.'

'He's fucking weird all round, that doctor of yours.'

Some unfamiliar sound wakes me. The door shuts downstairs. Heels are scoring the pavement; a car door bangs. I guess it's Carl she's meeting, or some new prey, but she doesn't want to imperil her position with me by telling me so. And then I am not so foolish as not to realize that a dangling suspicion on both sides is part of the appeal. The photos were a lure, and I am proving, perhaps, in some ways, to be a tricky customer.

We go back to our bunker ways. But things are not quite as they were. She has taken to bringing me small presents: first editions, obscure DVDs, my favourite wines. She has new speakers for her iPod. All this despite the fact that her three shifts a week barely earn her enough for anything but cigarettes, booze and chewing gum. I've begun to pay for all the coke and all the weed. I find myself scanning my bank statements on line almost every day but there's no sign of strange withdrawals from the British accounts. Always, as I do this, a sense of disloyalty mingles with a fretful anguish.

Having galloped headlong into her studies, Tina has now got stuck, repeatedly catching on the same question of artistic intent. 'Yeah, but did he mean to do all they say that he meant?'

It's a tricky one, of course. What can we gauge of the fantasies guiding hand and eye? I talk a little about optics, direct her to Gombrich's essays on the ambiguities of reading and reading into, on the tricks of the pictorial plane. She is still puzzled, nagging, bovine for her. Eventually, I find a Picasso quote – 'It is the other who calculates' – about the unconscious dimension in the artist. I explain that just as the gaze must beware first impressions, expectations, so the brush, the hand, are guided both by aesthetic intention and the blind wishes of some other, outside the artist's will. 'If you like, it's like answering an unspoken call.' This seems to satisfy her.

She has infected the house with her arrhythmia. Having caught some alteration in me, she responds with a restless hyperactivity, cooking things we never eat, fidgeting around, inspecting the house, given to much sullen, fretful pondering. She borrows my clothes compulsively but, sensing herself to be under scrutiny, she takes huge pains to always make her comings and goings clear: where she goes, what she does, who she phones. As if she were performing a more ingenuous self. Her animistic nature has run rife. All household objects are now imbued with hostile spirits. She has broken a small picture frame, perhaps intentionally, of myself and Jake in Morocco, and both our mobiles. And then, there are the other people over the wall in the unlit street. Footsteps send her continually running to the dining-room window. 'I swear I saw a guy jumping over the wall,' she says, quickly correcting herself. 'Not Carl. A dark, slim guy.' And I glimpse suddenly through the gauze of doubt: the gifts, the suspicion, the fantastical projections. On constant guard against tendencies in herself, she sees them all around her and buys gifts to atone. The drugs (she is losing weight, taking them behind my back, I believe, as well as with me) can hardly be helping.

One of her chief targets is Kim. She is due in today. The sun is streaming accusingly into the garden, highlighting the huge, glittering dock leaves, the thickets and tangle of dying rose bushes. I look away, flitting away the thought of Jake's disapproval.

I don't want her to be in when Kim comes in. Kim, large and solid as sandstone, already a little sceptical and circumspect, has taken an obvious dislike to Tina. Whereas she would normally begin her afternoons chatting with me over a cup of tea, now she is all curt answers and much over-industrious pressing down of the iron. Perhaps it's something to do with the way Tina has taken charge and Kim has divined this. To Kim she is a usurper, a ligger. Tina, for her part, is watchfully hostile, convinced Kim is spying on us.

'She's always listening, poking about, following me around with her gorgon eyes. I don't want her in there – period,' she says, unaware that this is clear evidence of something to hide. I tell her in vain that Kim is totally trustworthy, that she has been with Suzy for two years. 'Oh yeah, and what d'you think she does when she goes to Suzy's, hey? That Suzy sniffs up gossip like we do lines, and that Kim she racks 'em up for her. All about us.'

When Tina finally deigns to emerge, resentfully torn from her bed, she spits, 'She's only a flipping cleaner. She's got the evil eye, get rid of her.' After much banging of cupboards, rattling of spoons and silent scrutiny of her teacup, she claps her hands. 'All right. Let's go to the National. You've never taken me there.' I decide to chance it, to make light of it. (Given what she knows of my malady, this may be her sweet revenge.)

'You know why I haven't. But I'll try. I'll chance it,' I say.

It's a glorious June day, wafer-fine cumulus clouds. I decide to drive in with the car top down. Traffic clots everywhere, almost halting to a stop. An ambulance flies past; sirens follow. Tina trawls through the radio channels. 'Sections of the West-way have been closed off after an incident in Hammer-smith . . .' She flicks through, unperturbed, to an indie music station. I weave through side streets. Strange, how quickly the topography of terror has reduced itself to traffic irritations in specific localities, so that to anyone on the other side of the city Hammersmith might just as well be on the Iraqi border. On the grass verge outside the gallery, two Rastafarians bang softly on drums, young tourists lie around, resting their heads on their rucksacks, soaking up the sun, putrid pigeons parade with their lazy pickings. There's a long queue for the security search but out of the sun's glare, I feel no apprehensiveness. I suggest that since the place is so vast we should head for the relative peace and quiet of the smaller Dutch rooms. 'Just make notes on what grabs you and we'll talk later.' She nods, eager to get on.

She begins too close, fairly gobbling up the painting, a cartoonish squiggle of concentration etched on her brow. I tap her on the shoulder, whisper quietly, 'Don't try and take it all in: you won't see anything.' I smile at her. 'Let the signs come to you.' She makes a physical effort to relax, slinging her shoulders back, and begins pacing slowly around, stopping and scribbling in her red notebook, wisps of hair falling busily around her face. Every so often she looks aside, or round, smiling when she finds me.

Walking around with my sight slightly averted, fragments, details blur past as if in jump cuts. Tiny flat grey fish on sand, boats in misty seas, a cat being fed from plates, a parrot drinking from a cup, the shimmer of green and gold skirt, the pond before the Westerkerk, vast skies everywhere, vast skies riven with thunderclouds. And one of my favourites: van der Heyden's *House in the Wood*, white raised statues gesturing to one another before the large house in an enigmatic dialogue lost to the humans on the path beneath them.

There is nothing still about *Still Life: Pewter and Silver Vessels and a Crab*. The arrangement of objects, trays, flagons, glasses, as if inexorably moving towards the table's edge, is a moment of precarious suspense – of imminent fall. I listen out for the familiar hum, but nothing. So far so good. But then I am not meeting them straight on. We walk through to the Central Hall.

We are in the Central Hall, before Moroni's Knight, *Cavaliere del Piede Ferito*, dismantled armour lying at his feet, ruins behind him. Moroni's use of black is almost as good as Bronzino's. She's alongside me. She's not so much looking as absorbing the picture before her with a burning power in her body, and I'm reminded of that first time in the cinema, how I became weightless in the particles of light shining which seemed to obscure and create us. And today, it comes to feel the same, except the rays originate in her, flowing towards the image before us. I lose myself in them, just as before. She turns and whispers in my ear, 'Just let your eye roam, let the dead come to life.' It's one of my mantras, my father's mantras, which I've often repeated to her. She turns back to look at the funereal dapperness of the knight, his lofty, sad, equine austerity, his wary, examining, sidelong glance. We both look at each other at the same time. 'It's Jake,' I say, moving on to the left, on to the Titian.

I'd always walked straight past it before. There was something off-putting about the browns and russets, like a disguise, a smokescreen, uninviting to the eye. It has a private feel to it; he'd kept it to himself for years, never leaving his studio. No real central focus as such, except perhaps the goddess's dominant, forward-flung figure in the foreground, the pert exposed breast, the hound's shape in imitation at her feet. To the right, in the middle distance, that agitated, violent scene, just before Actaeon's mauling by the hounds, paws flinging him back. His face (rather ridiculously) turned into a stag's, melting with the brown foliage as he clutches desperately behind him for support. I absorb the murky brush strokes, the claustrophobia of the narrow colour range, repeating itself everywhere, in the clouds shaping opaque monsters, on the ground, giving the scene such relentless tonal closure, despite the apparent openness. In the middle ground, the fretting bending trees, expressionistic in their fearful movement. And there, in the gap, beyond them, a tiny solitary rider, it seems, watching. I sit on the trestle seat, feeling the russet foliage shiver and shift as everything moves in a dreadful flux. I am in its hair's breadth of time. Tina sits beside me. 'Is that what he did, spied on them?'

'Yes. The intruder had to be punished. No mercy. According to Ovid it's not Diana but one of her nymphs who does the deed.'

As we make our way down the long stairs, she takes my arm and whispers, 'You were all right in there, weren't you?' As if it had been she who had been the cure, the agent. And she was, I believe, as we emerge into the shade of lush green trees, the square and its life, its statues before us. I feel a giddiness; as if someone had suddenly removed my crutch.

In the car, Tina answers my mobile and I realize, too late, it is Jake. 'Yeah, yeah, she's fine, yeah, it's Tina. Hi. I'll get her to call you.' The call makes no sense.

'Why is he calling on the mobile from LA? Did he say it was urgent?'

She's smoothing back her hair against the frenzied wind of the road. 'You're worried I answered your phone to him, aren't you?'

'I'm not.' The traffic is almost at a standstill. I do a U-turn but when I reach the end of the road and turn right, there is a police cordon. The idea of bombs seems so unreal on this beautiful day.

Like all the new bar-restaurants in town, The Lounge resembles a spoof seventies film set with its long brown wood-and-steel bar. I have trouble edging round the tables; the cream circles of the floor carpet are moons misting at the edges. Outside the house, things coalesce and break up; dimensions blur. I make an effort to focus. Suzy beams her crimson gloss smile, glancing in the mirrors above the banquettes, strategically placed to reflect the new arrivals. Slim and tidy, grey shirt done up to his collar in the manner of architects all over the world, Nick gazes over with his limpid hazel eyes as we weave our way towards them.

'He's cute, like a squirrel,' whispers Tina.

She fairly vaults into the seat next to Nick, opposite me. I sit next to Suzy. In the mirror I see I've overdone it on the cleavage and, judging by my gurning jaw and jabbing eyes, on the coke spliffs.

Nick is appraising my belt. 'Snakeskin. How apt.'

Suzy laughs. 'Really, Nick. He gets away with murder with that sweet look of his.' She publicly endows Nick with a roguishness he doesn't possess but it flatters him. She does her usual thing of taking charge of the conversation. We quip and gossip about mutual friends; this excludes Tina for too long. Tension forms like bad weather. Suzy has decided Tina is both too pretty and too insignificant to court, but beneath the polished indifference burns an intense flame of curiosity. Tina responds with an irking, bovine sullenness.

'Well, Zara and Tom are finally splitting up,' Suzy says. 'God, you should see her, Chrissy. She looks dreadful from hanging out with these young music types. In and out of rehab. All puffy-faced, with manky short hair, camouflage gear that's way too young for her. Looks like a dyke.'

I break off some bread, which I decide I can't eat. 'Tom knew what he was getting.'

'Mmm, surely marriage is about a process of accommodation on both sides,' says Nick.

'Oh God. Just because he's cleaned up, and she hasn't, suddenly she's a demon. It's absurd to expect anyone to change.' I seem to have flapped in on some huge wing of rage. Nick colours and looks down at his plate. Tina looks up, startled. Suzy points a glass up to his face. 'Nicky, taste this wine. Are you sure it's okay?'

'Mmm. Not corked. Let it breathe a bit.' Nick turns his attention to Tina while Suzy continues to gas away at me. I hear Tina mention my name and grow apprehensive, particularly since her face is growing crimson from the drink and a pretentious refinement is creeping into her voice. I am beginning to wish we hadn't come. Nick's sane presence conjures up a different, more worrying dimension to reckon with, as if Jake had sent a deputy. They are discussing the Chapman Brothers' alterations to Goya's *Disasters of War*. Tina manages to bring out a puckish side in Nick. 'Oh, come on,' she says. 'Goya himself said there are no rules. Everyone robs what they want.' Her elbows are on the table, hands outstretched by way of punctuated emphasis. I recoil as I recognize my own gesture in her, so bold now, out in public, before my friends.

'They're riding on the back of Goya. It's just sensationalist tactics. Puerile.'

'Wrong.' Tina stands, drunkenly wagging her finger before

jolting and upsetting the table as she leaves for the loo. Suzy grasps ill-humouredly at the corner to steady it and we all watch the glasses right themselves with relief.

Nick's eyes dance with mischief. 'Terribly taken with you. Very bright, your new project.'

'I love that word, "bright". So only the educated middle classes are allowed to be "clever".'

'I wasn't being patronizing.'

'No, I know you weren't, Nick.' I touch his sleeve briefly by way of apology. 'By making her my new project, you could argue I'm being the patronizing one.'

'Maybe you're her project,' Suzy adds, her drollness on the cusp of disapproval. 'She's even talking like you.'

'Well, whatever it is, she's done me a power of good. No more blackouts. I had a whole morning at the National. Nothing. I can start thinking about work again.' I go through various options.

'I hardly think your recovery is anything to do with Tina –' Suzy arches one eyebrow as she catches sight of the returned Tina, swaying as she stands, listening, at the side of the table. The waitress comes up to take our orders. Suzy gives her precise instructions ('No butter and no salt and can I have the vinaigrette on the radicchio on the side . . .'). Tina stares with mocking disbelief. 'She'll probably forget it all the minute she's out of sight,' continues Suzy. 'Tristram Baxter hires them for their looks.'

'So he owns this as well?' says Tina. 'Comes into The Castle sometimes. Creep; always eyeballing us.'

'He's a very good friend of mine.' Suzy eyes her sharply, directly, for the first time. 'Tina reminds me of Lucia, you know,' she says to me.

I blow out smoke lengthily, fencing off Suzy's tactic. 'Lucia was a strawberry blonde. And Tina's much prettier. Remember, Tina, I told you. The story of how I became an overnight monster.' Tina throws me a conspiratorial grin. No, it's more – there's something deliberately cunning there.

Suzy stabs at her hard piece of sourdough bread with her butter knife. 'And how's Jake? We never see him these days.'

'Busy doing LA,' I answer. The food comes. We go on to discuss LA. Nick saw Jake on a recent trip. Suzy and I entertain ourselves by listing all the plastic surgery we will need just to set foot in the Château Marmont.

'Don't forget the knees, knees are this year's bums. Wrinkly knees are a dead giveaway,' I say.

'So will you be joining Jake there?' asks Suzy breezily. I grow concerned by a louring shadow on Tina's face. I toy with my food, begin to deflate with a fidgety dismay; a grainy, flat static overcomes me. I feel I will flop down, face flat on the linguine. I sneak my hand under the table, squeeze Tina's thigh and make meaningful eyes at her. Suzy's head moves a fraction to the side. Tina hands me the coke wrapper beneath the table. When I return from the loo, it opens, a barrier at the back of my skull, a pilot light woosh. Suzy lights a cigarette jerkily, her mouth yielding to the force of vinegary gravity. 'Watch the cleavage.' She is pointing at my décolletage. I automatically do up the undone button.

'It looked better before.' Tina leans forward, biting at her lip, takes firm hold of each half of the shirt above my breasts and, after a halting moment, tears at the top with efficient swiftness, ripping the button. I give her a low, level smile as I gather the shirt inwards.

Finally, Nick interrupts quietly. 'Girls, girls. We'd better call it a night. I'll ask for the bill.'

When the bill comes, I insist on paying, foggily aware that we have misbehaved. Suzy barely says goodnight to us. In the cab back we pass through the sulphurous dark streets in complete silence. I am suspended on a transparent freedom, removed, up above the world. My voice comes out smooth and polished as a new coin. 'Here, you pay with this. I'll open the door.' The house is unusually silent. Expectation sits like a parcel in the middle of the dark hall. Tina says woozily, 'I'm sorry about the shirt.'

'That's okay. It's yours, remember.' We break into long, uncontrolled, convulsive laughter. Tina makes her eyes pop out like Suzy's. 'Of course, it was unfair to blame her about Richie. He was a junkie. She's tricky but not bad. Anyhow, she'll be back to her old self soon, to her old life. I've no doubt about that.'

I listen with a desultory air. Suzy must have said all this during one of my refuelling visits to the loo. It occurs to me I must take care with Suzy. Though gossip for her is a desperate method of charm, an offering for her listener, her ego when humiliated can conjure proper threat. We lie with sluttish tipsiness smoking weed on my bed, catching up on the latest *Big Brother*. Tina becomes unduly agitated, smoking continuously and ranting at the television. 'Fucking freak show. Morons.' It has something to do with my private ruminations, that I am keeping thoughts from her. She picks up Jake's photograph by my bedside table, squints a little and puts it down abruptly.

She's intoning softly, 'And so anoint thine eyes with eye salve, that thou mayest see.'

'Remind me, where is that from? I know it's the Bible.'

Tina shrugs. 'Carl's always sayin' it. Used to be fostered by a preacher. Carl worshipped him. Still goes to see him.'

'Where's his real father?'

'God knows, dahlink. Dead in a ditch somewhere.' Tina flips herself sideways to face me on the bed. On the television, there is much tinny squealing and squabbling.

'I don't actually say "dahlink". That's your version of me. Anyhow, and what do you see with your anointed eye?' We are leaning on our elbows towards each other on the bed. A whisker of cognition passes between us.

'I see what you can't. And I see with my little eye . . .' She jumps up and twirls round the room, ending on the other side, by Jake's chest of drawers. She opens drawers in quick succession. 'Jesus.'

'Don't touch anything.' The TV ads begin their raucous manic ranting.

'It's unreal. So fucking neat, socks here, all cashmere, in colour order, jumpers down here, all folded just so; and look, the cufflinks, all in a row. Belts rolled up.' She picks up a leather belt and unfurls it like a whip. She picks things up and puts them down, taunting me.

'Tina. He will freak.' I switch off the TV and it sinks down into its slot at the end of the bed. I have a better panorama of her actions. 'Leave everything as it is.'

'Total weirdo.' She is examining a paper of some kind, a bill, or letter. Now she fishes out a box – of syringes. 'What's this?'

'He's a doctor.' I lie back, giving up on the struggle. 'Actually, he injects me in my sleep.'

'What? Why?' She begins to walk over.

'So I'll succumb, be cured, transformed, pliant, perfected.'

'Creepy, like all doctors.' The bizarre, the vulgar grotesque, such things feed her thirsty soul. She'd do well in the contemporary art world. I get up and inspect the drawers, tidying them.

Back on the bed, I pat her on the head.

'Grrrrr.' She turns and bites my hand quickly.

'Biting the hand that feeds you,' I say, my hand smarting.

'You're not really going to LA, are you?'

'Over my dead body.' It occurs to me fleetingly that when tidying the drawers I didn't see the document Tina had been reading.

★

She's preparing the evening meal in the kitchen. She's been imitating the female star of our favourite gardening programme. As the garden grows in its own wild way, our skunk logic dictates that we watch several series of gardening programmes to plan and decide its eventual fate down to the smallest detail. She holds out the onion as if to the camera and begins to slice it with fast, dazzling precision, giving instructions on the best method of slicing. I am at the table, reading, drinking wine. Outside, the evening is dank and foliage-ridden.

'You're mixing up your programmes. That's the gardening woman. Too much spliff.'

Tina's chopping is accelerating, the knife in her hand an extension of her arm. Then the arm stops, the blade glints out towards me. 'You can talk. Look at you.'

I survey the garden. Two bushes in front of the sloping lawn have grown, almost obscuring the view of it. At the bottom of the lawn, entangled, intertwined branches hide most of the fence except for one dark hole, an opening, like the eye of the storm. 'I need to get a gardener before Jake comes back. Otherwise it's –' I do a slit-throated gesture.

'He doesn't scare me.'

'He's the provider, the law.' I replenish our glasses. She begins to rap on about what Dylan said about the Atlas Mountains and how we should head for Essaouira first and then come back on ourselves. I continue with my book.

When the meal comes, I can barely eat. I light a cigarette as Tina continues to extemporate ad nauseam about Zac's Moroccan trip.

'Look, the pasta's going all cold, Belle . . . eat a bit more. All you do is drink.'

I look down at the pasta, specked with the weird pink flayed skin of the salmon. I plonk the fork down, hold my stomach. 'Can't take any more. I'm getting fat; you keep trying to fatten

121

me up.' I realize I'm angry again; one vein surging in my neck.

Tina grows morose. 'There's nothing to you. I'm fatter than you.'

I am a little more apologetic. 'Yes, well, you're young.'

She pushes her plate away. 'Oh, so you think I'm fat then.'

'Oh, for God's sake. This is ridiculous. I'm allowed not to eat in my own bloody house,' I say, getting up and scraping back my chair, lighting a cigarette.

I want peace. The drink is souring, acidic, inside me. Jake returns tomorrow. I must separate from this mood, from Tina, in case I cannot transmute back into a semblance of who I was. We have not had any coke for two days. But it only means I get blind drunk. Tina took great pleasure in telling me that coke sticks around, oozes through, no matter how many baths. It stays in hair for years; doctors can tell. She comes and throws herself heavily beside me on the sofa. 'Oh goodie, *Posh Pads*.'

'Look out, you clot, you've spilled my drink on the rug.' The words strike out, vicious as stones. There is much mortified scrubbing at the stain. Her aggrieved agitation makes her all the more oppressive; my own crabby state worse. She takes to making unfunny asides watching the TV. I realize she is growing a little scared of me. As I am growing a little scared of her.

I get up, yawning, the half-digested food in my stomach a furry coagulating mass. 'I feel moronic. I'll go and read in bed.' Tina's hurt looks are straight out of a silent film. I go upstairs. But the feeling of obtrusion persists there. I hear her in a prolonged conversation in her bedroom, in a quiet, agonized tone, wafting in unintelligible tendrils of interference through my ears. All I can make out is a repeated 'she' and I suspect that I may be the topic. But who is her interlocutor? Not that wretched Charlotte, I hope. But anyhow, anyhow, I must cut down on all my conjecturing, and on my unguarded, spaced-out confidences. Heaven knows what I bang on about. I blank out hours from a whole evening and it is Tina who will remind me of things the next day. I puff on the spliff. No more abdominal ache. Silence at last. I drift off; drift back.

I hear a scrape of shoes, a cough, outside. I get up, move the blind. Out there, on the corner, opposite, under the orange light, I see a man smoking; his hood lowered. I check the time. It is 11.18 p.m. I push the half-closed door. 'Tina.'

I can make out the edges, the crumpled bag on the floor – like a dark creature guarding her, the body wrapped in soft mountainous folds, the whiteness darkly incandescent, the edge of her chin, the closed, blank line of the eyes. Her head rises, a startled, senseless moan escapes from her mouth.

'Carl's out there in a hoodie,' I say.

She stands gingerly, long sublunary legs under her t-shirt, walks through silently to my room, to the window.

'No one's there,' she says. 'Carl doesn't wear hoodies.' The figure is gone. We are both shivering above the vibrant lamplight, the darkness behind us. I hear a faint hum, like radio static. 'Liar,' I whisper.

'Why are you angry with me?'

I go to lie down in the darkness. 'Knowing he's coming. It shatters –'

She sits on the bed. 'Leave him. Is it the money?'

We are both looking at the photograph of him, in the shadows on the bedside table. 'No, it's not that. I can't. It's not that simple. I can't expect anything else. Because of me.'

Tina's flesh smells of milky sleep. She lies beside me. We are in smoky hues: indistinct, unknown. We start whispering, tracing a figure on the wall, shaped from the raking light of the outside lamps. Tina points out a huge face, its cheeks, temples and forehead all hollows, its grotesque grin like an Aztec mask.

'What does Carl make you do?'

She talks up to the ceiling. 'He likes watching me doing it with someone. Like he wants to see the worst that could happen, control it. Once, he made me put coke on his friend's cock and suck it and then he fucked me from behind.'

I'm resting on one elbow, tracing the movement of her dark lips. Her hand begins to pull up my t-shirt, glide round the contours of my breasts, so I feel the softly deckle-edged rubbery chill of my nipples as if they were hers. She lets out a slow gasp. 'And with girls, he liked them to call me names. Like cum-soaked slag . . .' Her laugh rolls softly in my ear. She turns over to me, saying, 'I wanna eat you out.' We snicker, recalling the video attendant's words. We kiss deeply, with swift, avid tongues, fingers grasping at the hair around our napes, tugging at the roots with a preying urgency.

I wake to a long bleating on the answerphone, signalling its burden of messages. A few are from Jake, sounding resentfully concerned. I never called him back. When did he call? Two or three days ago? I tear the plug out. Tina has gone to work. In the middle of the night, in that grainy incorporeal light, a pair of eyes surveyed me unblinkingly. I remember little except a deep-water fluency. As if our desire, our hunger, were some preordained underwater ceremony. I put on a tracksuit, eager to leave the house. I run errands, return a few hours later, all pinging, heightened exhaustion. I wonder at my own perverse timing – the night before his arrival. My heartbeat judders, registers a sound. Noises from the kitchen. Not Jake. He is due in the evening. I suddenly remember it's Kim's day.

'Hi, Kim,' I call out. Kim may have noticed Tina's t-shirt, in the wrong room, the unusual crinkles and puckering of the sweat-drenched sheets, stains. Houses reveal their owners in forensic detail when you clean them, bring order to them. She appears with a grave, impassive stone face. 'I didn't go in her room. Like you said, in the note.' I notice it's three o'clock, near the end of her time, but she's finishing up downstairs last, against her normal routine. I curse Tina inwardly for infecting me with her paranoias. I take a shower, avoid Kim's scrutiny. But when Kim takes her leave, as I pay her, she hesitates, as if to say something. I fill with a sudden coldness. She closes her mouth tightly.

I'd looked at Jake's shadow, the dark blot, in the photograph, as her fingers sliced into me like soft scissors. I'd felt the immediate trickle of my own warm juice; ceded, lost and panting to her conducted rhythm. We'd weaved and turned. Tina had suddenly stopped, crawled up the bed, eyes lit with a hard white focus. She looked at the photograph on the bedside table. 'He's looking,' she said. 'Good,' I said. We rolled obscene words in our mouths, like a half-learned language. We lay, panting creatures, legs entwined. 'We have to go soon,' she said. 'Morocco.'

Footsteps. Weary, slow limbs, up the stairs. I move them, like silvery statuary in the darkness, run my tongue slowly down, surprised at the flesh, salt, must, brine. Or is it my smell? The window is full of tracks of rain, making random, convoluted paths. My eyes are the wrong shape. The bed is made up, pristine. Jake's photograph is now back up, upright. Kim must have put it straight, taken the drinks away, the overflowing ashtray. Unease itches through my body.

'Hi,' says a voice behind me. Tina's head is tilted expectantly to one side. I pretend I am snoozing. She turns silently to leave and I notice some brochure in her hand, with sand dunes on the cover. She bangs the door shut.

7

I've searched the entire house for Jake's vintage Raybans; he wants them sent to him by Swiftair. Tina has probably 'borrowed' them. She made a great, nonchalant to-do about leaving the house at the last possible moment before his arrival. Now Jake has left too. I needn't have worried. He was constantly on the phone, in hushed tones, or on his laptop, over-engrossed, too engrossed even to notice the garden, let alone the signs of our fevered coupling. I wondered for a brief second if he was talking to a woman.

Anyway, the Raybans are an excuse. I'm seeking unspecific evidence. I haven't seen her for three days and as I turn over things in her room, I'm turning over questions, doubts – suspicions.

Her bedside table. A bus ticket, a set of keys for elsewhere, nail file, biro, mascara, a half-melted scented candle, my copy of *The Death of the Heart*, my Gombrich, its spine submitting to advanced wrinkling, one of her red art history notebooks, full of notes.

In the margins, scattered phrases: 'see how the paint is applied with a stabbing technique to intensify the sense of violence'; 'the flawlessness is part of the chilly fascination'; 'the elongations and distortions of ecstasy'; 'as usual with this genre, inviting the eye to wallow in what it purportedly condemns'; 'the effect, like a blinding limestone glare'. I recognize them immediately, my unmediated musings cut and pasted, from ear to paper. I put the book down, look in the small drawer beneath. Scraps of paper with names I don't recognize (three male, one female) and phone numbers, condoms (old or current?). A note, folded in half, not in Tina's writing: 'Don't turn youre (sic) phone off to _me_ again.' The underlined 'me' – it can only be Carl.

I tingle with the apprehension of discovery. A card, for a clinic, with only a 'customer number', no name; the anonymity suggesting drugs or sexual disease. What is that glinting? Platinum cufflinks – Jake's. What would she want with them? I leave them there to check if she will return them. An old postcard of a valley scene, the kind given away free in bed-and-breakfasts, the Mawddach estuary, all heather and unnaturally blue water, soft feminine hills in the distance. On the other side, slanted, spidery handwriting: 'Dear Tina – Bloody rain – north Welsh are mizerable gits but that's my lot. Come and see me soon. Always your Dad.' The postmark is two years old. I am about to put it back. It's so glaring I nearly missed it. The card is addressed to Tina Devlin, not Tina Vaughn. It pings up, circled, in a cartoonish bubble: the name Carl mistakenly used at Jonty's party. So, her real name is Devlin. Strange how my ears heard it back then but my consciousness blanked it. Yet now I am more unanswered, unsated. My eyes pick at the cornicing in confusion.

The mirror opposite the bed reflects my face, blanching into the disturbed folds of sheets which seem sculpted to her phantom form, as if she were a statue recently emerged from her drapes. I leave, circle the house, shaping furious clouds of cigarette smoke. I think of all the different reasons why she might change her name. Her mother's death might well have unhinged her, sent her off on a spate of general misbehaviour, shoplifting – or drugs. Now this is more likely, considering her ready supply. And I think back, of course, to the day in the gym, the dislike of form-filling . . . the name change is most probably illegal.

I open the French windows, their hinges squeal. I stand just inside the garden. Doubt pollutes the air around me in tiny droplets. The garden heaves with so much overgrown verdure, weeds thrusting through cracks in what was once a patio; the unruly long-haired lawn. The late-evening light has the quality of blurred, thick, rubbery green glass. Somewhere, from an open window, comes the sound of a newscaster's voice about the police surveillance operation. He moves on, to a famine. The cricket score. From the left, occasional jarring laughter, the scent of charred flesh in smoky tendrils from a neighbouring barbecue. A blackbird flaps out from behind me, followed by a second, then a third. I go back into the house, sit in the gloom, on the high-backed chair. The shadows grow out from the corners of the room as, above the rubber-band hum of distant commuter traffic, I hear footsteps stop behind the wall. Someone is there, murmuring into a phone: I can almost feel exactly where he stands, through the marble chimney-place.

Jake was behind me. He always breathes in reluctant sharp stabs. He left my cardigan on, the red one, and the pendant. Brusquely for him, as if sensing my impatience, he turned me on my side, then face down on the bed. His fingers hovered, then rested tenuously on my neck, scraping back the hair. His cock grew harder inside me. And she wafted into my mind: Carl fucked her, shanks illuminated, in sledgehammer grunts, lifting her cold lunar leg. I felt the thrust. At some point I was all three: being fucked, fucking violently, watching. Jake's strangled breathing brought me back. I arched my head just so, to the lamplight – he gave an agonized yelp, one hand clapped tight to my shoulder. Earlier I'd heard her sneak into her room, and leave afterwards, in the middle of the night. She'd heard us.

I wake with the sensation of something landing and squatting on my chest with a heavy malignity. Some neglected corner of me seizes on a logic that shreds itself as soon as formed, carried away from itself by taunting gusts, a red, spiked pressure pushing outwards. The phone rings shrilly like the phone in a dream. I go in, and tear out the switch before the answerphone comes on. A thought slaps me alert. Tina's notebooks. She has red for art, but I've seen a black one. Her diary. A box under her bed – tracksuit on top – here it is. It is one of those half-page-a-day diaries and there is a childish touch – she fills each space for the day and no more; cramping her writing if she has more to say, or travelling up the side of the page.

So here I am, in the room next to hers. I knew even before we talked. One sign after another. I don't care what Charlotte says – I know, I see her. Rescue me, she said. It has to be me.

The entries are not regular.

Busy, busy working then cooking for us. Loads of puff. She tells me things, trusts me. Says I can tell you everything which is well weird cos she's ice-cool, hiding, like she's always behind tinted windows. That's why people fall so hard for her. Her husband, letting her get away with murder. But she tells me more than others. Life personified, she calls me. We're going to Morocco – her favourite place. We'll stay there till she's better.

A more recent entry.

I almost ruined it yesterday. And then there's that bitch Suzy with her jelly eyes always looking to stir it. She's one of them. She was in for lunch with a friend and they were both staring me out – that red smile like she's smeared blood on her lips – all chatty, asked me to sit down for a bit – telling me how B loves picking up 'fresh blood'. Mentioned some drunken guy, a tree surgeon, in the country and how he started ringing and bothering her at night. Like I was another one. Yeah right, Suzy. Word up. Bitch.

C texting all the time. Trying to ignore him, told him to quit stalking us. He said we're bonkers, he's got business on our street. He knows where to find me – he hates it, me and her. But he knows I'll be needing money now I'm hardly working – having to do him favours.

(What favours, I wonder, with a sleazy sexual rise.)

She was all antsy and quiet today – didn't speak for nearly two hours. Stared at the kettle when I came in the kitchen – blots me out – I start going back to my old ways – too much shit. But I know it's not me – he's been here. And those pills he makes her take – I'll make her ditch them when we get to Morocco. She told me, there's no danger, no fusion with him. I know why she married him.

There are rants against a work colleague plotting against her, a furious convolutedly jealous diatribe on Tristram Baxter trying to chat her up, enquiring after me. (She knows we once had a fling.)

Carl met her at that party and he was slagging me off but she's loyal. Calls her whore of Babylon. Now he's working for that Suzy. He's building up to something.

In the next entry, the writing is slovenly, tilted.

Waited for ages, on purpose, to go back to the house – B all over me – but he's been here – she's gone weird, changed. Two nights with Tania and Mark. Mark had to pay me like before, made me pretend she was a tart too. We were well mashed – he had a big cock and she's good, not one of those girls who want it all done to them. Showed B the pix – turned her right on, though she didn't want to let on.

Saturday night it was all going down. Carl had picked up the girl at the wedding. Sam was well into her – they gave her the whole medicine cabinet. Carl was banging on paranoid about some geezer in a black VW stalking him. Mark was robbed and I know it's Carl, getting revenge for the other night when I went off with Mark and Tania. Got someone else to rough Mark up and steal his wallet.

He's back in 28 hours – why she's so evil tonight – acting all bored with me – I started flipping out – like she'd slapped me or something.

Sex with B. Horny, weird. She said I was her hands, her mouth, her eyes, her missing senses. She wants to leave him but she's scared cos he's controlling her. But she freaked out next day – Carl's been in constantly for the last two days in the pub like he can sense it. Says I gotta help him again seeing as I owe him nearly 400 now – he's doing the stuff with Jermaine now. Charlotte came in, with all that story about B.

Don't know why I came back late at night, why I didn't stay out – I know she wants me to avoid him – I could hear them, through the wall – it was disgusting – I was her, breathing in, hating him. I got to get her away.

I put the diary back and wipe my hands absently on my jeans, as if wiping away the fragile grubbiness of her existence. It's all mess, and youthful delusion. Dear me, she wants to save me. But she's not stealing. Rather, have I not been the thief, invited this obsession, filling her mind with my ideas, my whisperings? All for what – an injection of blood, hope?

I'm in the kitchen when she comes in. I smile, resolved to eject her politely. She is unforthcoming, opening the French windows to let in a very slight breeze. The sky is alternating between blue and slate. She has two Selfridges carrier bags. Shoplifting, probably. Or a new provider – the hapless Mark, no doubt. The bell rings insistently, three, four, five times. Tina makes to move. 'I'll get it,' I say. I open the door to be met by Charlotte's rubbery mouth working convulsively round her pasty, sick-horse face. She hasn't registered me. I call out, 'Tina.'

Tina hurries to the door. 'What's up, Charlie? Where's Boris?'

'I–I–I've lost him.'

Tina brushes past me, coaxes her in by the shoulder.

'No really, I–I–I . . .' She looks fearfully at the doorjamb. She comes no further than the hall. Eventually, we gather from a painfully halting account that she opened her flat door to someone and Boris ran off down the stairs. 'I've been l–l–looking for him for hours.'

Tina puts her arm around her. 'He'll be back in a minute, homesick. Probably sitting at the door now.' Charlotte nods like a marionette, temporarily encouraged. Nodding still, her misty, faded porcelain eye lands on me, acquiring a white dot of growing panic. As if she has suddenly woken up, realizing she is in hell. Tina guides her into the dining room. Charlotte follows, mouth half agape. I linger outside but can make little of Charlotte's prattling.

I go into the kitchen. At last they come out again. Tina pops her head round to explain she's going to Charlotte's. The door closes with a long, jarring clang that stays, vibrating minutely, as I pace around the lower floor of the house.

After a couple of hours, Tina returns, throwing her coat on the chair. 'He was there at the door, the bastard.'

'I don't want to know. I'd rather she didn't just show up here. She gives me the creeps and I know she maligns me.' I take ice from the freezer and throw cubes into a thick, round glass and pour in some vodka.

'No thank you, Belle, I wouldn't like a drink. Bit early for me.'

I rattle the ice in the glass. 'I didn't realize you followed such stringent etiquette.'

'Don't do the sarky posh bitch on me now, I'm tired.' She slumps, then pulls herself straight, to root around in the fridge.

I turn, crossing my arms. 'So. Tell me why Carl is always lurking about. He told Suzy you owed him money, that you have a crack problem and that you steal from him.'

She gets up, takes the cellophane off two thick gleaming fillets of tuna. She walks to the counter. 'None for me, thanks,' I say. A sudden bang as her fist hits the chopping board. She deliberately lets the two fillets drop to the floor. They tremble on the pale tile, two clotted, dark red hearts. She bends to pick them up with a sigh, dumps them in the bin and turns, fixing me with a blank, white violence. I respond with an involuntary shiver.

She's washing her hands in a thin silvery rope of water. Through the soft drumming, she mutters, 'Your mate Suzy is a shit-stirrer.' She dries her hands and looks for her cigarettes from her bag, takes one out and then, slowly, with deep, deliberate exhalations, goes to sit across from me. 'He always does this to me.' Her face comes close, eyes paling with rage. 'I keep telling you. He hates it when I get away.' Tina's voice falters, in a note of weariness. 'Sometimes he wants to make a couple of grand with a quick drug deal or a bit of furniture – full of big ideas, he is. Gives me loads of charlie to show off, winding me back in. Then he gets miffed, says I gotta pay. That's where all the charlie was coming from before. But I do him plenty of favours.'

'What kind of favours?'

Tina's face collects into a stoic smile. It's a good perform-ance. 'Favours.' She flops forward, leaning on her pointy, vulnerable elbows. Light-headed now with the stiff strong drink cooling me, I suddenly don't much care about their petty intrigues and slurs. 'Sounds just like the art world. Fix me a spliff, Candy.'

Tina shoots me a grin. 'Fix it yourself, Helga.'

'Oh, I'm bored with them. Let's get rid of them. Strap them both to the chair.' For some reason, this reminds me of last night's dream. 'Listen. There was an aeroplane crash in an underground tunnel. It was a huge passenger plane and the lights had gone out. I walked through the aisles in the gloom. The only standing survivor. For the rest, all I could hear was a constant moaning of pain, the moaning of people dying and severely wounded. Row after row of men with their arms or legs cut off, dying, severely wounded, quietly moaning. Until, two seats, one in front of each other, in each one a woman. One has long blonde hair and she is masturbating, so that her moan rises above the dying ones, in an arc of pleasure. The other one I cannot see. It might have been me. I wondered if someone would come to their rescue, and woke up.'

'Wicked.' Tina looks on gleefully into the air before her, visualizing the dream, her elbows all askew, and the detail of the pointed, awkward bone elicits an automatic lurch, of pathos or pity, or love. 'Oh, come on, let's have a line.' I have no money in my purse. I take out my card and hand it over to her. 'My PIN is 7707. Will you remember that?'

She takes it from me with a lengthy, questioning look that slowly transforms into a smile of relief.

We've gone back to our bunker ways, hardly going out, eating less and less, what with all the coke. Days are off-limits, though. We must leave ourselves some space, some limits. Now that I'm paying for all of it (Carl is off-limits too, she says), it sometimes gnaws at me that Jake will notice more money being withdrawn.

She has taken a week off work. The phone begins to ring again; but no noises. Just a cutting off when I answer. Tina is all a-jitter; saying it's not Carl (he likes her to know when it's him), that it's Reza, the boy from the shop, who has taken to skulking on the street corner, watching out for her. I suggest to her it's the delusions of cocaine. But even without it, Tina's habit of hovering, as if trying to anticipate my signs, my moods, worsens. Or she will fall into a broody reflection, her eyes taking on a watery pallor with some imagined slight, stretching to their outer corners. Sometimes she holds something in her hand, turns it round and round. Jake's cufflink. I don't say anything. In turn I respond by an exaggeration of my glacial side. What we share is an ability to take minute readings of each other. So it builds up thick in our atmosphere, in the house, this sense of an old story drawn up long, long ago, by something staring back at us from some invisible hiding place. We've taken to using the unused rooms, wandering into them and chatting on the floor. Tina likes keeping an eye on the yard. The house has now welcomed us back into its dusty, neglected corners with a bemused tolerance.

She's caught on that we mustn't cross the line again, to sleep together, but still I say nothing about her moving out; half-afraid I will be scooped out, emptied. When she is absent, I shrink into myself and feel the choking dust enter my nostrils and throat. I am half-afraid, too, that she will react badly, disastrously. For she has become jealous of any conversations or dealings with the outside world. When she is out, I fight the urge to read her diary. She has still not put back Jake's cufflinks.

I'm trying to record exactly how it was with the benefit, the objectivity of hindsight. The sun was pale, high and dazzling, the day promising to be hot. I dressed carefully, opting for slim, low-slung black linen trousers and short, gauzy black kaftan top. Even then, I was trying to please his tastes.

I could hear the interminable yawns and bumps of Tina getting up, pictured the childlike puffiness in her face, the adolescent torpor with which she lit up the first fag, heard her irking morning bronchial splutter. I do recall, as I pencilled the eyeliner on my lid, stretching my eye, how bad I looked, the skin a thin, putty-like mask. The dark puffs beneath my eyes had turned into toad-like growths in the mirror. I was thinking of the tightness to Jake's voice the night before and how I used the usual weapon with him. 'Oh, I'm fine. Tina's here keeping me company.' I've mastered it well with him, the art of defensive reproach. Tina was there, slouched on the sofa beside me, humming lightly, on purpose so he could hear her, I thought.

She rapped quickly on my bedroom door (something she would not have bothered with weeks ago. Funny how a night of intimacy brings hesitancy, doubt); came in with a towel around her. My blinds half-drawn, I was making up in artificial light. But I sensed a bristling awkwardness, noted purple marks on the milky flesh of her upper arms. 'Don't know what to wear.'

I carried on at the mirror, hiding my shock: when had I invited her? (The amnesia will suddenly strike just as a memory will suddenly thwack at me.) 'Wear my cream suit.' She looked hesitant, about to speak. 'Don't do your morning slug routine,' I said. When she emerged, wearing the cream trouser suit and a thin asymmetric vest, I saw a chain round her neck with a little Gothic cross.

When she saw me looking at it, she said, 'Carl gave it to me.'

'Strange,' I said, fingering the chain briefly. 'He badgers you for money and then he gives you that.' But I was felled, taken aback by her glow; felt the worn cheap cloth of my own dullness.

It was very hot. Letting the car roof down, I noticed a black Golf reflected in the wing mirror and driving it, someone who looked like Reza from the corner shop. He had sunglasses on, but Reza, I thought, was hardly old enough to drive. The black Golf rang a bell: Tina had mentioned it in her diary. But she seemed not to be aware of it. She was unusually subdued, fidgety, chewing gum and smoking, brooding on something.

To hide my displeasure at her coming along at all, I told her about school exeats and Sunday lunches, when Dad would always appear with some woman. Sometimes Jimmy would be there too. I told her about Barbara, a redhead with a thick-lipped smile, who intrigued me. She lasted a few years. She would grow gradually louche, her coppery hair falling about her face a little, her cheeks two spots of red from the drink; the spots of sin, I'd think, with the melodrama of the Catholic schoolgirl. Every so often she'd redo her lipstick with obscene absorption in front of a small hand mirror, right at the table. My father would watch with apparent amusement, mutter something about vanitas. Brandies would come and she'd narrow those green eyes, the mouth twitched into a private sign, and his wolfish smile would spread over his face and he'd ask for the bill. His other hand was on her thigh beneath the table. Perhaps this only happened once, yet it remains, imprinted, in my memory as a repetitive scene.

I'd think of Lucia then. Lucia would have known, I thought. Was it Barbara's funny little jacket? Her large quivery mouth, her faint lisp, or was it the way she looked at him behind a strand of hair falling loose and forward? My childish mind had seized on a sophisticated truth; that's why he liked them smart to begin with – to watch them get messier.

For all his sensual habits, the racing, the women, the wine, and let us not forget the art, he has a bemused imperviousness to people, disguised as worldly geniality. I rarely saw him angry; his humour simply turned vicious. Once, he glanced over my shoulder as I studied Rosso's *Cleopatra*. 'Now this,' he said, his voice catching, lowering in register, 'now this –' It was as if he had arrived at the very kernel of fascination. But it was a controlled, varnished fascination. And it drove my mother mad with envy. 'Always looking at dead stuff, dead people.' He'd always correct her: 'Dead Dutch people.'

Falling back on my thoughts over the river's white glare, I caught sight of the big wheel, so poised, so still, its pods glinting in the distance, dot-like humans inside. People sat at cafés, the traffic slumbered lazily through. Time itself slowed in the hazy swish and pale wash of summer, and its illusion of never-ending.

'That's why I turned to art,' I suddenly thought aloud, 'to be his favourite, to drive Jimmy out.'

Pinpricks of heat spread through the roots of my hair as we crossed the white bridge, the river water blazing in an undulating white shroud. The after-effects of last night's skunk.

'What did Jimmy do about it?' She eyed me accusingly, as if I'd forgotten something crucial, something obvious.

'Retreated. Took smack. Takes after my mother's family. Do get rid of that gum.'

I was pulling up. Outside the restaurant Tina flicked away her gum resentfully and gestured at the newsagent's. 'Getting some fags. See you in there.' I saw the black Golf again, swerving past us.

There, in the cool, shady interior of the old-style trattoria, was my father's silvery forelock, like an elegant school-boy's, bent over a magazine. I stood there for ages before he became aware of my presence. 'Ah!' He stretched up elegantly in his pale linen suit and white cotton shirt. It hasn't left him, the early sixties glamour, Savile Row suits, dark sunglasses, the elegant, shrouded libertinism – politicians and rent girls in cramped basement clubs. At least, that's my fantasy of it.

'I have a friend with me, she's buying cigarettes.'

'I'm on the Menetou, it's the only drinkable white here.' His whisper was loud and actorish, hand held up to his mouth.

'I'd better watch it; I'm driving.' (Curious, this, why I 'behave' in front of him; he wouldn't give a damn if I drank him under the table.) He'd searched for the waiter with that equable, patrician air as if born to butlers, but then, it was largely how he fed us after her death – in restaurants. Sunday lunches and early suppers before the au pair put us to bed. An avid frequenter of restaurants, he assumed these were treats for us also. We only ate in when he was out.

His eyes wandered upwards, sparking, alighting. Tina slouched, looking down on us, smoking with desultory languor. Attitude personified.

'How do you do?' Flushed with courtliness, he smoothed down his hair. She sat down beside me. 'It's charming, that suit,' he said, and I noticed it was the same colour as his.

'It's Belle's.' She oozed challenge, calculation.

He glanced at me sharply before turning back to her.

'I'd kill for a drink,' she said. Tina had pointed at the mineral water.

'Absolutely! Would you care for some Menetou? Or an aperitif?'

She nodded vigorously at the wine. 'Fag?' She was sending herself up as some sharp little cockney in front of him; rather cleverly avoiding any imitation of me as she'd done with Nick.

'Oh, all right,' he groaned. 'Just one.' And so began the first of many conspiratorial grins. At some point I'd called him Daddy, which he hates. I wince now to think of it, how pathetic was my need not to be excluded.

'Tina's living with me for a while. She had a bully of a boyfriend.'

She seemed to react well, turning confidingly to him. 'Yeah, Belle rescued me. I was out on the street, no keys, nothing. Appeared like a goddess or something. In the middle of the night.'

'Yes, well, there always was a touch of the self-appointed goddess about Belle.' He'd carried on, 'But what does he want, this bully?'

'He stalks me cos I'm getting away from him to study. Belle's helping me with art history.'

'Well, you're in good hands. So what's hit you?'

'Well,' she began, curling her mouth outwards, 'I like iconography, what d'you call them, emblems. Like Envy, Invidia, eating her own entrails.' And here was the moment when I became certain, am certain, that she had been looking up my father's work behind my back. She listed at least three of his passions. 'I like Brancusi, Hals, Rembrandt, Goya, Henry Moore.' She paused. 'Rosso.'

He'd refilled her glass, remarking how she was obviously already forming a taste of her own. 'Belle's into a more mannered, polished aesthetic,' she intoned, her nose up in the air in a sort of parody of a posh art historian. 'Icy fascination.'

I sat back, a blanked, black presence, aghast at her flagrant use of the information I'd given her about him, watching the ritual of the ensnarement, the flippant frankness she intuited he admired. Seduction is a low art form, vaudeville. Especially the seduction of men. Tucking into her spaghetti, as she licked enticingly at a corner of her mouth with her tongue, he commented on how he loved to see women enjoying their food. She even managed to move the conversation on, ably, like a conjuror, to racing. 'My dad was a bookie for a while, went to all the races.'

'Really? What was his name?'

'You wouldn't know him – I'm white trash.'

'Oh, so am I, white trash, from East London originally.' His eyes actually watered with stray nostalgia. 'Anyhow, I'm afraid I've succumbed to the lure of cable television's racing. Do you still go?'

'No. Only used to go occasionally, when he showed up. He buggered off when I was a nipper to devote more time to his hobbies: the turf, the pub and the feminine sex – in that order.'

He'd chortled, his food, for once, almost neglected on his

plate. How easily, how casually, she seemed to affect, unshield him.

'Yes, what is his name, Tina?' I was seeking revenge. Her head had flung round, the green eyes narrowing to two small, dull slits of menace. I responded with stillness, shock. Turning back to him with a smile full of winning weariness, she held out her glass. 'Yeah, well, pour on, Leo. Families, who needs them?'

He warmed to his theme as the bottle he held plinked wine into her glass. She went on, about her scant early memory of the form, the draws, the trainers, the turf. Then they came, the inevitable invitations – to Goodwood and Ascot. They carried on smoking, drinking, laughing, voices gradually rising, as if someone had wound up their mechanisms too tight. He wanted to know more about Carl, grew protective, concerned, even offering the service of his lawyers.

'Hardly necessary,' I interjected. 'He's very much a part-time stalker. Tina seems to thrive on it.'

Tina had gurgled blackly. 'Leo, the desires of the heart are as crooked as corkscrews.' One of my father's favourite quotations – one she'd heard me use often.

He cleared his throat irritably. 'Belle, what is the matter? You look strange.' He has a cutting way: I should know, I've inherited it, that dismissive flicker of boredom with anyone not playing the game. Tina scraped her chair back to go to the loo. His eyes followed her receding figure. 'She's delightful, perfectly ravishing, that extraordinary curve of the mouth.'

I thought of my own unremarkable mouth. 'Thought you might like her.' My wit so often deserts me when with him. But back there, I could barely fashion words. I let him carry on with his paean.

'Ah, here you are. We were beginning to miss you.' I wondered if she had taken a line though we are supposed to be 'off'. She was too much now, a life force sucking up the surrounding air, tits triumphantly poking up as she embarked on recounting some overheard fragment of conversation between the couple seated by the loos, mimicking their polite hostility. She followed this with accounts of the monumental fights between the owner of The Castle and his young, wilder wife, to which the staff were all unwilling auditors. 'He called her a silly frigid bitch the other day. So the silly frigid bitch . . .' And at this point, leaning forward close to his cheek, hair falling louchely over her face, she whispered to him the story's end, and he was nodding and smiling back at her.

My gaze clambered desperately over the diners at the other tables, clinging to their ordinary pudgy faces, their quiet chatter. I rested my eye on a poster of a bullfight, some years old, gazed at the circular images of the bullfighters, probably long dead. The yellow and red and black began to stain, the colour running. I looked away, aware of some woman at another table staring at me. I forced myself back. He was in the middle of one of his interminable anecdotes. Tina choked on her wine as if it was the funniest thing she'd heard all year.

I'd stood up abruptly, muttering about not feeling well. Tacit looks were exchanged between them. His fountain pen was admired, one more cigarette was smoked, as he told her, grandiloquently tipsy, how some wise man had written a book on the sublimity of smoking. He must lend it to her. He'd opened the door, full of gallant flourish and kissing of hands, another invitation to Goodwood, Tina pouting, cigarette dangling from a negligent hand.

Then he'd sauntered off, one hand in pocket, the other holding the *Spectator* which he drummed, marking out some musical rhythm, against his thigh, the old roué bounce in his well-shod feet.

In the car, I concentrated on driving fast. Finally, as I braked at a zebra crossing, she said, all ingenuous innocence, 'Whoa, Belle, you'll get done. There's a speed camera up there.'

I drove on, angry at the anger she had provoked in me. 'Perhaps you could move in with him after mine. Not sure what his mistress will say. What is it you want exactly? You're a bit sick, aren't you?'

She banged her fist against the window. 'That's fucking rich coming from you. Don't you remember last night? Your game.' She turned a tired face to me, pulling off one side of her jacket to expose the tops of her arms to show me the bruises. 'No, you don't, of course. Just drop me off here.'

I screeched to a halt. The car behind swerved past hooting, with protesting, wind-sucked voices.

I was all the more furious for not recalling last night, for letting her have some nameless advantage, for the suggestion that this lurid, grubby little scene with my father was somehow connected. I let her out wordlessly. Hurrying off, wearing my suit, she looked back once at the end of the road, a mean line of intent on her mouth as she produced her mobile to make a call.

I saw Reza when I parked the car, serving in the shop. As usual, he looked past me, scanning for her. So it couldn't have been him in the car.

In the house, some electronic gadget was beeping incessantly. The sitting room was a mess. I began tidying up the empty fag packets, the scrum of half-drunk wine glasses, full ashtrays, the sticky pools of drink stains on the table. I opened the bin in the kitchen. Something red caught my eye. My red cardigan, shorn into elaborate shreds.

The sky is the flat colour of vapour. I yearn for vast deserts, limitless skies, open, endless water, not this blighted closeness, this crouching chain of houses with their blinded windows. We decide to chance it, and go to the Park; her house is close by if it rains.

A few other people are also out strolling, flicking glances

up at the ripening sky. I listen to Suzy's steady burble with relief as we skirt the mini-golf course, its shrill yellow flags drooping in the dense air. There's more cover at the northern end, the doleful horse chestnuts looking as out of place in the dinky park as the old Irish boozers in the refurbished Castle. A sign on a rural-green background proclaims we are in an 'imitation woodland walk experience'. Perfect cylinders of chocolate-coloured logs are carefully scattered around, some layered and shaped into kit-like benches. Cars swish by in the street. Behind the trees, the inscrutable red-bricked facades of the houses; as with people, one learns more from the backs of them. We walk fast, branch and twig cracking beneath our feet.

'Is she stealing?' Suzy asks. 'Well, you know what Carl said.'

'Not exactly. A few things go missing. She "borrows" things; young people do. I lend her my clothes freely; but Jake's things she takes secretly.' I stop myself from telling her about the shredded red cardigan.

'Is she on drugs?' In the distance, I spy a small boy clinging anxiously to his swing, looking ahead with queasy fear while his father pushes him, higher and higher.

'Well, who doesn't take them at that age? We do smoke some grass at home; very occasionally coke. But when she's out, who knows? It isn't smack. I'd know.'

A thin branch whips the side of my head. I put my hand to it, break it off and whisk it about in the air as I talk. 'I can't decide whether she's mad, devious or what. I mean, she exaggerated about Carl, to get in, to manipulate me. But, yesterday really –' Cold settles like steel in my spine. 'We had lunch with my father and she . . . she was quite – disgusting – all over him – my father!'

'Mmm. Does she do that with Jake?'

'No. They haven't met.'

'Really? How extraordinary. Never?'

'She thinks I should leave him. She has a pathological hatred of doctors. In fact, she seems to believe she's rescuing me –'

'Things are getting out of hand – to judge by the other night at the restaurant. She's obsessed with you – flirting with your father might have been to provoke you.'

'I don't know why I, why I did it . . . invited her. I know that in my way I used her – I do toy with people – but she seemed to be doing some good – but no, it's something else . . .'

'Chrissy, it's nothing. Another of your crushes. She's a nobody. Just try not to treat her like . . . that tree-surgeon guy you were doing.' She halts, making it clear she almost said someone else. 'Say she has to go, and soon, blame it on Jake coming back more often . . . she won't know.'

'She's not that easy to dupe.' I want to say, angry as I am with Tina, that no, that is not it – she is not 'nobody'; but I know Suzy doesn't wish to hear this.

'Never mind; there are rules, you must be nice, she must be grateful. End of story.'

The subject is tacitly abandoned. Suzy's lack of imagination, her pragmatic toughness, has appeal under stress, her sureness of having authority firmly behind her like some uniformed bobby at her gate renders the scenes in the house, my existence with Tina, a grotesque, souring comedy – easily zapped away to another channel.

Suzy goes on to fill me in on her forthcoming family holidays and tells me she longs for an adult trip. She suggests taking an early autumn break, in a friend's villa in Essaouira. I hesitate, recalling Tina's Moroccan obsession. But by then she will be long gone – she won't know.

It begins to spot with rain. As we stride back quickly towards the gate, we spot a commotion: two park guards in yellow-and-black jackets. One holds a dog. A woman is pacing small, jagged circles, over by the animal farm. A few people look back as they pass.

We edge in closer round the path. I realize the woman is Charlotte, jabbering, drops of rain flattening her lank hennaed hair and exposing those thin spaces of white scalp. One of the park keepers holds her dog, Boris, by his collar. The dog is barking excitedly. Just in front of the gate, on the ground, I can see a small mess of grey fur, the wet leaves of grass around it delicately spotted with blood; a filmy, dead, button eye. It's one of the farm's rabbits. Boris wags his tail at me, a fine film of rose blood spotting his teeth. I see that Charlotte has both her large-knuckled hands round her cheeks, her mouth open wide but silent.

Suzy is asking what has happened, and the keeper says, 'Someone left the door open, it got out and he was just there, went for him.'

Charlotte walks over, places her arm on mine, in bewilderment. 'He's really not like this, he's the sweetest thing. He–he–he–he's only playful, and the door was left open, it wasn't his fault, he just ran off quickly, they're naturally like that and –'

She goes on in this vein, eyes staring intently at the tree beside me, before halting, startled, removing her hand quickly from my arm. 'Where's Tina?' Somehow, she is back to some weeks ago; the two incidents have converged in her mind. I blank her, silently panicked. Her mouth is half-open; then it leers a little as she crouches towards me, sensing my panic. She whispers in my ear, 'I know. It's obvious, isn't it? You reek of it.' Closing her mouth tightly, giving me a firm nod, she steps back towards the wooden fence.

'Come on, Chrissy.' Suzy takes my arm. Buried in the grass blades, the dead eye seems dully, sadly alive, trapped in the dead body. Back outside on the pavement I say, 'That's Tina's friend, that madwoman with the dog.'

'Doesn't surprise me.' Suzy looks down at her watch. 'Oh

heavens, is that the time? I must pick up the children, I'm late – yeuch, and wet.'

The sky is ripening, turning. At her front door, under the porch, Suzy puts both hands around my cheeks; an unusual gesture, as if to kiss me. Shuddering, still hearing Charlotte's whisper, I say, 'I forgot to tell you. She changed her name, her surname –'

Suzy shakes her head reprovingly. 'Get her out of your mind – and out of your house.' I feel an intense stab in my gut, as if I'd betrayed myself. And then, the perfect, corny timing of weather – an eerie silence, the nanosecond before a bomb hitting its target. Then the early report of the thunder, the giant furniture being heaved around. Big drops, merciless, fast, the titan gnashing of teeth as the second clap seems to open almost above my head. A few fat drops splash on my hand and cheek. The muffled excited squeals of children, hurried footsteps. I stand beneath a doorway watching the water collect in the gutters and pavement, the rain's tripping sound like that of a huge exodus of tiny beings. Puddles, miniature clear grey torrents, form miraculously in the rustling tropical hiss. I look down and see that I'm soaked through, my cream cotton jacket and jeans darkening.

Inside the café, across from The Castle, I drink a coffee seated at an imitation rustic table with a huge slab of butter in the middle. At the other end, a bespectacled man reading a paper winces discreetly at my damp state. I look out on to the shimmering street behind the vapour rising from my cup.

I recognize his rolling walk immediately, the rolled-up jeans, boots, denim jacket, and the sunglasses, the vintage Raybans – Jake's. Why wear them in this weather?

He enters The Castle. They both come out, Tina wearing an apron, the tilt of her head, eyes raised urgently, betraying some urgent discussion. Even from here, I feel her like a toxic shock. But I'm calmer now. Their hands lock; something, money perhaps, is exchanged. He pulls her a little towards him, kisses her and laughs, walking off. She goes quickly back in. The puddles reflect the windows and houses like a miniature, fairytale world in reverse, looking up from its own dappled bubble – on the electricity cables, the precarious poise of silver beads of rain rising up like a long string of tiny liquid lights.

8

The bath is as soothing as the prospect of seeing Paddy this evening. A blob of water shakes violently at the tap's rim, falls, as the door slams hard on the entire house.

Always, such a hard slam, clump, clump on the wooden floor. But my anger has receded. I must achieve equanimity, generosity. After all, this is the inevitable, souring ethic of parasite and host – a machinery set in motion by my own whim and idleness. I need time to think about how best to proceed. It is the past, a past quite separate from her, that is making me worry now, fear consequences.

I picture her turning on the kettle, taking off her coat and throwing it over that one kitchen chair she always throws it on, lighting a fag, wondering where I am with that fretful, glassy-eyed frown into the garden, pointy teeth chewing at her mouth. But it comes up through me; the need for whatever jolt I get from her. I run some more hot water, catching a surprising glimpse of my flushed pinkish thigh. I have begun to think of my flesh as ashen compared to hers. I'll get out with barely enough time to dress. Tina will hear me; her ears are over-zealous sentinels.

I hear the creak and thud of her approaching footsteps. She opens the bathroom door, all swimmy-green stare above that wide smile. 'Here, I bought you something.' Her hands reach out with an offering. I glance over the rim of the bath. 'Tina, you mustn't. I don't know where you find –' unable to keep a peevishness from my tone. It is the bust in green glass of the child's head with its stupid blank eye. She has seen me look at it. It will be repellent here, in the house. I don't look at it.

'Thank you,' I say. In the mirror I see her mouth quiver and gather itself straight.

'That thunder. Fucking wicked!' And now, she has put the bust on the shelf. She has taken off her shoes, is stepping, fully clothed, into the water. I get up, spluttering, angry, grabbing a towel. She sits, glassy-eyed, in the bath, staring at the tap. 'Sorry,' she says flatly, 'I'm out of it.'

I recall Suzy's words of caution. I breathe in, out. 'Tina, I need to breathe; it's been fun but Jake is over again, Friday and –' But I can't say it, ask her to leave. It is still unfinished.

She shrugs. 'Cool,' she says. 'Me no vexed,' emitting a manic giggle as she stands and begins stripping off her wet clothes. 'Wouldn't want to get in the way . . .' I flinch at the thought of her deriding my marriage as she slithers around with Carl on sweaty sheets.

Everything in my bedroom looks the same and yet always, the sense of her after-breath, her print on my things. Later, when I am about to leave, I enter her room. 'By the way, where did Carl get his Raybans?' She is sitting wearing a t-shirt and jeans, at the edge of her bed, her diary beside her. Taken aback, she stands, her lips dismantle as they try to formulate an answer, and then she bows her head, and something in the tilt, the parting all askew, the old-gold hair falling forward, undoes me.

'It's no big deal, Belle.' She stands, hands fidgeting mechanically in and out of her jeans back pockets. She sighs and rolls her eyes up to heaven.

I grow withering once more. 'Oh yes, it makes me look like the petty one. But it is a big deal. Not just about manners and trust. There's something wrong with it. With me, for letting it all happen.' I look over at the cufflinks on the bedside table. 'Your little deceits, all of it.'

She is standing, imploring, 'I love you, Belle . . . you know, you know why I'm here, to –'

I'm putting on my jacket in the downstairs hallway when she appears again at the top of the stairs. I see her looking down, hand gripping tight to the banister, as if afraid she'll fall. She has changed into a mini-skirt, piled on the dark eye shadow. She looks like a demented doll. I ignore her as I gather my keys, bag, open the front door. Out of the corner of my eye I glimpse something, a calcified shape, like ectoplasm, swirling, falling down the stairs. But she is still up there.

I shut the front door behind me, a branch from the magnolia brushes my face, its thick flowers bend their heads in the glutinous air. My car is parked, as usual, round the corner, opposite Ali's corner shop.

Through the window I catch Reza's sharp turn of head; an agonized desperation to his mouth makes me realize she hasn't exaggerated about his lurking. He's in the grip of a sickness. I haven't been in for ages; it is Tina who shops, fetches, immobilizes me. Immobilized, for I must let go, use the past tense. In the rear-view mirror, I don't look too bad, some feistiness returned to my face. But that black Golf is there again. I recognize the number plate. I can barely make out the man inside – he's on a mobile. Not Reza's car then. Perhaps he too is like Reza, a lovelorn stalker of Tina's, I think ruefully, half-seriously. Perhaps he's following her rather than Carl.

It's a relief to be elsewhere, to see Paddy waving his frantic, mock-idiot wave through the plate-glass, ceiling-length windows. Standing at the bar by the entrance, his hair is the usual exclamation mark. He's in shirtsleeves, a lilac shirt with blue waistcoat – ever the dandy. But close up, frantic lines etch his kind eyes which seem hidden behind a veil of cloud.

We're on bar stools, elbows on the bar, heads inclining towards each other, gossiping. And it's true – Paddy, more than anyone I know, gives me back a rare thing, a likeable version of myself: mirthful and generous. Our thoughts used to meet, touch hands in mid-air, and clap themselves with glee. (As it had been, briefly, with Tina: but no, with Tina it was the skidding, immature intensity of schoolgirls.) We gossip about old acquaintances, recent shows, the fallout from the recent infamous art warehouse fire, and the extent of the damage. Paddy suspects foul play; a Mafia-style plot from a rival collector. I venture something more banal, more invisible; a mad warehouseman, perhaps, with a lunatic grudge against some piece of artwork or artist. We entertain ourselves going fancifully through the various possibilities. Which one might it be?

We drink too much, as always, oblivious to all at the bar, swept along exultantly by all the talk and the thickening darkness outside, the sensuous phosphorescence from the street and the plate-glass frontage looking out on to the glittering pavements.

He is casual, drumming the fingers of one hand on the bar counter. 'I met your lodger.'

The spell breaks. I begin to fray, caged in by her.

' – she's very beautiful – delightful and somewhat excitable.' Paddy knows more than he is letting on.

'How did you meet her?' Dread rises in my gut.

'Oh, recently, in The Castle. Tristram Baxter introduced us. He rather fancies her.' I feel nausea, panic at the exposure, at Tina's silence about meeting Paddy. But perhaps she didn't connect him to the Paddy I knew. I breathe calmly. I say tentatively, 'It may sound barmy, but she helped, being around. I don't get those blackouts, I feel better, less dead.'

Paddy says, relieved, 'Ah, so it isn't serious . . .'

I take my time to respond, shifting as a dark-haired man eases himself into the banquette next to me at the bar. I opt for frankness, I trust Paddy above all. As much as I can trust anyone.

'Deadly serious in that way that highly immature relations are.'

'So you've gone about spoiling her in your image,' he says. I wonder a little at his interest. It isn't like Paddy to analyse emotions in such detail nowadays. My marriage to Jake brought out no apparent jealousy; though perhaps the odd allusion to regret, in his cups. But then it's hardly his place; he was married when I met him.

'Yes, I guess, in the sense of messing up, and teaching her, all my old excitement. It's been empty. I seemed to stop wanting for a while, I missed it.'

'You could come back, you know. I'd like that.' Then he joked, 'You could help me haul it out of impending bankruptcy.'

'Yes, perhaps. In a few months, perhaps. I'll think about it. But what happened, Paddy? Why can't you tell me you've been in trouble?'

Paddy keeps his flushed profile to me, his nose showing its telltale network of red veins, his mouth too loose. He has begun to grow into his own caricature. 'I don't know, Chrissy. Maybe I felt a bit deserted by you when you left. I understood, I mean, I saw you black out, totally, when Guy's show was going up. But still we were a bit of a team –' He sighs, tugging at his chaotic hair. 'My father's being done, for handling stolen artefacts. And everyone's to blame, the auction houses, but because of his reputation he'll be the scapegoat.'

I don't remember anything of Guy's show going up but I remember rumours of his father befriending batty widows and selling off their art at a huge profit to himself. 'I feel sorry for him, but you know, I'm ashamed too, ashamed to have his name,' he adds quietly.

Perhaps she too was simply ashamed of her father's name; perhaps that's why she changed it. We cannot return to our previous banter. I enquire about his child, his wife. I have a rosy picture of them all in their Dorset barn, the joyful family, swinging on flowery swings in some eternally lush sunlit meadow. We fall into an unusual silence, the space between each other's private grief, nettled, tangled. The bar is too loud, the smoke is thickening. The man beside me irks me by constantly flicking his head down, checking his mobile on the bar – too often. I glare over at him. He stops, glances down into his glass with gloomy panic and a touch of shame. We leave, earlier and wearier than we would ever have done in the past.

Dark inky clouds are glued motionless to the violet-black summer night sky. Paddy turns me round by the shoulders. He pauses, grimaces, points the finger at me. 'You are well over the limit.' He looks round, steps out, hand lifted. A black cab appears, orange light dazzling in the dark. Paddy turns to hug me with that hasty English warmth of his. He says, 'Come back. You need to.' I sink back into the black cradling comfort. So much space, compared to that clammy house, to the street. The perfect, shrouded ride for my thoughts, to consider, for once, my immediate future, whether a return to the gallery would be risky in more ways than one. My mobile shows three missed calls from her. I delete them without listening to them. Our wires need to be snipped for good.

In our street, I don't recognize my own front door.

The lights are all off, which is unusual since it's a strict house rule to leave them on. Perhaps she was distraught after our scene, and forgot. Once in, I press the hall switch hard against the enveloping gloom and stride through, throwing all the lights on. I'm making a noise on purpose. Immersions, lights, fridges, radios, TVs, hi-fis, none of their usual low rumour. I'm clumping about, vague and unnerved. The answering machine has no messages; when I left it had three; it must have been a power cut. As I wait, swaying woozily against the sink, listening to the throttled hiss of boiling kettle, outside, through the French windows, the woman, head bent, arms extended on the counter, has straggly hair and blank eyes. So it was Guy's show, the first blackout, all those wax models of himself. I don't remember.

I turn the light on in Tina's room, holding on to the cup of tea, and catch a vision of her on the bed, diamond pendant in tantalizing relief, squinting slightly, and I am straddling her, knees either side of her body, and slowly, methodically, cutting through, blade against red cloth and bare flesh. Her irises are bruising, swoony-dark, as she follows my movements, her mouth slightly open. We both listen to the gentle purr of the ripping cloth. The kohl from her eyes has smudged, her eyes are flying. I am beneath her now.

I blink.

The bed is made, everything suspiciously tidy. The red art diary is on the bedside table. But the other one isn't in the box. I search methodically, inside trainer boxes, in each drawer, even in boots. A click downstairs. My heart jolts in its cage. No one. The vase is not in its usual place. I stick my hand in, tip it slowly on the bed and shake it out. There it is.

I can't stop it, this whirring round my head, whirring, whirring, like this house. Charlotte said, get out – I'm thin (v. good) but I look shite, like some fucking ghost, big circles round my eyes. A right minger – but she looks fine. One minute she's all over me, the next she says she needs to breathe.

Last night – what she said. Freaky, but I was right about us. But the other stuff, the weird game. I know it was ragga cokespliff madness – but then the next day, with her dad, it all went apeshit – she was making me nervous – hinting.

Let the signs come – like answering a call. It's all there, in the paintings. They speak for her. I hear it.

I stop abruptly, put it back into bed. Enough.

*

I wake feeling as if I have been dredged from the bottom of the river bed, my forehead wet, saliva drooling on my chin, my mind struggling through the wetness. The dream featured stairs and stairwells, leading down to more stairs and a stairwell, again and again. But I knew there was just one big concrete door, locked, at the top. It's 9 a.m. I pick up the phone and ring Suzy. Tina is out till tomorrow evening.

'Chrissy darling; up so early on Saturday? What is it? Have you spoken to her yet?'

'No, I couldn't. I nearly blew it.' I don't want to admit to having read the diary. 'She's clingy. And in the house – last night I thought someone else had come in. She might do something.'

'Mmm. I doubt it. Not everyone's weak like Richie.'

I stay silent, gathering the pace of my breath, willing myself into tranquillity as I've done so many times, putting the machine in operation.

'It's none of my business of course –'

It strikes me, Suzy knows. Kim. 'We slept together once. Big mistake. You know how it was a bit odd with Jake.'

'She must leave. Soon. It's all so unhealthy.'

'But I can't seem to stop myself being awful. I don't mind if she takes or steals something – it's as if I actually want her to do that . . .' I stop. Why do I neglect to tell Suzy some truths yet blurt out perverse depths? But perverse depths inspire Suzy with confusion and brisk dismissal, and the infinitely more perverse logic of common sense.

'It's just a thought, but why not get Carl involved? Get him in to finish off the work in the house, it will help ease her out. He's very good, you know . . . she'll be off in a flash.'

'He deals drugs – Jake might freak. Anyhow, he's weird about her.'

'No, no, he's not a dealer, he just knows people. He's a hard worker. And let's face it, can you trust what she says about him? I'd sooner trust him. Yes, he's your answer. He speaks her language.'

I hang up, suddenly recalling I need to collect the car before it is clamped. On the way to the bathroom, I notice Tina's door is closed, which means she is in. I listen, outside her door. It's too early for her to be awake; she can't have heard anything. I can hear the city stillness of an early weekend morning, the faraway roll of a beer barrel, the solitary motor stuttering to a start. I dress quickly, phone for a cab. The morning is calm, the sun hazy behind a veil of mutable cloud.

Lucky, lucky. No parking ticket. A good omen. I have begun to interpret in omens. I feel triumphant, exultant. Back in Ladbroke Park, I have lunch in a café, among pruned trees, spindly shoots growing from lopped limbs, like tree-hands in some German fairytale, fingers grasping, scratching at the air.

I read the sign on the church. 'After the first birth a second birth'. Oh, the pathetic illusion of a second birth. Yet I want to believe it this mid-afternoon, one side of the street in shadow, the other all golden vanilla sheen. And I continue, standing for a few soft, floating minutes, in its liquid light, head turning dreamily.

On my way back, outside the shop, I notice Reza, nervously guarding the pavement.

As I come to the house, through the thick panel of glass in the front door, I can see, as if through antique spectacles, the figure of a man, flattened, like a cartoon character that has been knocked over and gathered itself up in a flat shape, still moving.

As he nears the door, the nose grows huge and long, the eyes round and hollow, until all I can see are the holes where the nostrils were. Jake. He's back earlier than expected. The bags are still in the hall. He smells different, musky, sweaty even. He is jacketless, in shirtsleeves. He is looking at me full of excitement. 'The contract's through for everything.' We

157

decide to celebrate this evening. 'Let's ask Paddy along,' says Jake. 'I see, you don't want to be alone with me,' I joke. I immediately also ring Suzy and ask her to get Carl to ring me.

I've followed him up with the cordless still in my hand. He's standing in the middle of the bedroom: I'm at the door. His drawers have been flung back and emptied violently: t-shirts, jumpers, belts, in a heap on the floor. At first I imagine a robbery but no, I know. The worst of it is he looks round calmly, his face without a trace of a question on it.

'I was tidying up. I must have forgotten –' I sit, exhausted by the desperate lie. Shudders travel through my arms and thighs as if a force were pulling me down. When did she do this? Did she hear me on the phone to Suzy? Jake begins to tidy up methodically, in impenetrable silence. 'I forget what I'm doing half-way through,' I say, not looking at him, not helping, giving up.

He guides me to sit on the bed. 'It's time . . .' he begins.

'I think you're right – about that new prescription.'

I shift uncomfortably as I read in bed. Beside me, I can hear that Jake's breathing seems tense, unsteady.

I don't even bother to discuss the film we've just seen; I hardly watched it and he must still be pondering about the disarray in the bedroom, thinking God knows what. And I wonder why I don't just call her and tell her to go immediately, why I didn't tell him it was her. It occurs to me, in calmer moments, it might even have been a bad joke, meant only for me; but if she heard the conversation with Suzy . . . well, even then, it is a silly, spiteful gesture, hardly worth all this angst. Thank God for Paddy at dinner, regaling us with the hilarious tale of his eleventh-hour bail-out on the day the chickens came home to roost. Aware of Jake's constant vigilance of my face as Paddy poured me more wine or teased me, a fast acid shot of food travelled up from my stomach, back up to my throat. But we have got through the evening. I am waiting for the right moment to put out my light and turn over.

Jake's vision continues on guard. He fishes something out from beside him on the floor. It is a large black hair clip, evidently not mine, with one long, unmistakably golden thread of hair attached. He hands it to me. I look up briefly, take it and put it quickly on my bedside table. So close up, with his clinical eye, and ear, he must note, he must hear my own breathing mistiming. On the surface of the table, the hair clip pulsates, the sharp spikes pinging a low hum.

He looks up from the *Financial Times*. I say, just to say anything, 'I think I need to –'

'Mmmm?'

He moves his head in my direction and reads my face dispassionately. He turns back to the article on the Alternative Investment Market. At least it's not advanced research on wart removal today. 'What you need is a top-class neurologist, a second opinion. A psychiatrist.' He folds the paper carefully in half, then again, and tapping it twice against the bedside table says, 'And a change of scene, but, of course, I can't coerce you.' It's unmistakable, a direct threat.

Lucia was forever taking her clip off, putting it back on. She turned round, gravely, eyes daubed full of our ridiculous attempts at makeup. 'Mother says America's huge. Everything's bigger there. Ice creams, roads.' We cut flowers, roses and honeysuckle; there was the buzzing silence peculiar to the lushness of May heat. Lucia's hair glinted, a burnished gold in the sun. But she wanted to rob me, I knew. Her father was gone. I confided in her, I told her I'd kept some of Mother's clothes behind Father's back. I took the dresses out carefully; the scent lingered, that old powdery pressed-flower smell. Lucia tried them all. We put them on, smeared ourselves in makeup, solemnly put them back in the wardrobe, then ran out to the garden, exhilarated. She sat on his lap, she called him Leo the Lion, and she looked at me with that mean line of intent.

And she led him away, by the hand, to his study, where she wanted to know something about one of the little statues. He chuckled, following, pliant and captive. She pointed to one. 'Tell me the story of Medusa,' she said, looking up, fixing him with that repellent, radiant look she gave when she wanted to make a new friend, cast a spell on someone. His voice had grown warm and fond. He said, 'Well done for knowing who it is,' and I wanted to say that I'd told her the day before, but I couldn't speak or move and she knew, watching me, her eyes turning to narrow slits. And he explained the myth while I stood in the doorway thinking my eyes had been turned to stone, a cold and hot dread pinning me, sitting on my chest. I couldn't look away or move. We were never allowed in there, Jimmy and I. She wanted to know what had made Medusa so angry. She took off her clip, made her hair fall forward over her eyes. And he moved the hair back gently, and said, 'You're a curious girl, I like that.' She looked over, her mouth a mean line.

I dreaded the return to school; the next half-term before she left for America. I knew that she had to filter her anger through me; that I had to pay. For a few weeks, she was breezily, nominally, still my friend. Then, she turned her charm manically on several girls, among them Alison Jeffries, my silent enemy. After that, not a word from her, just the odd pitying smile. They began to avoid me, to sit far away in the dining hall. And then that afternoon in the library, when they made their way purposefully towards my desk and sat down. Lucia, Alison and Kirstie Hardie. They kept their books closed before them. Nervous and fearful, I played up, joked and entertained them in loud whispers under the sleepy super-vision of Mrs Cadwallader at the far end of the room. I was warding off the moment. Lucia sat furthest away. Then Alison began to make birdlike nods, opening her eyes wide as she listened, in a parody of lunacy.

'Go on, wear it,' she whispered, in a semblance of a catatonic state.

'What?' But I knew, by the composed tilt to Lucia's head.

'Now, Christabel dear.' Alison leaned forward, with an expression of kindly, matronly concern in imitation of Mrs Cadwallader. 'You must understand that a normal girl, well, normal people, find dead people's clothes spooky. Under no circumstances should you force your friends to wear your mother's pongy old clothes. Only weirdos do that, dear.' I didn't look at Lucia; I didn't look at any of them. And without another word, all three of them got up, Kirstie making a great to-do about stifling a giggle. Even now, I torture myself for not being brave enough to say that they smelled good, my mother's clothes.

I never replied to Lucia's letters from America, not really apologizing, blaming Alison Jeffries. I'd got used to absences by then, with Mother having gone. Gone, not dead. The past bites back. And betrayal forges a lethal intimacy, so much more tenacious than the bond of love.

My thoughts dance and flicker over the surface of the page of my book. Why doesn't Jake yell, 'Enough'? Perhaps he pities me. I will get into his inner thoughts. He makes his decisions for me, without me. Why do I sense that he notes every muscle, every stray change on my face?

In the morning, the space beside me is empty; only a small, barely discernible indentation on the pillow gives any evidence of Jake having slept there. He is sitting at the kitchen table, showered, lightly after-shaved in front of his inch-thin laptop. As I pass, I quickly squeeze his shoulder by way of good morning, feeling through to hard, unyielding bone. Only then do I realize he's quickly clicked away, to another document, a letter to his bank some two years old. The espresso pot on the stove is whistling, bubbling up into small explosions. I sit sideways to him, surveying the murky, dark green late-summer day, the dingy backs of the houses.

Once I have the coffee, I go upstairs and ring her on the mobile. 'You know Carl's coming to work here?'

'Yeah, brilliant idea, genius idea, Suzy's, isn't it?'

'I'll do a deal so he leaves you alone about the money.'

'Don't have to do me any favours.' There is a pause, cars passing. 'I'll be moving out soon.'

I must take care here. 'Tina, that mess you made . . . Jake's stuff in the bedroom.'

'What the fuck are you on about?' The line goes dead.

A firm ring on the front door. It's Carl. If it weren't for the sinewy block-bodied physique, the grown-out crew cut, he would be almost cherubic. And then of course, the eyes, hard brown pebbles, surveying, swivelling sideways, no hint of doubt. The jeans are fashionably low slung, there is a tattoo on his arm; it is a 'T' done in Gothic script, with a serpent around it inside a heart.

It is only when we reach the kitchen and I say, with Carl behind me, 'Jake, this is Carl. He's come to do the building work, give us a quote,' that I register that Carl is holding out some sunglasses in his hands, the Raybans.

Jake's long fingers quiver on his laptop as he turns to pay reluctant notice to Carl's gesture. I cannot see his eyes; the light plays on his reading glasses.

'Oh darling, I forgot to tell you, Tina borrowed them thinking them mine and forgot them and Carl picked them up.' I seem to be making a lot of excuses for Tina.

'Nice, very nice shape. Vintage, aren't they?' says Carl.

Jake casts him a politely chilly smile, before frowning back at the laptop. We move out of the kitchen and Carl whispers, 'Friendly chap, what? Right then, let's have a butcher's.'

'Suzy says you're a perfectionist, which is good because Jake, my husband, is the same.'

'Is that right?' His hard button eyes examine me up and down as if for faultlines.

We are in the third, back bedroom at the window looking on to the garden. Carl undoes the catch and opens it wide, grimacing, sending dust and air in alarm around us. 'The window's fucked. Needs replacing, look at the sill 'n' all.'

He brushes the wood away as if it were dust. Looking out, he says, 'Bit of a mess out there.' He strides centre-room, stops, arms akimbo, legs slightly wide apart, taking in the flowery Chinese patterned wallpaper, the faint tracings and mappings of mould and damp behind, the whitish squares where pictures once hung, the large plastic bags, unwrapped paintings and photographs, neatly marked in red felt-tip. A layer of dust covers everything.

Down in the dining room the sad, after-rain daylight reaches in through the dripping branches of the apple tree a few yards behind the window. 'Tina hates it here, hears voices.' He snorts, and strokes his white chin, up the line of firm jaw, almost square up to his ear, and then down the back, to his neck, in a form of display.

'So,' he says, softly whistling some tune, jiggling the keys hanging from his jeans, looking around. 'You could chop that tree out there to get light in here, bring some life in. Or go with it. Leave it dark, like an opium den, give the floorboards a dark stain, walls "Deep Boudoir Red".'

'Deep Boudoir Red! You must have been watching *Home Invaders*.'

'No. Never have,' he answers calmly. As I step forward, he grasps my bare arm. 'Watch it. See that?' He's pointing at a nail sticking up from a floorboard. 'Get your flattie caught in them and it'll go right through to the bone.'

He lets go of me; a current of hostile agreement runs

between us. I have that fleeting, odd sense again of having known him for ever. Behind the irreverence, there is a beady desire to impress. I wonder what Tina has told him.

'That Edwardian monstrosity.' I point at the marble fire-place. 'I hate it.'

'I'll rip it out, flog it for you if you like. Hollow it out.'

'Yes. Just a rectangle. perhaps a limestone surround.'

He points up to the stain. 'That damp up there. Needs cutting out, replastering. But there'll be mess, gutting, rippin' out. Mash it up. You gotta do damage to a house, to change it. People never want that, they want it all painless, like their lives, they don't wanna see the truth, how it all comes down so quick . . . and goes up so slow – for in one hour all great riches is come to nought.' He says this last phrase, suddenly but slowly, in the same soft voice he'd used in the upstairs room at the Medusa party.

I open the front door. He shifts the weight on his feet, eyes roaming outwards. He checks the street corner. Something tectonic moves in his block-bodied being. In a sudden hurry at something, he fidgets with his car keys. 'Call you with a quote,' he says. He gives me a quick wave, leaving behind a whiff of cement and petrol.

'Well,' I sigh, entering the kitchen theatrically, 'it seems we have a builder. He also knows a gardener. Any requests?'

Jake doesn't look up from his tippy-tap, tippy-tap. 'Are you sure we want him in here?'

'Well, Nick and Suzy recommend him. Builders are hard to find and most of them are bloody awful. It's you that wants things finished, done, perfect.' Jake stops, looks up quickly, tight-lipped, holding something back. I am his china doll, his brittle thing that might break, or worse still, even come to life. 'And. As soon as it's done, I'm going back to the gallery. Part-time.' I'm thrown a humouring smile as he clicks back on the computer.

'Good,' he says, looking down, barely surprised. 'Sure you're well enough?'

'I'll try very hard to be.'

'Do you think it's the right environment for you? I'm not entirely sure Paddy is out of trouble.' He has closed his computer, changed his mind about something. 'I wouldn't make any hasty decisions,' he says softly, before picking up his keys quickly from the table. 'I've forgotten something I had to do.'

All day I pop in and out, running errands – as I come out from the deli, Carl is standing just behind me, arms crossed in front of him. 'Got the hump, have we?' I glare back at him. 'I'm just sittin' over there,' he points at a bench outside The Castle, 'just finished your quote.'

I perch hesitantly on the edge of the bench. He is facing me, legs splayed apart, with the bench in between.

'Right. You got two rooms, the hall, scraping paper away, prepping, staining the floorboards, rippin' out the fireplace, treatin' the damp, paintin'. That'll be three weeks for me and three, four days' work for someone else scrapin' – he leans down, out of the breeze, to light up a pre-rolled – 'three weeks; cost ya three G labour excluding materials. Pay me half up front. Rest the end of the job.'

'Two thousand five hundred and I'll pay cash.'

He holds up his free hand. 'Joking, aren't you?'

I must take care not to give in too easily. It's important that he feels he has won. He crosses his arms again. 'That's my price.' We barter on for some time until I say reluctantly, 'Okay. Three thousand.' A pause for effect. 'Cash. And you let Tina off her debt to you.'

'Fond of her, are we?' he asks very softly, his hand absently reaching for the 'T' on his arm.

'Well, she needs to find a new place. You won't get your money back otherwise.'

'Ah, so that's it, sure, I see it, I get it. Sorted.' He curls his lip by way of a quick smile. 'Got a small job next week. I can move that. Start next Monday. Nine o'clock sharp,' he calls out, mock-admonitory before a dusty black BMW hisses slowly to a stop in front of him, and a man with a baseball cap, his eyes half hooded, gets out, leaving the door open. The music inside, I recognize it. A man ranting about his name, half-stuttering his rap. It's one of the tracks Tina listens to.

When I come back in, Jake has already left, several hours earlier than usual, for his flight. It should bother me but the house feels cool and quiet. The coolness of a vestry. I hear a snap outside the front bay window. I turn to see a blur of long hair, face floating bodiless through the glass, then vanishing in the twilight. The front door opens. She stands at the door.

'Was that you spying at the window?' I ask.

She replies evenly, as if to a fractious child, 'Just checking you weren't with Jake.'

'No, he's out of the way.' She remains at the door. I say, 'Carl's starting Monday.' She does not react to this. I continue, 'Better the devil you know. You don't owe him that money now. All right?'

Her brow constricts, then smooths out with shining, beatific calm. 'I'm looking around for somewhere else.' Her voice is unusually flat.

I cannot settle; it is so hot. I fancy I hear her murmuring into her telephone for ages upstairs. I walk up, ice tinkling in my tall glass. I watch from the doorway as she struggles with a tight top coming over her head; a tawny light from the late sun glazes her skin. Pale as alabaster. She has lost her pinkness. She turns around, adjusting the bottom hem, bringing it down. She has new jeans on – tight black drainpipes. Closer up, her face looks lightly bruised, mashed up as she would say, the lips heavy, the slanted eyes turned a little more downward than usual – as if crushed with some abrupt new dissipation.

There's a new photograph on the bedside table, of a child, with a woman behind. I pick it up.

'Ah, family photo. I was beginning to wonder if –' I halt, sensing this is a bad idea.

The colour has faded, browns pervade. They are in some room, an edge of window in the corner. The woman is sitting on one of those ugly heavy brocade sofas, and a white-haired child plays on the floor in front with a doll, small scissors in hand, cutting her hair. The woman is in shadows, looking into the middle distance, distracted; she is slim, dark, but the eyes are the same slanting shape as Tina's.

'She's got your eyes.' I stare at the child, the creased cuteness of the features, absently run a finger over them. I put it back. I perch beside her on the bed. I wonder about mentioning the mess in Jake's room but it seems insubstantial now. Instead, I hear myself saying, 'You don't have to hurry straight out, you know.' She lies back, eyes shut, her face locking in a strange agony. I move my head near her chest. A current begins in my temple, like a fast throbbing prod. Tina's hand begins to smooth it automatically and I slacken. A pool of tenderness, at last. Beside her is a newspaper. I pick it up. The headline says, 'Arrests made'.

'What do they think, when they're blowing themselves up, the minute before?' she says.

Her mobile goes. I can hear shock in her voice. 'Look, all right, Charlotte, I'll be there.' She sits up, groaning. I listen to her confused jabber about Charlotte being trapped somewhere by Boris. Charlotte has a knack with bad timing.

9

His hand swipes at a half-broken branch before him, wrenches it off, flinging it down at the ground to his right. 'Still in our dressing gown, are we?' A man pops his dimpled head round Carl's back, red eyes abrim, as if avoiding full-blown laughter, beneath a baseball cap. He has the fleshy mouth and rubbery, cinnamon-hued skin of a Bacchus.

'Jermaine's helping me out,' Carl says quietly. 'Don't worry, he doesn't bite. I'll be needing some cash, to buy materials.'

I leave them to it; head for the cash-point. On my return, they're both looking industrious in the back bedroom, moving around, whistling, making preparations. Carl roots around in a huge, clinking workbag of tools in the middle of the floor. He is the inverse of Tina, curiously feline, his body hardly making a sound as he walks. I hand over three hundred pounds. 'My husband would like receipts.' Stuffing the money in his front pocket and moving towards the front door, he turns his head and says, 'Naturally.'

By late afternoon, the sound of the scraping machine, the strong wafts of scalded damp paper, send me out into the sapping heat of the day. People move exhaustedly, broken down, like the mechanical soldiers in the junk shop. Sounds diffuse into surrounding traffic, metal pipes clang in some nearby construction site, the high-up gonging bringing to mind the height of cathedrals. Five messages on the mobile. I leave them, assuming them to be Tina on the Charlotte crisis. (It's her way to call numerous times if I don't pick up the phone.) My resolve is weakening once again. This I cannot make out: why, why ask her not to hurry to move out? It's beyond logic.

Everywhere, the stairs, the floors are covered in white sheeting. The newly uncarpeted floor in the spare bedroom is littered with shavings, large and small, as if a vast manuscript has been shredded by a bored child. Layer upon layer of paper, blue, pale crimson, floral, reveal themselves on the wall, each glimpsed behind the other.

The men are coated in tiny flakes, whitened by the plaster dust. I make my way round them, continue, round the bend in the stairs, past the bathroom and into her bedroom and there, with the door ajar behind me, the electric tingles begin again. Before she leaves I need an answer. There's something I seek, want. I begin by looking in the vase, but I know by now that Tina's habit is to move it around. I open the wardrobe and look at each shelf in turn, patting the jumpers, the clothes. Beneath the bed, nothing. She must be carrying it around. Not the holdall, or rucksack, or the vase. Her parka is hanging up behind the door. No diary – instead there's a miniature spirit bottle. Its top is pinpricked and burnt; its bottom gutted out. Makeshift crack pipe – hardly surprises me, she's not been in now for three days – someone is approaching now; I leave the room.

The afternoon sun comes in spikes through the slats. I realize I have not eaten since Jake left yesterday morning. I feel giddy as I enter the dining room. Footsteps behind me, his firm, prowling tread.

'Done for today.' Carl sounds light-hearted, almost gallant, a little preoccupied. Jermaine enters behind him. They look archaic, half-angel, half-satyr, in white plaster, as if they had appeared, ready-formed, from the walls themselves. In the dying light, the plaster from their hair forms a cloud of motes slowly escaping through the window, up to the streaked red-and-grey sky.

'Carl tells me you used to work in the art trade. Know some of them, drank in that pub in Spitalfields with that geeky pop band.' Jermaine reels off a few half-famous names. 'They didn't half go for the beak. One of them went to score, got kidnapped by the dealer who locked 'im in and went out again. He was nuts, right? Rang me, like I was gonna know what to do.' He is full of inquisitiveness, this one, the opposite of Carl, his attention focused on my work, my history, my family history.

Carl sniggers, one corner of his mouth curling, the pink of his gum gory against the dusty face. Tiny beads of sweat settle around my collarbone and forehead; the heat seems charged with a curious static. And they in turn seem like two people trying not to catch each other's eye; in on some private joke. Then the door slams and Tina enters, scowling slightly. Her long-eyed gaze sweeps over us scathingly, as if establishing the scene through a wide-angled lens. She settles on Jermaine. 'Turned labourer's mate now, have we?'

'Aren't ya gonna say hello?' says Carl, full of dismissive intimacy, his spliff faintly trembling in his whitened fingers.

'He-llo,' she says, thrusting her face at him for a second before turning away in disdain. His edges seem to fizzle, as if she produces shocks in him. Her wide lips are white, flat. She looks through me. Something is different, wrong. Picking up her handbag, she stomps her way over the bare floorboards of the hallway.

'Listen to her. Stomp, stomp, stomp.' Carl's ovoid head nods three times in parody. The men burst into a complicitous guffaw, Carl bending over to roll another spliff, Jermaine keeping up the patter. They seem curiously reluctant to leave, as if half-expecting me to do so first. My mind distracted by Tina's presence upstairs, I catch the tail end of something – 'Yeh, the youngest boy, whassisname, Reza, his brother told me.' Here Jermaine starts giggling, holding on to his half-paunch with his cigarette hand, 'Heeeh, heeh, the dad found girlie mags on 'im. He's sent him off to Pakistan. A spell of religious rehab. He's got it all upside down, with all that Islam one side; fit birds on the other. He was the one stalking our Tina; getting a boner for 'er.'

Carl flicks ash on to the floor from his spliff. 'Yeah, creepy, hangin' round the street corner out there. Worrying, mon.'

Jermaine lifts his thumb up to Carl. 'Know what you mean.' He shakes his head, and they both laugh knowingly, their blokey cackling rising, small spots of saliva glistening on their teeth, their laughter like an echo chamber. Carl follows with a story about a mugger he caught the other night, round the corner, attacking an old woman. 'He was young but a big fucker; the old dear was down on the ground. I chased him, said, you wanna get a head up, yeh? Kicked the shit out of him. You know what? I enjoyed it. You don't do that. I said to him, don't care if you're black, white. You don't do that.' Carl's knees are jigging up and down, his crotch pointing up as he leans back on the hind legs of the squeaking chair.

'Someone did that to my mum, I'd kill him,' says Jermaine reasonably. The silences lengthen and linger in the encroaching twilight. No air comes through the windows. They nod at each other and start busying themselves rearranging some paints, and I leave for the sitting room and turn on the television. They leave very soon after for some unspecified appointment. The door opens. She sits on the other sofa, composed. 'Charlotte's in hospital,' she says.

Her voice is flat, matter-of-fact, lacks its smokiness; her eyes have a calm, hallucinatory clarity. 'Boris just went mad, he wouldn't let her out . . . she was trapped in there. I was knocking on the door and she wouldn't open it cos she was scared, and I told her not to be silly and she started unlocking it and he just attacked her, I could hear it all going on. She managed to open it, the door. Her face was just like – '

She stops, gulps a little for air, twirling her wrist round with her other hand. 'He was still attacking, mauling her, so then I thumped him with my rucksack but he was still at it. Got hold

171

of a lamp and hit him hard. Yelping and blood. The ambulance came for her. They had to put him down but I – I haven't told her. We waited hours, 'er leg bleedin'.' There's more. She pauses for a moment, watching me waiting for what's to come. 'I had to go back to sign these papers. The police.' Her voice acquires a very soft burr. 'They said I had to sign more forms. To section her. Been back tidying the blood.' She looks quickly down at her hands.

'Well, it might be for the best,' I say quietly, wondering how she coped signing those forms, being filed into computers. 'Pinned down' as she calls it. She comes and sits down, leaning towards me, but I feel intransigent, indifferent, not even a tiny flicker of pleasure at Charlotte's fate. No consolation, no solace. Something ticks in me with its own hard volition. Tina's face is too close, a huge golden buzz.

I turn on the television. We listen and watch in silence – it's a reality show in which a woman's best friend and mother are collaborating with a team of specialists to find her a perfect romantic partner among the many applicants. The first choice of man is a narcissistic fitness fanatic who purports to be a Buddhist. 'I live my life and follow the paths that come . . .' The friend comments, 'He gets through the girls too quickly.' Tina stands in fury. 'Fucking crap this, you can't shop for love. Jesus, people – ' She bangs the door shut.

The house surprises me, so powdery, phantasmic, as I walk round turning lights off, giving rise to a feeling of being outside myself, watching myself doing simple things, as if by rote. Not long to go, I think, not long. A week perhaps.

She's already out. As I'm brushing my teeth after my shower I sense his silent presence outside, on the landing. When I open the door, he's there, wiping his brow, regarding me almost tenderly. 'I need to get the right paints. Why don't you come with me, it'd be easier, we can work it out in the shop, show you the difference in the shades and what not.'

At the builder's merchant, he plays Jack the Lad, exaggerating this for my benefit. The Irish foreman's red, jovial face turns indulgently to him. 'And what would that be that I was reading about your friend; there's something else in the paper today, that singer? Some trouble with a pretty young girl –'

'Oh, that. Rubbish. All made up,' says Carl with nonchalant aplomb. 'Pop stars. They get that all the time.' He adopts a flaccid, girlie pose, emits a half-shriek: 'Ooh, help, he spiked my drink and raped me.'

The sun has come out on the way back; we stop in front of a shop, I buy ice creams and the newspaper. We sit in the car, licking our ices with relish. He finishes his quickly, wiping his fingers on his paint-spattered combats, switches on the ignition, turns his head slightly, one hand casually on the wheel, the other resting on his knee, as if he were sitting in an armchair at home, and drives on.

As he drives, he looks out at the pavement, eyeing up a young girl with scrawny legs and a too-short skirt, following her censoriously with a shake of the head. He adds, 'If it wasn't for me she'd have ended up like that, like her friend Stacey, crackhead, half on the game, banging the yardie boys for the pipe, doing tricks for some Albanian fuck.'

'How long have you known her?'

'Too long!' He guffaws fondly. 'We was kids nearly.'

'She's a bit confused on her past. She told me you lived nearby, then you were fostered. Sorry, perhaps I shouldn't –'

He swivels the car round, holding up the traffic. 'Gotta be careful doin' that. There's cameras everywhere now, you noticed? Yeah, nah, it's cool. I went away sometimes, when Mum went on her binges. Came back. I was all she 'ad. My main foster-parent was an ex-soldier, an Evangelist. Kept banging the drum, preachin': "For all is vanity and vexation of spirit."' He edges the car forward. 'But he had something. Did me good. Still see 'im. His own son was a cunt, you see.'

'Do you believe in it?'

'Yeah, some. The Lord's vengeance, sacrificing your son, the burning crystal lakes, angels, all the stuff with the number 7. The wisdom, man. "When goods increase, they are increased that eat them, and what good is there to the owners thereof, saving the beholding of them with their eyes." Wicked stuff. Yeah, can't say I 'ad much time for turning the other cheek. Bit daft that.' He drives with surprisingly slow care, given his nature, frequently glancing in the rear-view mirror. But I imagine he can assume terrifying speeds, assume invincibility in the right mood. 'Tina moved in with me again after that twat Aaron. Then she buggered off somewhere with her dad, who wrote to 'er out of the blue, didn't work out. Back she came.' He turns his dark sunglasses, very like Jake's Raybans, to me. 'She can create trouble in two seconds.' Wounds are his battle scars, frozen, vengeful purpose; whereas Tina spills over with her electrical charm, lashes out unpredictably, prey to the jerkings of her mutant, patchwork being.

As if reading my thoughts, he says, 'She's had a hard time of it.'

We join the congested Broadway, sticky and grimy, the shoppers bumping against one another in the somnambulant heat, baring their newly uncovered, putty-like bodies like penitential millstones across the road. I try to sound casual. 'The change of surname, was that necessary?'

His head spins round. 'You know?' He turns back. 'I was there when she was filling in the form to change it. Said to me she wanted a new start. Can't say I blame her, after what happened with Bob. Then her mum.' He stops to let someone get across, looks in the rear-view mirror with concern.

I'm reluctant to ask direct questions and show him that I know so little. It will make him enjoy clamming up. So if there was a form, then it was legal, so my theory about her aversion to signing the form in the gym is partially right – the aversion goes deep, like a transgression. But it doesn't figure. Devlin was her father's name, not the stepfather's, Bob's. But then it would be typical of Tina to make a gesture, a radical new start. 'The mother's overdose – she seems confused about that too,' I say. I adopt the best tactic with him – appeal to the self-appointed, autodidactic guru. 'What's your opinion?'

He muses at the wheel for a while, a little hesitantly, as if letting me know that he has worked out I don't know much more. 'The mum was always ill, depressed, clinic, pills. And then, she couldn't take it, the trouble.' He adjusts his sunglasses. 'It was a mistake, an accident –' he halts '– the mum . . . Tina's got nobody really. I mean, look at it, you wanna chuck 'er out now, don't you? Why do you think I stick around?'

'It was only meant to be a temporary arrangement. There are enough men out there who'll take her on. She's very beautiful.'

'Or women,' he says. 'Whoever, whatever. New home, new personality.' He's turning the corner; checks the rear-view mirror with a fast grin, as if practising how to smile. 'She's a funny user,' he continues, 'always trying to be someone else. Even did it a bit with that Charlotte, picked up some of her ways. And then with you – way you two have been carrying on. Tell you what –' he lets out a chuckle sideways, as if at an imaginary audience in the street.

'Well, I know, fun time is over. My husband, he –'

By way of response, Carl turns to me, lifts his sunglasses once to reveal his deadpan stone-eyes, and lets them down again. 'Oh yeah. Him.' Again, the way of unnerving me so I am unpicked, wanting to do the uncharacteristic, to explain, to mollify.

'So here we are again,' he says, all mock nursery-jolly, lifting out a bag with various hammers, saws and paint-spattered chisels from the boot. They clank softly into the house. Behind him, the black VW rounds the corner. I haven't seen it for a few days. Carl is back out to fetch the paint, noting me watch the car. He follows it hawk-eyed as it goes down the street.

I look at him rather than the driver. He looks back again, frowning, before entering the house.

Tina is at the kitchen table, head in a newspaper. She shoots Carl an intent look, a message. 'Jermaine went out half an hour ago. On a job. Said he had a look next door in the dining room.' Carl nods as he starts moving paint pots into the dining room while her face begins to take on that unnerving wide-eyed paleness, fleeing outwards from itself, as she pretends to read the newspaper.

I busy myself folding towels neatly; aware of some private silent dialogue between the two. Now Carl is at the door, his brow lifting slightly. She gets up quickly, follows him out, and they move next door, out of earshot. I make out hurried exchanges; none of their usual snarl and swipes. She leaves, popping her head briefly in the door to say goodbye. And that's that – I'm left floundering in the refracted hot rays coming through the French windows.

The sun is diffuse and high; the streets scorching under nearly record temperatures. The traffic, all noise abated, has surrendered to the torpor. I am sipping a frappuccino after doing some errands. People are missing. Of course, Bank Holiday weekend starts today. Last year at this time we went to Capri where we decided, finally, to move. Jake is fine about Essaouira with Suzy – as long as it's somewhere away from the wailing, he said. But he hardly mulls over such things any longer. Now he humours me, as if the future were my own fanciful country.

As I round the corner, I see a commotion outside Ali's shop. Two policemen are restraining a spluttering, white-haired man holding a plastic bag. 'Filthy fuckin' robbery. Fuckin' suicide bombers.' He leans his head into the doorway. The police begin to escort him away. In the shop, Ali stands impassive, looking straight ahead of him as he serves the next customer. The red-faced man is ranting, spittle and froth coming from his mouth. I skirt round him. I wonder if Ali misses Reza.

We have all been quiet. Tina has come in and out, only using her bedroom and the bathroom, communicating in withdrawn nods and hellos, her manner almost serene. She is staying out till late at night.

During the day, I chat a little to Carl who has turned furiously efficient, lost in the work. His talk consists of outraged monologues against the 'poncy fucker on the radio'. Carl turns out to be an expert on troop movements, supermarket Mafia tactics, the Islamic mindset, farming subsidies, the probability of hurricanes. I force myself to do errands for him, be out, but in the evening I cannot quite leave the house in case she returns. Relieved yet emptied, I drink a little, speak on the phone to friends, go to bed early, take the usual pills, thankful for the strangeness, the transformations in the house. I hear her coming in mid-sleep and turn over, her arrival registered like a page turned in a dream.

The house is altering daily, like a sedated patient; dust-sheets still reign like vast floating bandages. The smell of fresh paint, of burning and scalding, of metal and dust has taken over. The hallway walls have been scraped so that the exposed dark plaster reveals dark scarring and pitting like primitive cave marks. He is almost over-zealous, pointing out small things not on his list – the switch in the bathroom, the shelves in the kitchen, the garden tap outside. He is now showing me a crack in the corridor. He taps it rigorously, follows the line of the cracking to where it peters out, above. 'I need to dig in, widen it first with a screwdriver, cut out, open it up and then fill it, replaster.' He claps his hands free of dust, gloating over my long-suffering expression. 'People make me laugh – want it all quick and painless – no mess,' he scoffs. 'But it ain't like that.

Nothing is. Any change – revolutions, wars, there's mess, right? That's history for you.'

In the afternoon, as I walk past the dining room, I see Jermaine is back for a day, burning off the wallpaper. He breaks out into song with exaggerated gusto. I stand surveying them in the doorway. Carl carries on, ignoring me. Jermaine looks round, winking at me from his crouched position, like a lit-up corbel, eyes bulging with unnatural light.

Kim is passing, clucking at them. She's doing her best to clean around the mess, emptying the kitchen rubbish bag, taking it out of its metal holder with a competent swipe. Her mouth is, as always now, a crimped line of diplomatic silence. Her hair looks different, with new golden highlights, complicated layers. For some reason this unsettles me.

The telephone rings. It's Suzy. 'How are things?'

'Fine, fine. She's very quiet. Hardly around. Looking for somewhere to move out to.' I look round. Kim is standing in the hall, wiping the sitting-room door, and from her quiet humming I know she is listening. I move away as I speak. 'Yes, all under control.' I walk away upstairs with the phone.

Kim is coming up behind me, with something in her hands. The green glass head.

'Did you mean to throw that out? Looks all right to me.' She's watching me for my reaction. Tina must have picked it up from my bedroom and thrown it out. It can't have been Carl or Jermaine. The blank eyes, the lying position in her hands, something lurches inside me, as if I were condemning it to die. Aware that a long time has passed, that I am sweating with indecision, I say, 'Yes, yes, get shot of it.'

She is leaving. I urge more money on her, saying it's too much of a mess; dirtier work than she is used to. We are both aware that it's an obscure bribe. I compliment her on her new hairdo, and she registers embarrassment, evasiveness, before turning, holding up a carrier bag with a large round object inside. 'Do you mind if I keep it, the head? My son will like it. I'll pay you –'

I say, 'Don't be silly, Kim – have it.' Again, the over-punctiliousness confirms it – her guilt. Tina is right. She's been talking to Suzy.

We sit next to each other in the kitchen, looking at his list of works left to do, any additions. Tina enters with a subdued 'Hi', her eyes ringed with indigo circle, their green irises dulled, filmy, the hair so greasy it is almost brown, and loose from its ponytail in dank wisps. She puts a can of Coke in the fridge. I haven't seen her for days. I've been in a mild stupor all the time, slowly achieving indifference.

She comes over to the table, picks up an orange from the bowl of fruit. 'Rotting,' she says. She dumps the whole bowl into the bin and places the bowl in the sink, running water into it. Carl ignores her. She is carrying her red art notebook and I realize I haven't tutored her, guided her, for weeks, a month.

'Fucking skinny. Too many rocks,' he says when she leaves. So she is not spending those long nights with Carl. But he knows her movements. I haven't encouraged a conversation about her since the one in the car. I don't want to open the box yet, not the whole way.

The evening heat feels stale with the lingering clamminess of the day. Carl is at the sitting-room door. He has changed his t-shirt, washed his arms, face and hands. Normally, he is proud to be powdery, enjoys coming towards me like a moving, lapidary challenge.

'Fancy a beer?' he asks softly, a surprisingly sweet smile on his lips.

'There's beer and wine here. In the fridge. Bottles and bottles. All there is.'

'You never go out much, do you?' His tone is that of authoritative reassessment, as if, having noted my quiet, intro-spective ways, he is reconsidering his original opinion. 'I'll get it.'

His insistent, caressing monologue mesmerizes me as the shadows lengthen in the kitchen and his face takes on a charcoal glow so that the voice, the words, seem to come from elsewhere. He speaks highly of Alan, the man who fostered him. 'He was wounded, shrapnel, in Northern Ireland, and then "they" treated him like shit. Poxy pension. No gratitude. Had a son who went to some poncy university, called the army the "killing machine". But some people have to do those jobs, don't they? There's got to be some order or the whole thing would come down, bosh, like a bad wall. Keep sharp, he'd say to me, look, fix on the detail. Make it your business to stay one step ahead, know what's really going on.'

His words continue with the soft rat-tat-tat logic of an endless procession of snooker balls. 'Told me I'd make a good scientist. "You're empirical," he said. I love all that stuff, atoms, particles, neurons. Stuff to really blow your head. Like take the eclipse, there I was standing watching it in Cornwall back in 1999 and I thought, now I get it, time is non-existent. Death, nature, that's one thing; time is another. You know, our existing calendar, right, it adds 11 minutes, 14 seconds to each year. In 1582, the days from the 5th to the 14th of October just disappeared. Bosh. It just jumped. They were trying to put the clocks right. And people were like up in arms about it. Like they'd robbed them. Awesome.' His voice warms with wonder. The room fills with his flinty, asphalt sweat. Now I hear stories of teenage tough gangs and racist rucks and how he tried to avoid them. He lifts his shirt, shows me a thin white scar to the right, on his muscled stomach. A few tiny, gold-red hairs grow up from his groin. 'All doing the brown, they were. Brown's for losers, y'know . . . Now and then, a spliff, a line or two – gotta wind down, ain't you?' All the while, as if guarding the relaxed voice, his box body turns and tautens, listens for signs.

'So many blokes I know just get fucked up but you gotta work, ain't you? Always do stuff. The devil makes work for idle hands, hey. Look at Sam, eight years ago, in a band, number one, awesome at Glastonbury. Then they break up. He's thirty-two, wasted. Just chasin' pussy, boning, and schlonging – lovely woman back home. He's not makin' toast. Other night, he wouldn't let Tina off. She can't stand 'im but he can't help himself, see, no control. Doesn't get it, notice, clock the details. Someone likes you or hates you, there's proof, it's there, in some detail. It's forensic, right? Like, take you for instance . . .' He looks at me, his eyes filled with close, sombre intent.

At the same time his mobile begins to go off in his pocket. 'Word up.' He moves into the corridor with a growly short laugh . . . 'Listen, mate, life is grace under pressure, right? Answer the phone to 'em, speak to 'em, don't ignore 'em – unless you want a tack in the gut. No, don't worry on that count. Wrong car. Yeah, yeah, all right, we'll see . . . Jeezus. Too much sufferation, mon. What? She's got nothing to do with it – yeah.' He listens for a while longer. 'Yeah, not a good time. Yeah, yeah. Cut.'

He returns, picks up his beer. 'See. That Sam I was talking about, likes weird shit.' I think ruefully about Tina's tales of Carl's sexual proclivities, his need to control his jealousy through the presence of a third party, and wonder how he squares this up with the censorious morality. But in Carl's mind there is no illogic. All his actions, his thoughts, have an adamantine exactitude, rightness.

'He's a boy, not a man, get my drift?' He lifts the bottle at me and tips the rim lightly against his temple for emphasis.

I smile with what I hope is an alluring feyness, but it feels stiff, desperate.

'By the way, how did you end up with Jake's sunglasses?'

'Yeah, well, I took them from her.' He throws out one loud laugh, like a bark, scratching his arm absently on his 'T' tattoo. 'To get my own back. She's always nicking my stuff . . .'

'Is that how she gets money?'

'What money? Oh no, she doesn't do it for money. Nah, she's not got her mits in the till. No, no.' He rubs his chin playfully. His denial sounds overstated.

'Why do you think she does take things?'

'Well.' He leans back against the chair, splays out both legs in front of him, blond brow puckering with reflective wisdom. 'Well, look at the logic of it, right, the detail. Number one: there's things she just borrows cos she thinks she's got a right to them – CDs, t-shirts. Forget that. Red herring that. Number two: other things she takes and keeps behind your back: photos, knick-knacks, weird little things mostly. She can't help herself!' He's all wide-eyed clarity suddenly. 'It boils down to her thinking there's something she ain't got. So she fixates and takes something she can hold in her hands, and she relaxes. Seen her do it, watching her, the details. Now it's you she's fixating on.' His tone seems softly sadistic. 'When she first met you it was Belle this and Belle that. Like it was fated. And the name being the same. Like it was a sign.' He fake-writes a message on an imaginary wall in the air before him. 'Got it in her 'ead she has to . . .' He ends the sentence by thumping the tabletop with his fist twice.

A thought occurs to me. 'What were you arguing about that night I let her in? Back in the winter, you had a fight out there, on the street.'

He throws a cocked eye up to the ceiling in an effort to remember. 'Yeah, yeah, I got it. She was doing a number, her usual number, only worse. We were on our way to a mate's round the corner. I was locking up the car. Then she comes back and starts acting up, takin' off her coat. It was freezin'. She just left the car, walked off into the street out here, and I thought, she just wants a fight. She's acting up. Crazy hoe. So I left.'

He lifts a packet of Gauloises out from his top jacket pocket. I am thinking of an image in my mind, of having seen Gauloises somewhere else recently, elsewhere, but the image refuses to settle. He looks up, one eye narrowing at the smoke. He has carefully edited that event. I sense that despite all his resentment, his sly digs at her psyche, he still protects her, holds back on information.

'What I'm trying to figure out,' he's still speaking in the same flat tone, 'is you. Well, no, I've figured you out. But why get her in here, living here? Asking for trouble.'

'There's been hardly any girlie action if that's what you mean. You wouldn't understand.'

'Oh, like I'm too thick, am I?' His hard eyes are two vibrating dots of hate.

'On the contrary. You're rational. I mean, there's something not to understand. I don't understand it.' I beam back at him a little helplessly.

His eyes pummel at the air above me with short, sharp stares.

I'm keen to placate him. Too keen. 'You're right. No doubt you've seen it all before. So, when are you starting next door, in the dining room?'

'Next week. Monday, Tuesday. Told you. Where's your head? There'll be a lot of ripping out, filth.' His leg jigs up and down. He has scented what's coming. I stand up, put my hand to my head theatrically, though the feeling of glutinous walls, a sloping floor, is real enough. 'God, I'm smashed. I'm going to have to call it a day.'

Carl cracks his knuckles, hurriedly picks up his cigarettes from the table and sticks them in his denim jacket top pocket.

He adds, injured scorn eyeing me up and down, 'Not much stamina, have you?' His hot, alcoholic breath fans my face. His eyelashes are unnervingly light. 'Best be going. I'm due down the pub anyway.' Carl's pride does not take to being cut short, to polite dismissal. There is much lengthy rooting and clunking in his tool bag in the dining room. He emerges with a wrapped blue plastic bag.

I wait, holding the front door open for what seems an age while he fumbles for his mobile at the threshold. 'Happy weekend,' he says, with his back to me, looking up and down the street before crossing. I close the front door on him. I should have been going out this evening with some old friends and Paddy, but I am somehow fearful about leaving the house. Even when they are gone for the evening, I feel a presence encroaching. I undress, struck by the frailness of my legs. I no longer look at my face. I stand, look out on the last rays of summer dusk coming through the grimy building-dusted windows. Clouds clot together, and after a while lengthen and thin, disappear beneath the horizon, into the redness of the bleeding sun.

I catch sight of Carl coming out of the corner, from the side of the boarded-up house. Then he's gone. His car is still parked in front of my house. Now I remember a packet of Gauloises on the floor of that house, just inside the side window. I imagine it serves as some sort of drug kiosk where they meet the dealer, get the wrap, say, 'Yeh, blood', smoke the crack. Hence that first night. Just as I flick the blind back, I notice the black VW driving away; its number plate has various Ks in it. Reckless with the drink, I dress quickly, grab a torch and stumble outside. It's not yet night but a mantle of violet and grey seems already to shroud my movements.

I crouch in, making my way through the open side window, avoiding getting my clothes caught in the broken glass at its edges. There's a feral, rotting smell. Things are left to die here. I hear tiny insect scuttlings. I shine the torch, shiver as it lights on some quick, furry thing flying past. I walk tentatively. A floorboard bounces, clunking beneath me. On the floor I see something glinting. A tool of some kind, a paint-smeared chisel. A cigarette, the whiff of Gauloises. I pick up the chisel, heart racing, wedge it alongside the loose floorboard to lift it. Dust filters up to my nose, settles on my hair. There, a long metal box. It opens. Inside, Carl's cheap blue plastic bag, inside that seven wraps already made up. I put everything back the way it was. A shadow crosses outside as I stand back up, stamping down the floorboard.

Back at home, I sit drinking in the dark. It explains much. Carl's stash – his hoard. So his vigil of Tina, the sightings of him in the night, were linked to this. How fittingly pragmatic of him to be guarding his hoard and Tina at the same time. That's why she was only half concerned, only half serious about his stalking. She knows. I should ask them all to leave at once, but somehow I haven't the stamina. Not only are a few wraps of coke fairly insignificant, but the episode brings me back to her web of deceit, of intent. I wonder why I didn't push it further with him earlier, seek out more – but I wanted him away from me.

Now I see it's all rather predictable, banal grimness. Carl's drug-dealing, Tina's story – an abusive stepfather, provoking her mother's suicide. She changed her name, her own father's name, to forget the whole thing. To punish her own father. Fine, now I know. I have the answer. Soon, they'll all be out.

I feel heavy, like a dying fish slithering in dank waters. The shredding effect of the drink and the pills, as always, gives me an erotic charge; a wayward desire. I slither into depraved corners, with visions of Carl fucking Tina with spiteful thrusts on the rubbish-strewn floor of that dark house.

*

Morning. Silence. Saturday. Of course. Outside the door, a note. 'Dear B. Found somewhere – not sure what day. Might take week or two.'

So it is resolved; she is going of her own free will. I must make the last few weeks amicable, free of storms and reprisals. There's a message from my father on the answerphone cancelling lunch. Something about a book review due on Monday. This is very last-minute for him; his voice is flat, curt. Not only is he not one to change his routines or plans, but his excuses are usually produced breezily, full of the righteousness of his cause. It is becoming an addiction, my suspiciousness, but still I cannot brush away these fears flapping at my edges.

Like giant fat green spiders, the bushes in the garden have become its rulers, grown in fantastical scale against the shrinking web of lawn and trees. Relentless growth always unnerves me. I long to hurry it away, long for the wood-and-fire breath of autumn, the old gold of the trees, the cleansing chill of the winds. I have, I realize, a free day, a weekend free of home invaders. The house itself is in estranged, anaesthetized silence, nerves slackened, in shock from the changes. A thin film of plaster dust has settled, immovably, everywhere. An absurd thought comes to me: this house will never be other than what it was. It will return, the old house.

I pick up my old notebook from the kitchen drawer, surprised to find it still there. Just banal lists of things. It seems so long ago, before she came to stay. Make a list. Number 1. Add to Carl's list – redecorate Tina's room. 2. Sort out garden. 3. Ring Paddy. Work. 4. My birthday?

Next to it, the laptop Jake left me when he bought his latest model.

I open it, sign in. An email from Jake. He emails now, calls only once a week at an allotted time since he complains I never pick up the phone. 'Do you need me over? How's it going? Up to you.'

I click 'reply'. 'The house is mayhem. Leave it a couple of weeks when it'll be finished. I'll keep you posted.' Downstairs, I straighten the wedding photograph, tilted from all the tapping and banging.

The weekend passed. Suzy and I had Sunday lunch with a mutual friend and to Suzy's disappointment, I carefully avoided discussing Tina, assuring her she was leaving. I made myself busy on Monday, looking for furnishings for the top back bedroom. If Tina came in and out, I didn't notice. I'm becoming used to her absence. I feel saner too, if a little flat.

I tell Carl the back bedroom looks great. I don't tell him it feels strange, like a mirage, a world apart. 'I'll start in the dining room Wednesday,' he says. Tina comes in. She mutters a 'Hi' and races upstairs in her usual manner. She avoids my eyes as I greet her, bounds up the stairs. Carl's mobile goes off. He waves a perfunctory goodbye as he heads out for the evening.

In her room she's struggling with the zip of her jeans, flapping her hands as she does when in a panicked hurry. 'I only got ten minutes.' I am aware she might want to borrow something out of habit.

'Would you like to borrow something?'

'No thanks,' she says. A new wall of reserve has set up in her, a febrile secretiveness. I leave her to it.

She has put her hair up, carefully made up, pale pink lipstick, in line with the dress's style. It's a black dress, not unlike my Balenciaga, but shorter. She is in the slingbacks I bought her. She looks stunning, transformed, cool and somehow antiquated, black-and-white; an early sixties film star. I cannot quite get over it, as if she had emerged from the screen. The worst of it is I am assailed by a pathetic shrinking. I straighten up, recover my balance. 'Where's the party?'

She smoothes down her dress. 'West End.'

'Bit early. It's only six-thirty.'

'It's some drinks thing.' She is making a big show of looking for her keys. I immediately suspect that it's an art opening. It's Thursday, a common day for them.

'Splendid,' I say, the freeze between us solidifying, settling. I am getting it back, the tranquillity, the imperviousness. One has simply to breathe, flatten any glimmer in the eye from within oneself. 'Have fun at the opening,' I say. She shoots me a quick, alarmed look, and says nothing.

I am in her room. I have woken in the middle of the night. I realize now that my mind seeks clear, cool certainty. Now that I am not befuddled by drugs, I want to know if I'm right, simply that. So I am here again to read a diary that I can't quite believe. Diaries never tell the truth since people edit their own thoughts or wishes. She's getting negligent; it's on the bed, as if she has forgotten to pack it in her bag at the last minute. There are no new entries. I pick up the novel she's reading. I like the cold painterly opening, the ice, the discussion about the young girl, the intruder in the cold marriage. Strange how the book, a favourite, prefigures, like all books, something in one's own story. Except that you are never the character you imagined you were when you read it. Who am I now? The brittle cold heart of the winter park. The older sophisticated woman. And she – well, hardly the innocent, but whether a force of accidental chaos, or devious? Well, it turns out she is tough, tougher than I thought. Moved on. Reinvented herself with my help. All my worry was for nothing.

The A4 red art notebook is there also, on the bedside table. All those notes, the glossary of my sentences, my comments; her careful academic annotations on the opposite right-hand page. And on the left, reproductions, printed from the net mostly, carefully sellotaped to the top of the page and folded in half. My suggestions. Woodman, Cranach's St Christina and St Ottilia, the latter offering those repulsive eyeballs on the book in her hands. She dutifully read all the experts, the cultural critics, on the influence of the secular, the grotesque in medieval religion. Now another sellotaped copy: the *Rokeby Venus*. More notes. Munch: *The Morning After*. I thought she'd like that, the woman, supine, drunk on her bed. Another page. Munch again. Then one I didn't suggest. *The Dead Mother and Child*. No notes on this one.

She has done something to it. The child at the front and the dead mother in the background on the bed – their faces are cut out, very neatly, as if she has used a coin over them. The mourners' faces are intact. I am shivering a little. It disturbs me, this. It's the neatness more than anything. One more page. Last entry. Those brown tones, I recognize the Titian. As I unfold it, a footfall, a creak. Through a raging flood in my ears, I make out rustling, a foraging sound, somewhere beneath, the odd suppressed cough. The dining room. I put on my dressing gown, creep out quietly.

The grainy dawn light is about to come up. In the penumbra, the scarred wall pulsates heavily. I pad quickly, silently, in bare feet down the stairs and I can see already the dining-room door is not properly closed. I push it gently open. The room is lit by a slither of moon, by the ochre lighting from the street corner. She sits in the high chair, head obscured in the wallpaper, dark dress scrunched up. Headless, a lit cigarette waving in front. On the floor, I slowly make out papers, photos, a box. Her head inclines forward, those pale orbs flaring. I make out the stuff on the floor, my notebook, my handwriting on letters. Strange, they don't feel like mine.

'I saw it. A list.' Tina leans over, lifts the notebook from the floor. ' "One. Add to Carl's list – redecorate Tina's room." You use people up. They're just fresh blood to you.'

'You're off your head. Please put the stuff back when you've finished with it.' Poise is the thing; composure, not to let their need, their spirit, encroach.

Tina's laugh is different, laconic, someone else's. I realize there's a brick loose in the fireplace, a plastic bag in the hollow. She follows my gaze. 'Carl stashes the big stuff there, the rocks of coke. Makes tickets to go out to sell some in the evening and puts those outside, in the corner house. Safest place here, he says.' She laughs. 'Help yourself.'

I say with resignation, 'Perhaps you'd ask him to remove it.'

'Perhaps not. Can't. You see, he thinks the usual place is trouble. There's a guy in a car always round here, he thinks he's a cop or out to get him.' Her voice is drawling in the darkness. 'I know who he is –'

'If you don't watch it you'll end up like that father of yours, smelling of booze, ligging fivers off people. Is that why you don't want to see him? Why you changed your name?'

'That. Is. Not. Kind,' Tina says, pronouncing each word with slow staccato, head moving slowly from side to side with each new word.

'Well, you know me, I don't do kind.'

She blows her smoke out with exaggerated poise, holds out a long arm, finger pointed at me. 'You chose me. That's why I'm here. I know why.'

I stop short, my heart pounding, concentrate on the nail-heads glinting in the moonlight. I prefer the other, overexcited lunatic Tina. But she continues. 'Richie's letter. Charlotte told me. He said everything in this letter to Lucia, how he regretted leaving her and how miserable you made him feel so he wants to kill himself.'

I smile. 'Wrong. Your fantasy. He was a hopeless junkie who overdosed. It's not certain he committed suicide. Death by Misadventure. Even Lucia told people the letter was ambiguous. I did chuck him, humiliated him too – he couldn't stop talking about her. To wind me up, that was his one source of power, because in the end he realized he was a pawn, a tool in our battle.' I stop, regard her, suddenly aware of that first night in the sitting room; feeling the same incoherent intimacy, absurdly, in my dressing gown.

'As you say yourself, Belle, just because something's a fantasy doesn't mean it's not real. You don't remember things, do you? Or won't. Don't remember what you tell me. And Lucia, you went weird on her, didn't you, after your mother died, and she left for America with her mum? But she came back, didn't she? You both went to the same college and the whole Richie thing went off.'

I am alarmed by her knowledge but shield my disturbance with a bored sigh. 'Lucia betrayed me when we were children. Years later, she followed me to my college. I shouldn't have forgiven her. She steamed in, as she always did. When she scented someone's interest, she had to take them away from me – like Richie, jump in first. So I swapped the tables, yes, took Richie away. I don't need to explain myself to you. It's an old story.'

'Dead and buried, hey, Belle? Don't think so. There's a lot more. I came along. I remind you of her, and it's all come back. You told me, don't you remember? That night before we saw your dad – about that night, that night you went to Richie's.' She stands, her voice clotting, her body buckling slightly. 'You should feel guilty but you just feel this coldness. I know. We need to get away to Morocco . . . to the heat . . .'

'You don't know. You see, there's nothing to save.' I close the door. I take two Halcions to ensure sleep.

Morning. A text. 'I'm moving out tonight. I'm working today.' The black diary is back in the box under her unmade bed. Unusually, the entry has run over, over several days.

Time not on my side – Carl says the bloke's not after him – he's going in with Jermaine on something bigger than last time. Her dad could tell I was upset – we had dinner after the opening, after I got rid of Tristram and Paddy. I told him about us and he remembered how she went weird after her mum's death, turned all nasty and jealous with Lucia. All the pictures, the Woodman, the Munch woman, the angel in the cemetery, they're all her, all her messages . . .

I put the book away, calmly, for the final time.

Tranquillity can be practised, perfected, even if something is waiting to pounce. Sometimes you look it straight in the eye until it submits. At other times you flatten the gleam in your eye, deflect it. It depends on the nature of the beast. I think of statues, for example, how they scare people, inspire awe, fury, because you can't stare them out. They look back blindly. Conversely, flesh, if you watch it enough, grows smoky in hue, petrifies, until it is no longer a threat.

In the distance I hear a stalled small aeroplane, no, a lawn-mower. The noise is circular, a muffled, endless loop without variation. The house is totally hushed. I enter the dining room. All the boxes are neatly stacked up, chair in the corner. She cleared up, at least, before she left this morning. The last room, the last room and then – all over. Tonight she goes. And she doesn't know everything, I sense she's guessing, pretending. I sense that from the diary. No rain for days: the ground is parched, cracking. I walk around. Carl has done a good job plastering the walls. Not a trace of imperfection. He has an eye for 'detail' as he puts it. How easy it is to alter space, mood. She packed up last night. Full tote bags. A few clothes hang in the wardrobe. Mine.

Carl is down in the dining room. 'Where's that Tina then? Saw her in a flash car with some shaven-haired git.'

'Tristram Baxter probably. An old flame of mine. Rich –

she's off.' I no longer care what I say. Confusion, pity have now solidified into a numbed callousness, into necessity. Carl wipes some sweat off his brow with his dusty arm and turns to the wall, probes it with his hand, before striking at it hard with a hammer. A piece of wall cracks and falls. I retreat into the cool sanctum of my bedroom. I am fine in the mirror, colour returning to my face, sanity to my mind. The room vibrates with the gentle but persistent clinking of glass.

The light inside dazzles. For a while I think I am in the wrong house. No dust-sheets on the stairs. The hall wall is a cool Caspian blue. He comes down the stairs with an easy, hospitable manner as if I were the guest, he the host, those stone eyes. 'She's back.' In the kitchen, through the panes, I see a torso in the garden, all waving, bare arms wrangling with bed linen on the line. She opens the door and enters, her step faltering as if unsure of whether to stay or keep moving forward. It's easy, politeness. Don't make her an enemy, not now.

'So you've found somewhere?'

'Yeah. By the river.' She seems demure, voice soft, eyes dimmed, head bowing. I cannot connect this with the other Tina, the other night. 'I'll stick to The Castle for a while, then try to get a job closer to there.' I wonder if it's Tristram. She shifts her weight on to one leg, laundry still on her arm. 'Charlotte's bad. Pumped full of drugs in the hospital.' Then, out of nowhere, 'I'm sorry about looking at your things. But you read my diary . . .' She shrugs, moves off. Has she only just noticed or have her entries been taunts, deliberately edited deceits?

She is in her room. I can hear her tidying up, singing to herself in her lullaby tone. She has put the laptop in my room. The screen quivers at the sound of the thumping; the whole house is quivering. Suddenly, a cataclysmic rending, a thunderous clunk and then another, louder and louder, from the dining room.

'What's that?' I go down to the hall where the noise is intolerable. Carl and Jermaine are crouched either side of the fireplace like caryatids. There's a gouged area around the frame. Carl takes a crowbar and continues to pull the stone back. There is that smell again, of corky damp paper and uncovered plaster. The room is a small storm of dust. I turn away, shut the door, coughing, and return to my bedroom. More rending and cracking. He has moved up to the damp corner and it feels as if he is going to come up through the floor directly to my right. But I can't leave the house, not while Tina is in. I check quickly through my jewellery cases, Jake's drawers, then I stop, repulsed at my petty soul, infinitely worse than her lunacy. The cufflinks are back on his chest. St Christina, indeed, giving away her tarnished silver and gold. Jake's silver and gold. But Jake won't whip me or drown me or shoot arrows. He may, of course, divorce me. I email Paddy to discuss when and how to return to work.

It is early evening now. I hear Tina next door, singing. I pass by, and there is a smell of nail polish. She is varnishing her toenails. I stifle a surge of anger at her nonchalance. She may be playing for time. The two men have cleared up. The air still carries dust but the floorboards are swept of rubble. The crab is gone, leaving a cavity, exposing bare dark brick, in a long, downward lozenge shape. The fireplace, too, has been completely gutted, the columns, ghostly hollows edged in white plaster or paste, and the centre gutted down to just bare brick cavity. Such a shallow space. Fireplaces always promise more, a fathomless pit. I notice the bricks loose inside. Where the stash is. Soon it will be gone, along with them. Carl has followed my gaze. He seems keen to distract me. I know why, sonny boy. 'Yeah, we'll render and plaster that up properly next week.' He has swept up and Jermaine is using an old mop to wipe the dust.

'I've got the rest of your money here, one thousand five hundred.' I say, handing it over. 'That just leaves five hundred next week.'

'Oh, yeah, ta.' Carl exchanges a smile with Jermaine.

'Drink?' I ask.

They both smile. 'Not 'alf.'

'Come in the sitting room – you can use the bathroom to clean up.' I don't know how long she'll take to go; I'd like the shield of their banter.

Jermaine is on the tan sofa. Carl is on the end of mine. Both men are on their best behaviour, all polite, circumspect chuckles, jumping up like eager flunkies to light my cigarettes, replenish my wine. They speak about the house, the work. Jermaine gives off a genial air of green-belt suburbia, riverside pubs, football matches cheered around neat barbecues. Except for a nervous tic, a constant perusal of his phone on the table. As if responding to my silent scrutiny of him, he holds up his mobile. 'Used to do marketing, a long time ago, for a cell-phone company. Had my own outfit, executive life. Jacked it in.' I believe him, the chuckling voice, full of warm reassurance – a good salesman's voice.

One of Carl's eyebrows is scornfully turned up. '"Good morning, madam, my name's Jermaine, Senior Sales Rep for Harrow North."'

'Should have stayed. They offered me shares. That was before the whole mobile thing really went through the roof.'

'Yeah, but look at you now. It's done wonders for your looks.' Carl's manner is that of young master with indulged idiot servant. Doctor Frankenstein with Igor. Jermaine waves his hand pacifically at Carl, picaresque grin spreading.

Tina comes down, dumps something heavy, a tote bag, in the hall.

She hovers at the door, turning to me, her eyes full of deep green colour. Emotion, I think.

'Drink before you go?' I ask, holding up the bottle, wondering why I am prolonging the agony. But the truth is, something is blocking my throat, pressing on my breastbone.

She stands, her face registering confusion, conflict.

'Go on, get a glass from the kitchen,' I say gently.

She returns, sits down on the tan sofa at the other end from Jermaine. We are all smoking a spliff, which Jermaine has rolled with the swiftness of a conjuror. Which explains the perma-red moistness to his eyes.

'Hear about Charlotte's dog? Shame her being animal rights and all.' Carl responds with his soundless snigger. Tina wedges her legs up against the far side of the sofa, arms wrapped round herself.

'Yeah, heard what happened to him?'

'Shut it,' says Tina quietly.

Jermaine raises his eyebrows, puckers his lips. 'Ooooh.' He knows this is a good story and that if Carl can't tell it, he will. 'That Tina over there saw to that. Bumped him right off.'

There is silence for a few beats, then Carl's shoulders begin to heave with the effort to suppress his laughter.

'Tina the Barbarian,' says Jermaine and now the laughter is uncontrollable. Tina's face is aflame but very still. Amidst his splutters, Carl catches her expression, and for the first time since I've known him, his face registers anxiety, panic.

'Jesus.' Tina leaves the room. After a few minutes, I follow her into the kitchen. She is standing with her back to me, before the French windows, undoing the clip in her hair, and the light seems to come through her, she seems so fragile now, evanescent. There is too much to say, nothing to say. I return back inside. Tina follows a little later. Picking up on our tension, Carl bristles and stretches. He takes to lighting up my cigarette, tells me joke after joke, showers me with courtly, respectful glances. I sense a tactic, an ensnarement of her. Tina is smoking and watching, smoking and watching, with a new, unblinking serenity.

I don't understand why she lingers, but we are all lingering.

Jermaine asks me questions about the kind of artists I like, whether I collect.

Carl says, 'What gets me is they're not doing anything new. What's that guy's name who did that famous toilet, right?'

'Duchamp,' I say.

'Anyway, all that stuff was done like nearly a hundred years ago.' Carl continues in this vein of firmly held conviction.

'Yes, but all artists respond to artists before them. It's what they do with it, whether they retranslate the image their way . . .' I say.

'Daylight bloody robbery. Having you for a kipper. I like to see work's gone into something. I mean, you can see with Picasso, he can draw, that guy. Call me old-fashioned but I can't see the point to that bleedin' bed by what's her name, Tampaxes lying around or something.'

'It's conceptual art,' I say politely.

'Yeah, well, that's supposed to be about the idea, right?' Carl doesn't wait for me to respond. 'So where's the brilliant idea in that? Bit obvious.'

'Yes, but if you take something out of its context, put it in a museum –'

Tina starts humming. Carl responds by saying, 'Oh sorry, am I offending the expert over there? Have you noticed how she's talking all posh now, Jermaine?'

Jermaine gets up chuckling, flicking at messages on his mobile, adjusting his low-slung jeans under his emergent pot belly. But his mind is elsewhere. 'Gotta shoot, nigga.' He adjusts his baseball cap and I notice he is virtually bald under it. 'All right, ladies, arrivederci. Oh, I think I forgot me other t-shirt in the bathroom.'

He's nodding at Carl; I wave goodbye, stoned, a little vaporous now. Tina sits, following Jermaine and then Carl out of the room with an intent look. She seems to be trying to hear their conversation. No doubt some big-boy deal. They are muttering. She frowns, eyes fixed on the floor. The front door slams and Carl returns. He sits back down next to me.

'Does Jermaine never take his cap off?'

'Yeah, maybe he wears it cos he'll lose his scalp if he's not careful.'

'What do you mean?'

'Bad debts to the wrong people.'

'To yardies?'

He points a firm finger. 'You're sharp, you are.' I have a feeling he's taking the piss.

Tina says firmly, 'He deals charlie but he's fond of the pipe . . .'

Carl is trying to pre-empt something. 'He owes his suppliers, him being a little fond of the old pipe, so he's working with me, lyin' low. But he's all right, Jermaine, he'll come through.'

'Well, now you've told me I'd rather not have him around, just in case.'

'Jermaine's got good customers in the pop world, the art world. Even the yardies are impressed – they all read *Hello!*' He waves his hand at me. 'All right, chill, I'll keep 'im out. But last thing any dealer's gonna do is play havoc in a nice household. Long as they kill each other, nobody cares, right? Anyhow, just as well he's gone. He has the horn for you; he desires to copulate, mash it up.' He makes some lewd gesture with his fist.

'Lucky me, I've never slept with a man who keeps his hat on in bed.'

This amuses Carl greatly. Afterwards he watches me just a little too long. 'Can't say I blame him.' I return his look. And as the wine hits my tongue, cold and clear, a levity clicks into place. I am the clockmaker, the timekeeper. I am holding Tina. The timing, her going, rests with me. The choking eases in my throat.

'Got any on you?' I say mischievously.

'Yeah, sure – celebration.' He beams. 'We ripped it out well in there. Only three more days.' And as he puts his hand in his pocket through the dark, shiny denim, the colour of old artists' smocks, as he moves his hairless forearm, his whole body obeys his every move. Nerves tweak around the muscle by the tattoo, the significant 'T'.

'What's that tattoo?' I ask, knowing full well. Carl shoots a look over at Tina, who has her back to us, putting on a CD.

'Oh, it's an old one.' Now he is sitting with his thighs apart, leaning back a little, admiring something in his hand, like a chalky gem. It must be crack, a largish wrapped rock of it.

'I can get some charlie. Or we got this. Jermaine's tipple. He just gave it to me, owes me.' He darts a quick look at Tina.

'Don't mind a bit now, do you? We need a bottle.' Tina's face is placid, unmoving. 'Come on, T, you got one,' he says, looking at her. It strikes me with black hilarity that he goes through her things too. Of course. How else could he achieve his omniscience?

Tina focuses on the rock, then on Carl, her torso twisting with hesitation, like that of an animal scenting a trap, nosing slowly towards it, around it. 'Relax,' she says, looking straight at me, then at him, 'I'm moving out, remember?' It's as if I haven't heard it for some time, that thick, smoky, fuckable voice. She leaves and her steps sound slowly up the stairs. This strikes an odd note; she normally runs, up or down, to mollify her vertigo.

He leans over, puts his face close to my neck. 'Mmm . . . scenty.' Our eyes lock in a leering hold and I think of those saucy seventies film capers in which a cheeky-chappie window cleaner beds all the housewives. A cocky sneer, as he leans back. 'She's not really moving out, is she?' A muscle begins to tick in his jaw. He can't be happy she is off, out of his reach. He would now prefer the lesser of the two evils, that she stay here, with me. I begin to understand the mechanics of the evening. He was expecting a different outcome, the return of a sniffling, needy Tina, finally succumbing – all his.

'Gotta be careful,' he says, standing to look through the gap in the blind, perhaps thinking of the black VW, the fantasy or real cop. He turns back, switches all lights off except the lamp by our sofa, plays with the rock in his hand, putting it on the coffee table, picking it up. 'There's a guy hangs round here . . .' Tina enters and gives him a small liqueur bottle. 'Ah, perfect, all scraped and ready prepared I see,' he says.

The wrap is untangled with slow, tender care on the coffee table. Tina remains standing, hands in jean pockets. He puts the rock down; there is still more untangling to do. He picks up his cigarette from the ashtray and takes a long puff. Tina breathes heavily. 'All right, all right,' he says. She turns, smiling faintly, goes to the other sofa, coils herself in. Whistling and idly chatting, he is making his usual meal of it. I am unravelling, my senses coarsening. I need something to course through me, blowing away all this hazy grief.

He inspects the naked rock. 'Good stuff, crumbly, not like that plastic shit.' He picks it up carefully between thumb and forefinger. Gingerly, he breaks off a piece and crumbles it in his fingers before placing it in a small mound on the bottle-top.

'Here,' he says, pointing at me. 'You first, ma'am. I'll light it for you. Sit up, it's better. Now let me tell ya, do it slowly, yeah, hold your breath. When I say.' He burns the small mound of white grains on the bottle lightly. 'No. Just suck slowly out of the bottom of the bottle.' I wrap my lips around the carved-out base, sitting up on the arm of the sofa. He is now crouching beside me, caressing my hair back. The lighter flicks on. The noise of tiny twigs burning up close, and slowly, slowly, I suck in, watching the bottle fill with swirling smoke. A movement in my head, a powerful gust, stripping and flattening all before it with erotic clarity. 'Go on,' he whispers, burning it still.

I cannot breathe in any more. I move my head, wave my hand a little as if to say stop. He takes the bottle from my hand and quickly finishes it, in a powerful woosh. I flop back in stunned voluptuousness, holding my breath in. Tina is watching me, then Carl, who is busy with the bottle. 'Got a pin?' he asks. I am still sitting. Beads of sweat line my forehead. I am far up, locked in the tall, kissed reaches of my head. There is a sweetish smell, like burning plastic. My body sweats, begs for more. I lean my head back, eyes closed. When I open them, I let out an involuntary groan.

'Good hit?' says Carl.

Tina is watching me with the solemn curiosity of a child. He's about to serve himself some more, but hesitates. 'Okay, your turn.' He hands the bottle to Tina with some more rock on it. Tina takes it, and the lighter, from Carl, crouching before the coffee table between us.

'I can do it myself.' She turns to the side, her back to us, sits with head tilted and draws and draws. I watch, a beat of yearning rising and ebbing in me. There is a pale gravity to her actions as she hands the bottle to Carl and moves away from us, stands head against the wall by the door, eyes closed. Alone, removed. In mourning.

I hear myself speaking above me, in a cold, smoky drawl. My heart is racing but beginning to slow a little, hopping on one leg. I am bereft with pangs of lack, of not-having, of loss. Spikes of panic, rising. Carl has lit up and is drawing greedily, with practice, his expression determined, at furious work.

He talks in his soft, manic, insistent voice. In between, he nervously cleans the top of the liqueur bottle, clears the little holes. And so it goes on. Tina does not speak. Carl baits her in between directing himself to me. He thinks he can stop the gap, talk the emptiness away. Music comes very close to my ear, its beat separated into component, hypnotic swishes, then unfurls again. I take for ever telling Carl about the video shop manager who rang us up, about his fantasy. 'Must've been seeing you two together, put ideas in his head,' says Carl. Tina remains quiet, self-absorbed, moon-pale, her hair sticking to her head with that sweat at the temples as I've seen so many times.

It is all over, the sense of dispensation, of suspension. Loss sets in, in an itch under the scalp. Carl scrapes the bottle inside to get the dregs, scrapes them together, and we all have one final, desperate puff each.

'Could get some more,' he says. 'Or got a bit of k.'

'No,' I say. 'All over now.' I, the timekeeper, am impatient, edgy for the next stage. 'Let's have some skunk to come down.'

Carl is oily, obliging, charm itself. 'Whatever you want, my love.' He rolls a spliff. Tina looks pared down, reduced to some essential, pale core. She too is measuring out time with a heavy inner beat, dancing slowly for herself. Carl is beside me, watching her dancing too, her body forming a huge, sinuous shadow on the wall. He makes a second joint. We float on long pools of music and silence. The doorbell rings. He puts his finger up to his lips.

'But the lights are on, the music,' I whisper, swallowing hard.

Carl waves his hand at me to shut up, his face hardening. We all listen out. The footsteps go away. He stands, flicking the blind back minutely. 'It's okay, it was Jermaine.' Tina smiles at some private thought and he takes the joint from her and with a huge drag leans over to me, holding my head with one hand. 'Blowback.' He presses his mouth to mine. I am trapped, inhaling the smoke and his sweat, the flintiness of him. My heart is racing now. Carl laughs, taking another drag, leans over and takes me by the shoulder towards him, his mouth on mine as if he were saving me. 'Kiss of life,' he says.

'Tina, you too,' I say with a sing-song tone, as I sprawl on the sofa now, leaning back into a dim corner. I want to consume, be consumed. Carl's mouth gnaws at itself. Tina's mouth is rictus-fixed as she sits unusually straight, pounced, all her usual sprawl gone.

Carl's voice has acquired a metallic croak. There is a gathering thickness in the room, from the smoke, the silence. The beat, slow, rasped, insistent, is reaching my ears in an overpowering wave. I try to stand and Carl grabs me by the hips. I say, 'I think I need to go horizontal.' He watches with his hungry mouth as I walk out, my body liquid, my thoughts curling wafts of smoke. He follows.

He sits on the edge of the bed, with my hand under his hot hand, above his crotch. I moan, tantalizingly, feel him hardening. He bends over on to me and begins to whisper what he will do to me. He kisses me with his smell of petrol and flint. Muscles strain from the leather necklace around his neck. My cunt responds in spasms. A shadow above me. Tina's mouth is slightly open and fixed. The street lighting rakes over Carl's greedy arm, searching for my breast, ripping my top. He watches his hand as he does so, unbuttoning his jeans with the other. His breathing is dense, hostile. Now she sits on the edge, one side dark, the other amber-lit, eyes flashing in the still face.

Two joined fingers, pumping, stabbing hard inside me. I am feeling it and then not, in loops, stops and starts. Carl turns his head and begins undressing Tina slowly, as if for an examination. He stops for a few seconds, a solemn look across his features. I watch her long boyish arms move, and hear a whirring, as if a camera has been turned on. I have Carl's white, thick cock in my mouth; now I am licking moist female flesh, Carl touching himself. There are more geometric changes, manic adjustments, slippery bodies rolling like wild, hungry fish. Then a stopping, a flatness, numbness. Carl turns me over. A tongue working into me. I moan. Carl stops her, enters me with a few short strokes to savour it, and then thrusts in hard, hands holding me by each hip, on and on, until my mind floats down into a dark, soundless rending, and I hear myself moaning in odd animal grunts, and he comes in snarled breaths. She and I lick and nibble at each other's skin, our edges, as Carl smokes silently.

She is bent over the edge of the bed, on her knees, softly biting my thighs, and Carl is naked, standing behind her, holding on to Tina's hip with one hand and with the other working at his cock with his own spit. I hear myself whisper, 'Fuck her.' I watch him open her up, go in quickly. Tina shudders as if from the core of her, and I grab her old-gold hair and push her down further on to me. And I can feel Carl's thrusts through her face and tongue. He and I watch each other's dark faces; then Carl loses himself, clawing at Tina's hips, his eyes closing, opening, focusing on a ripple, some part of her back. Now his eyes close in a sombre moment in which his whole being seems to lock itself in. The movement ceases in a freeze-frame, petrifies. I come, shuddering, engulfed by showers of black dots. I open my eyes. Tina is moving strangely, supported on her elbows, and I back up a little in the bed to watch her. Her eyes are luminous, rolling back, her mouth fixed into a weird shape, still giving out flat little animal grunts, and I lean forward to kiss her as Carl pummels into her and collapses on to her, his head raised and straining as if just struck, felled.

Harsh breaths fill the room. I take Tina's head in my hands. Close up, I can see her tears smearing her face. I begin to say something. Carl returns from the bathroom. He's whispering, 'Behold, the whore of Babylon.'

Tina sits up in a sudden fury. 'Fuck you.' She leaves. I am suddenly cold and sober without her in the bed, anxious at being alone with Carl. I retrieve the duvet from the floor, cover myself and turn over. A soft wailing comes from the next room. Carl says, 'What's going on?'

'I don't know,' I say, after an age. He is tugging roughly at my shoulder. I sigh, 'Carl, I really need to sleep.' His hand freezes on my arm, as if he is deciding whether to squeeze, harm.

'Fucking women,' he says and quickly gets up. I can hear the muffled sounds, the quick zit of a zip, my door closing.

Her hoarse voice: 'Get out.' The thud of fist on human flesh. I get up quickly, reaching for my dressing gown. Carl is sitting on her bed and it is Tina, next to him, who has hit him. He looks up, stunned, holding his jaw, and then, registering me, turns and grabs her arm. They are figures in some hellish etching. The bare-torsoed satyr, about to strike at the naked girl, her other arm raised. Carl, panting a little, says, 'Go on, tell her, tell her if you're so bloody close. Tell her about Bob.'

Tina's free hand grabs his neck, squeezes with hard fury. He grabs and holds her other arm; just holding both arms now, staring at her. 'Enough', I say. He lets go. She crumples down sideways on the bed. Carl stands over her as her voice comes up, very clear and cold. 'You've done it now. Just go.'

He brings his hand up through his hair in a gesture of despair. I am suddenly weary, flat. 'Let her go. She doesn't want you.' Carl walks off quickly and I hear him prowling around in my bedroom, trot quickly downstairs. Finally, the door slams hard and loud. I go downstairs and she follows, barefoot, in her dressing gown. We set about cleaning up silently, methodically. We clear all evidence – the bottle, the ashtrays, the glasses moved by a mechanical, druggy energy. In a parody of our old days, our old ways. I go back upstairs.

She comes in. 'Why did you do that, with Carl?'

'Because it's goodbye.' I want to say, how else were we supposed to do it. I want to say much more, that I never learned to lament but today I'm close.

'He told you.'

206

'No, he didn't.' We are finally facing each other, standing. Some sense of decency, of truth, assails me at this late hour. 'I guessed about your mother, knew you'd changed your name. So what happened with Bob, your stepfather?'

Tina goes to stand by the window, with her back to me speaks matter-of-factly. 'They went for their night out. But they came back early and he came up. Mum was still out, talking to Jesse, our next-door neighbour. And he came up in the dark. Must've heard us and saw me and Carl on their bed, fucking. He called me a slag, everything, names – on the landing. Carl tried to stop him, shut him up. Bob shouted at him to go. Carl went. So it was him and me. We were on the landing, right at the top of the stairs. And he started pushing me in those short little jabs, towards the wall, on the landing, like he did to my mum, and called me a slag again, his mouth all twisted, disgusted. I ducked out and pushed him, my hand on his face, so his head hit the corner of a big mirror we had there. And he just went all limp, slumped down to the floor, eyes rolling up. The hall light wasn't on, only in the bedroom, and at first I just looked at him like it was a shadow, like it wasn't happening. And he was there, twitching, weird on the floor. Just him and me. I stood there watching his face, thinking of the way he spoke to her, jabbing his finger at her all the time. I just stood, watching, like willing it on. Then, later, Mum arrived. Ambulance, police. I was in trouble. But Mum helped me. Got me a lawyer, looked after me. She said I was innocent. But she was just pretending. She knew. I meant him to die. I should have told you, but I wasn't sure –' She turns, comes over. 'I was waiting to do it in Morocco. We haven't gone yet. We can forget about it, everything, there.'

I stroke her hair; awed, tenderized, by the moment. In her deluded, devious way, she had the truth about us. I recognized her. I saw it in her from the first. As her confused jottings said, she answered the call. Yet now I know, it's impossible, like an unnerving shadow. I must protect myself, even from her. I go downstairs, return with the purse, hand her twenty pounds, recalling that first night. Then I reach back in my purse, take out all the notes. 'Take all of it. For a cab. Leave the keys.' I lie on the bed. Tina does not leave. She sits on the bed, her husky voice cracking, quieter, in a macabre repetition of that first night she stayed. 'Now you know . . . let me stay one more night. I need to tell you something, Belle –' We are repeating all the stories, in one night.

'No. It's worse. It's too much.' I don't turn round; I don't comfort her. It will just go on and on. I am suddenly defeated, rancorous – she will bounce away from this. Move on to someone else. 'This time you're going to have to wake your friend. Tristram Baxter, isn't it? Thought you said he was a creep.' I turn over in the bed. Tina's crying ceases and I hear the air emptying of a departing body. The jingle of a set of keys dropped on the floor, outside my bedroom door. The second door slam of the evening.

The air chokes me. The drugs are powering my mind, a demented machine spilling out dark scenarios all on its own. That he will kill her, that she will kill him; or me. That she will return; that she won't return. When the door slammed I fell out of myself. Bitter tears cool on my cheek. I get up to get a glass of water, lost in the new flawless space, listening to the cheerful drumming tap. Through the upstairs window, I see a dark turquoise, cloudless sky as if conjured on a computer screen, the cars bathed in the orange night glow. On the street, a middle-aged couple argue. They are stumbling, drunk, continuing as they round the corner. A cold trembling I have only known once before, unfurling all my boundaries. And somewhere, as day intrudes, the glimmer of light in my mind. The strange scent we had. There is a sense of measure in it. Finality. Both stories played out and ended. My thoughts become automatic, concentrated, huddling around survival, pragmatic. I am tearing the bedclothes off; quickly, efficiently, opening windows, waving away the pall of stale smoke, putting them in the washing machine.

I am talking to Jake. It must be evening there again. He says, 'Keep them out. We need to talk. Not now. I can't, but I'll be there day after next.' So he's going too. I can tell.

I make all the necessary arrangements with Kim on the phone and drive towards Carl's house by the canal. Number 7 looks much like any of the other houses, squatting glumly in a street with a few short scrubby trees. The front door needs painting and the windows are covered by dirty net curtains. I change my mind, turning at the door to write a message back in my car. I don't want him in the house any more. 'Carl. Have to go away this week. Will leave some money with Suzy and phone you when I get back to arrange finishing the work – when it suits you.' He'll see through it no doubt.

As I'm writing my mobile's ringing and ringing.

It's Tina. A text. 'Please answer.' I switch it off. I drive and drive, I don't know where, automatically, unseeing. It's 5.30 p.m. I find somewhere, just out of Ladbroke Park, some pub on the corner away from the bicycles, the cars, the people jostling one another with their carrier bags, returning from the shops. Old men sit like turkeys, hands cradling pint jars on the table, watching a football match. But I am noticeable in here, jangled, when they roar and cheer and grumble at the screen.

The front door is just on the Yale; someone has unlocked the Chubb, disabled the burglar alarm. Not Tina. She left her keys. I am in the hall. The roll of the window opening in the dining room. The summer evening is shorter, darker. He turns, eyes dark and darting, jaw in a stiff lock. Of course, he has keys. I stand, still clutching my bag.

'So wassup?' he says, advancing, a plastic bag in his hand.

'Nothing,' I say. 'I've just got back from yours. I have to go away somewhere. My husband. You can finish the work another time, when you like. Not this week.'

'Oh yeah? How come?' he says, voice light, full of reason, advancing still. 'How come I can't do it while you're away?' I stand, speechless. He smiles angelically. 'You gonna offer me a drink then?'

'Carl,' I say wearily. He moves close to me, reeking of sticky plastic, of rock, that's what it is. 'Just a cup of tea or a beer. Yeah, I fancy a beer.' He adds politely, gently, 'Have one yourself?'; his voice has become guttural, staccato. I sit on the high chair, smoke a cigarette, ignoring his request, my bag carefully on the ground beside me. He wanders off, comes back with a beer, without his plastic bag.

A rambling tale follows about Jermaine doing a flit last night, and how it didn't occur to him, the real trouble he was in, niggaz with big Gs, wish he'd had nothing to do with him. All the time I'm wondering why he is at pains to talk about Jermaine: 'Jermaine, right.' He strolls over to the window, listens out for some noise. 'I was saying, he's on the fly, gave 'em the double, right, but thing is, he done me too.' He's framing Jermaine, that's what he's doing. He moves forward, stands before me, hands clasped, legs apart. 'Thing is, that man out there, in the black Golf, he must be followin' Jermaine. Tina says no. She says he's following you.' He stands upright, breathes a long, patient sigh. 'Anyhow, enough about fucking Jermaine. Off to Ibiza next week. Bought these jeans, like 'em then? Tell you what –' I have a sense he is pacing his own mind. 'Got some awesome charlie, fancy a bit?'

'No, Carl. I've had enough,' I manage to mutter. He looks injured when I refuse. He suddenly walks off into the hall, the kitchen. A few minutes elapse. I think of running out the door but I stay still, transfixed. I know him, I've always known him. He returns, a sudden spring to his walk. I smile politely, say nothing. He must not see my fear. He begins sniffing: he had some charlie out there. Perhaps he's just come back for the stash – a ray of hope. He follows my quick gaze at the fireplace. The bricks are orderly, put back. He slaps both his thighs with both hands. 'So then. Where's she gone then?'

'I don't know.' Perhaps that's it, he wants to know where she is.

'With that geezer, one of your friends? What's his name?' He comes over, leans in, face fisted up tight. I feel his hot, beery breath. He lets out a short bark of a laugh. 'Passed her on, did ya? You've had boy, girl, cock, pussy, you want everything, hubby's money.' He swallows hard, gurning, and stands again, prowling the floor before me in semi-circles.

'I kept thinking of her, got it in me head I'd look after her. Worked hard, kept me nose clean. At seventeen, got a job, Alan found it for me.' He halts, caught by a stray thought. He collects himself, wipes under his nose. 'Anyhow, I came back to get her. She was sixteen, I was nineteen. He caught us. Bob, he fancied her, way he always looked at her, from the side like, all sneaky. Got leery when he was drunk. Tina didn't like it but she never told her mum. He shouted, said she was like him, her dad, a waster, a slag. I was gonna hit him but I was thinking of her, see. Police came. They wanted to do her. There was an enquiry. Tina had to spend time in that fucking place, banged up all them weeks. When her mum died, she said, come on, Carl. Fresh start.'

He stands, calmed by his speech, looks down at me a little pityingly and says, 'You see, when you said what you said, to let her go, you were wrong. I'm all she's got.'

'I don't know, Carl.' I am too tired, too anxious to put on an act.

'You don't know?' He mimics my accent. 'Thought you were educated.' He clicks a lighter at my face before lighting up his cigarette. I see the tattoo, the 'T' on his upper arm. A smell comes off my pores, like very sweet shit, as I am snared, heart pummelling at its walls.

'Detail.' He exhales. 'You smell scared. You look scared.' The floorboards creak loudly as he walks on them. 'She shouldn't have been here but you can't just go and throw her out.' I begin to move to go. He taps me on one shoulder and says gently, 'That's not nice. Relax, let us conversate between us.' He barks out one short laugh again. 'You see, people like you – think you can do anything with anyone. I saw you at that wedding party, with your jewels. "For she hath said in her heart . . ." How's it go? Shit –' He slaps his temple. 'I forgot.'

I can't speak. He is feeling my arm. 'Getting a bit scrawny, aren't we? You two were bang at it, snorting and God knows what.' He is staring beyond me, trying to focus on something, his mind circling and halting. He turns his flat, reflectionless eyes on me. He is all quiet awe. 'Yeah, I know, I got it. You want me to do it, don't you? Rape you? Kill you maybe? That would be it. The answer.'

Something clutches up in my stomach. He throws me a look of contempt; puts his hand up to his head as if he has to think, concentrate. He picks his mobile out of his pocket, checks it, pondering. 'Okay, okay. We're gonna chill, have a bit of wine and spliff. That's right. Then, go out, have a laugh.' He slaps my arm with the back of his hand. 'Cheer up. Go next door to the sitting room, go on. Bit gloomy in here. Mind you wait for me.' I get up and follow him, my mind immobilized. At length, he returns from the kitchen with two full glasses of wine. 'Drink up.' I force some down. The wine tastes ashen, dusty. He is buying time, I feel it. Perhaps he is waiting to hear from Tina. Perhaps I should suggest I ring her to find out where she is. I drink, smoke and listen, as he pours me more wine, talks, fast and softly. All about Tina.

The snapshot on the wall next to the mantelpiece is a

hologram. It alters with the angle of vision. Now it's wide-angled, a nest of living round objects. I focus in on them, all glassy dead eyes. 'Now then.' He slaps me a little, playfully, round the face. I can barely hear him; he is far, far away, fuzzy, crackling. 'Don't go to sleep. Listen up, bitch. You and me gotta conversate.' Or is he now talking to someone else? I can't make out the words, only 'in fifteen'. More talking, sounds departing. The man lifts me, by the arms, under the sockets like a floppy mannequin. 'There, see.' He goes next door; I follow, somehow. He is doing something at the fire-place, lifting a brick, taking a round plastic shape.

'Oh no, don't look like that. Only huge rock of charlie; you like it . . . upstairs,' he says, 'we'll go up, change your top. Spilt wine on it, mucky girl. We're getting out, see. "For her house inclineth unto death and all her paths unto the dead."' He leads me by the hand, the petrol smell is strong, like we will both burst into flames. Along the top landing there is a hacksaw, hammer, resting against the wall. The walls lurch forward, then back, in soft ripples. The ceiling slopes in from one end to the next so that when we come to the far door, past a whole sequence of doors, to the end room, the ceiling is only a few inches above, pressing down. He comes to a stop. 'Go on, get it, and change. I'll see you downstairs.'

I push the door, which is heavy, like thick granite. I push harder. A cold air seeps from the dark room. I walk in and the heavy door clunks behind me. Where's the window? Ah yes, some thin, intermittent light coming from somewhere. I peer through the cold, half-lit gloom. I begin to see more. Canvases stacked along two walls, a chair, a desk, very messy. But over to the far end, it gets impenetrable. Now I can make it out. The double bed in the far corner. It's cold. I sit on the chair, stare at the bed. I can see now, in the penumbra in his studio. He is lying there in a strange, twisted way. I move up to the bed. Richie's breath is hoarse, rapid. There's a letter, beside him. To Lucia. I freeze. I pace back. Sit on the chair. I am watching him altering: his bulging blank eyes. Trapped. His face slowly turning frozen blue. There's no point calling anyone. Anyway, I can't move. Only watch, see. Sometimes you look it straight in the eye until it submits; sometimes you look and look, flatten the gleam in your eye, until you stare it away. Flesh, if you watch it enough, grows smoky in hue, petrifies. Such a waxy face. Cover her face, mine eyes dazzle. But it's not her, not my mother. I didn't see her. He wouldn't let me. It's him, Richie. When he rang me, what did he say? Why did I come? Oh yes, he called me Lucia. His voice was blurred, clotting. Close the mouth and the eyes, the sick, filmy eyes. But I can't. It seemed clear, when I turned up. It seems clear now. I need to go now, get in the car and go.

I'm shivering, the cold reaching into my head. I concentrate on the light at the corner but the constant flickering makes a hum, like a crackling, faulty radio, growing louder. I lean against a wall but it feels clammy and rasping behind me. I can only see before, the thuds and heaves in his chest. The face, the eyelashes stuttering, the final whistling breath. Flesh to stone. I must go. A panic that I have somehow locked myself in, and when I get to the door, I pull the heavy metal door knob but it's fixed, nothing happens. I try again. Again, it does not yield.

Someone is there; his t-shirt appears through the crack. 'What's the matter then? I was in the loo.' He has hard dark eyes, no light, no reflection, I can't see myself in them, not even a tiny spot. He nudges me down the stairs, half holding me. 'Where's your bag?' Is he rummaging around? The door slams as we leave. But all the lights are on, good. It's safe.

It's drizzling. My eyes catch fire. Lights tremble and overlap. I only have a black cardigan over my silk top and skirt, the wool fizzing on my skin, like wet, rank animal hair. Don't think about that. We are driving over a bridge, in a gold car.

He's driving. 'The pale horse,' he says. A wailing, mewing loud cat noise. 'Like the sirens, do we? Excitement.' Now through half-empty streets giving on to big tall walls, dark warehouses, heading for the main road. I say I am unfamiliar with this part of town. The radio is singing something about being just like you. Tina liked that man, the singer. I shut off from it, the song. It's easy. As easy as willing myself not to feel my skin. I feel a vast, burning rip on the skin of the air, the blackness of the day. Why is it so dark? Up near some arches, an evil odour. Three men with dazed fish-eyes on sleeping bags, their faces and hands caked in dirt. With their damp blankets and rags beside them, their stringy long hair, they are battle-weary Viking sailors, dredged up from a sunken boat. 'Imagine getting like that,' he says. 'Scummy.' Those dazed fish-eyes.

We're in a cab office, no, a backroom. Strip lighting. A fat, wheezing man is opposite us, sitting hugely on a small chair, a pending tray stuffed full of papers before him. He has huge specs which refract everything. He is fishing out something, a small machine, jabbing it towards me. I sign something. Now a machine: '7707'. The serpent vibrates and hums as it coils around the cross, the T-shape. I must keep my eye on it, have it within my sights. They put me on the phone. A woman's voice, far away. I answer, perfectly composed. 'Yes, mother's maiden name is Harding.' Carl says something, he is so far away I can barely hear him. Eventually I hear. 'For a car,' I repeat. It is still raining. Tiny droplets on the cables that cross the street, a pendant of shining pearls.

II

She is freezing, but the cold doesn't touch her. It's dense, dank, wood-cold. From time to time, the distant growl of some car growing louder. A rolling cloud is coming in from the left of the sky, over the grey bank. There is a flapping. A squawk. Now, coming closer, a clashing vicious machine roar, crushing all before it. She lies still. Beneath her the grass is wet, angry, alive beneath her. The machine roars forward, relentless, and then shudders to a halt. Quick, cushioned steps on the grass. Voices. Big dark boots. A Kagool, dark with yellow stripes. A face, leering down, sideburns. She moves her head up. The iron gate is there, a few feet to her left. The straw man.

'Are you all right?' says the man. 'I'll call an ambulance.'

It's been six, seven days. But she can explain nothing, link nothing. In this quiet, bland, beige, soundless room with a view of trees bending, turning brown. Sometimes, a memory appears perched on her shoulder. She bats it away. No dreams. The big clock, white with black lettering, continues to tick away with mechanical blitheness. At night, she hears it clicking. There were voices – a patient, a nurse. She opens the bedroom window for air. She leans out to see better and the sash window comes down like a guillotine, so quickly she barely has time to move out of the way. The shock stirs her from her lethargy. She picks up her orange cord jacket from the chair where it hangs limply. Its brightness mocks her. Tina used to borrow it. Around the collar, the coconut smell.

Outside it looks too vivid, as if someone has removed the

pane of glass: the grey light piercing, the sounds too raw, the green of the leaves gleaming and rubbery like the green of some alien forest. A fitful breeze toys with the branches. The gravel echoes to footsteps. A few tall old houses rise behind the wall. Here and there she glimpses a corner of a simple white facade, windows into which you can't see, reflecting the branches which appear in the glass like long strands of hair swaying under water. From the other end comes the forlorn grinding of machinery. There is some park, over the wall.

The sense of observing herself with surprise as she does ordinary things doesn't leave her. But she is there, in the mirror, with the chalky invalid pallor. The eyes are far away, somewhere inside. The smell of the place, medicine and carpets. She goes back to her room. Everyone shuffles around, as if treading water, eyes cast down. Everyone has the same blanched, used linen colour. They go very well with the walls. Wall colour: Corpse Beige. There's a dreadful painting on the wall, a sugary pastel water-colour of a guitar by a farm door. That will most certainly drive her mad.

Here comes Mr Specs, the doctor, the one who comes in and asks her endless bloody questions with a clipboard. 'Would you say you were anxious or depressed? Do you recall your first bout of amnesia?' Not really, since I suffer from amnesia. Didn't get the joke. They all have that air, like Jake, a detached concentration. This is Jake's idea, to keep her here, like in some Victorian novel. And then, as she takes refuge back in her room with its airless neutrality, a porter enters, his earring glinting, his hair with a blond tuft on top, like a vol au vent. He makes some comment about the food. She avoids his eyes and looks out at the tops of the trees. On the tray there is bruised, shrunken fruit. His voice sounds peculiar – chanted, not spoken. She smiles him absently away.

The phone rings and she sits listening to its purring jeer. She lifts the receiver.

'What's up? You're not answering your mobile,' he asks, cautious and pedantic. A doctor with an intractable patient.

Then, a little of her old spirit, her impatience, comes through. 'Have you spoken to anyone?'

'What do you mean?'

'Tina. I told her to leave but I'm not sure. All of them.'

'Look, I'll be there tomorrow. We're going to Morocco for a few days with Suzy. I'm off to a meeting in an hour. I'll phone you later. Eat. Stop worrying.' He hangs up. He is thousands of miles away anyway. She drifts weightlessly. Outside, the clouds are coal-black smudges. Always, when her mind detaches, in this drifting, Tina rolls into the foreground, blotting out all else as she gathers force. She dozes. It is afternoon or night or perhaps early morning. A dog barks a repeated protest outside. Suddenly a loud rap on the door before it bursts open. A woman. It is Suzy, her Lely eyes convulsing with drama. 'Jake rang me. He's terribly worried about you.'

The car ride back is quiet. 'Look, darling, has that Tina got anything to do with it?'

'No, I don't know. I don't remember the evening. I know I didn't have keys. I must have wandered around, strayed into the Park.'

'Why didn't you want to see Jake when he came to visit the other day?'

'Didn't I?'

'No. That's why he called me. He had to go away again for a few days.'

She turns to Suzy. 'I'll stay in a hotel. In London.'

'We are in London, well, if you can call Chiswick London – this is the A4.'

Suzy's words strike her as thigh-slappingly hilarious. She moves her head to the window to hide her silent laughter.

'Nonsense. I mean, she's not going to do anything. Carl

called me, gave me your keys, he went on to another job. Said you got very out of it with them; in the house, then you wanted to go somewhere, they lost you. You must have wandered out to the Park. Still had your bag with you though, I see. Everything in it?'

The house is silent when they return. Suzy says, 'Well, a great improvement. Space, light. A home at last. At least that's done.' Suzy turns, her face poised around a question. 'It's only the dining room left to decorate, isn't it?'

She switches the light on in Tina's room. Someone has been in, made some effort to clean up a bit. Tina's keys are on the bed. She arranges to change the locks just in case. She doesn't want to listen to the messages while Suzy's there. She opens up the post. When Suzy finally leaves she scans the bank account online: £13,000 taken out eight days before. She checks the credit card balance for her joint card: £7,000. And the other one: £8,000. All withdrawn within twenty-four hours. It returns – the man in the cab office or whatever it was. Or did she dream this? Was it all of them? Her too? But why so many messages from her on the mobile? It's more likely to be a cover-up, one of her usual ruses to appear innocent. She opens the drawers; she keeps the diamond pendant in the box in the top one. Gone. Some instinct warns her against phoning Suzy. She rings her father.

He looks fragile, his neck scrawny, looser in the collar of his shirt, his silver hair yellowing, the hand turning the whisky glass revealing more age spots. It has never occurred to her that her father will die. His regime, his routine have been upset and he is doing his level best to adjust in a civilized manner to the sudden demand save for the fast, impatient jig of the well-shod foot on his crossed leg. They are in his study among all the old books, the prints, the busts and statuettes. He has his back to his immaculately tidy desk. Maybe that's why he looks old, here among his things, the precious woodcut of *Susannah and the Elders* taking pride of place, as always. She realizes she hasn't been here for two years. It must be the drugs they've given her; she feels numbed, casual. She needs practical advice.

'So,' he says, the fingers of his free hand drumming the armrest of his carver chair. 'Are you absolutely sure it was her? It would be absurd – she's such an obvious suspect. She may be impulsive, wild, but she never struck me as a stupid girl. She was obsessed with you.'

'Well, she did get in touch with you behind my back.'

'Mmm. She was distraught. Young.'

'She used to take things.'

'What exactly?'

'Oh, it sounds petty. Sunglasses, cameras, she binned things, destroyed clothes. Jake's things, my things.'

'Well.' He is irritable. 'All that hardly amounts to grand larceny. If you feel so positive, call the police. But then, in my experience it's more likely to be the men behind crime, and nowadays they can do these things on the net.'

'Not the diamond necklace. Of course, there's always a doubt.'

'And it'll be hard with the police. They'll pick it up, that there was a relation there between you. You'll have to tell Jake. That's why more crimes than you imagine go unreported.'

He is watching her beadily. For once, she thinks ironically, his gaze doesn't stray when she needs it to.

She says flatly, 'You think I'm like her. Mother.'

He hesitates, unwilling to enter the territory. 'Yes, no. They always live in us. Sometimes, you're too much like me – icy at the core.'

She would like him to be on her side, to tell her what to do, what to tell Jake.

'Darling.' His voice is abrupt but kind. 'Perhaps you feel a little guilty, perhaps you may feel you provoked the girl in some way. Corrupted her, invited her in.' His tone alters to one of erudite rumination, as if he is about to begin one of his learned lectures.

'It sounds as if you think I'm to blame. You saw her. You told her about Lucia.'

He seems puzzled. 'Oh, perhaps I did . . .'

'You were nicer to her than to me. Lucia.'

'You were so odd, ungovernable, after your mother died. You know, once we split up, she wouldn't let go, she clung to you. You clung to each other. Jimmy was at school. When you also went away to school, she went to pieces.'

She thinks, he is blaming me for her death, not himself. 'I don't remember that; any of that. Why did you decide not to mention her for years after she died, get rid of everything except the few clothes I kept? Guilt.'

He remains silently turning his glass.

'Why didn't you let me see her when she died?'

He turns his full gaze on her, paling. 'But you did see her. You insisted.'

She gets up, goes to the loo, dries her tears, hot automatic tears, and methodically redoes her makeup, all without looking at herself.

The September air has the sharpness of autumn in it, a faint whiff of wood and chestnut, which makes her think of being driven to school. He looks defensive, baited, at the door. He squeezes her arm awkwardly. The windscreen is sticky from the lime trees. She tries to squeeze water on and clean it with the wipers but it just spreads the slime all over, and she drives home, with difficulty, through the smeared glass, tears smearing her face. The locksmith is there, waiting for her at the front door.

Jake thumps hard at the door because his key won't fit. There have been phone calls, abruptly cut off, a buzzing traffic sound and no message. And when Jake is there, the phone begins to ring, three, four times and she says, 'Don't answer it.'

She opts for a simple narration, in an unfamiliar, anonymous restaurant. She tells him she began to take drugs with them, tells him of the strange evening with an angry Carl, not knowing, even now, if he spiked her or what happened. Jake doesn't look at her; he hangs his head, fingers gripping the cutlery. Even now, she is moulding and bending evidence, omitting – is it to make him feel better or to save herself? He swallows, says quietly, 'I know most of this. I know a little about her history. Did Carl try anything the other night?'

Her mind is agitating elsewhere with some obscure knowledge. 'I don't remember.'

'We have to tell the police. You have nothing to fear after all, have you?' he says in the car.

He parks the car purposefully. He takes her stiffly by the arm and leads her silently towards the front door. She thinks someone is on the corner. The house seems to whisper quietly to itself but she is with Jake and a deep, numb exhaustion, a submission, begins to descend on her. Someone is hammering the knocker. Once, twice, three times. Again. Three times. They both sit up.

'Jake. Ignore it. Only Tina uses the knocker.'

But he gets up. 'I'll see through the spyglass.'

She follows him out to the hall, stands there, just behind. He opens the door. Her face is strained, thin, those pale slanted orbs jumping over his shoulders, pinning her.

'Yes?' asks Jake politely.

'Can I come in?' The voice is smokier than ever, hoarse. She steps quietly into the hall. She moves from foot to foot, her body agitated, but her face is like a mask. 'I've just been sacked at the restaurant.'

'You'd better come into the sitting room. Perhaps you can help us with some questions,' says Jake.

Tina sits on the tan leather sofa; Christabel is perched on the edge of the other one. Jake positions himself by the coffee table, hands in pockets, looking down at them.

'They fired me. They said I was lucky they weren't calling the police.' A garbled story emerges of a girl who stole several times from the till and after the last time, things were too hot and she left. But now they are trying to blame her, all because Suzy was in to see her boss. 'Suzy is behind this.'

'Well,' says Christabel, her voice ice-calm. 'Suzy doesn't actually know, but someone took my pendant from here.'

'You think it's me, don't you?'

She regards Tina, sinews stretched, legs arched, ready for the pounce. 'Not necessarily. But how do you expect me to react?'

'What? I didn't do it. Any of it. Maybe you did it, Belle. You were doing that stuff, binning things, forgetting you did it.' She rises to go over to the other woman.

'Tina, please, don't come near me.' She avoids the hurt, glassy stare.

'What about the missing money?' asks Jake quietly, following Tina's ash dropping on the rug.

'What missing money?'

She says, 'From our bank, credit cards. You knew the pins. You just said I didn't do any of it, so you know something else went other than the pendant.'

Tina responds with an anguished half-groan.

Jake remains standing, his hands joined behind his back. Tina sighs, hand grasping at the side of her hair, the old-gold mane grown limp and brown now. 'I had nothing to do with it. But I knew they were up to something. Carl was thinking of getting into stuff like that with Jermaine. I told him not to. But Jermaine's done a flit. He owes. And he owed Carl. He's fucked on the pipe.' But she is being cautious, slow about choosing her words.

'Tina.' Jake takes a few steps towards her. 'You were involved with Carl's drug deals.'

Tina is suddenly spiteful, her eyes turning. 'That doesn't mean I'm a thief. The man in the VW. The private dick, spying on us. He's yours, isn't he? You were spying on Belle, on us, weren't you? I saw him come in here, let himself in. I saw him talking to Kim on the street. He was recording us, here. That's why you put in a burglar alarm. I took his bill, which you hid in your drawer.'

Jake clears his throat dismissively, not betraying any shame or nervousness. 'You're running away with yourself. But yes, I was worried about Belle.' His head moves briefly towards Christabel. 'I didn't know any of you, she can be a little rash . . . she's not well.'

Tina throws him a look of contempt and turns to her. 'I thought you knew I loved you, Belle. Why I was here.'

She flinches and says, 'So if you knew about the guy, the detective, why didn't you tell me?' She recalls the nervous man in the bar, when she was with Paddy, his mobile phone wedged oddly close to her. Had she batted the thought away or had she simply wanted to ignore it, invite catastrophe?

'I thought it would be better for you if he carried on and left you. You need to get away from him. You're still here, with him, I don't get it –'

'I think you'd better go.' Jake moves as if he is about to show Tina the door. 'Belle and I are off to Morocco tomorrow and I suggest if you are innocent and know anything, Tina . . .'

'Morocco?' She rises and sways, as if struck by the word. Her voice goes low, monotonous. 'You told me. You didn't marry him for love, you haven't got the strength to leave. And he doesn't know about Richie, does he? You told me. Richie called you. You went there. Left him to die. You told me that night, that weird night you tore up that red cardigan. We're the same.'

She leaves the room, picks up her keys from the shelf in the corridor, and walks quickly out on to the street, not glancing back. She has lost her hearing, or at least sounds are far away, tinny. She sees the street, the cars, the houses vibrating, glimmering, as if alive. She starts the car, drives around a street, but now she is back, heading down to her own road. She feels tranquil, attains a calm, cold tranquillity in the speed. There is Tina, standing in the middle of the road. That hair. Those strobe eyes flashing wildly at her. The murky brown trees shake and tremble in the breeze. There are spots of orange everywhere. Jake is running over to the girl, grabbing at her arm. She leaps at him in one forward, graceful pounce, arms stretched out. He falls back, hands grasping at the air behind him.

She is looking through the windscreen at her. Their gazes lock in that hair's breadth of time. She walks quietly out. His head is at an odd angle, twisted, on the edge of the pavement. Blood collects in a large, widening pool under it. In the gaudy orange film, it looks black. She doesn't look at his open eyes. The houses crouch and tilt forward, silent witnesses.

12

It never helped to be back there, so near to everything, to you, my head so full of old images. I couldn't speak to you. I understand we couldn't. That time we met, before we had to go and see them again with the lawyers, you looked so wary and untrusting. It tore me apart. You said it would be best not to see each other; given the circumstances, the inquest. I remember the words, every word. Tell it simply, it was all very sudden. A terrible accident. (Another one.) But even then, we protected each other. Oh yes. There was love, friendship, there, even in the end. I did a good job of telling them it was my fault, I ran right in front, 'distraught', I said, and he tried to stop me. I told them I was drunk, upset. You couldn't stop. No time. But it saved me, that you'd hit him with the car, what with my history. And I saved you.

I moved in with Tristram but it was a horrible time. I hated the slimy way he rolled his eyes over me. I even thought about going back to Carl. Actually, Carl rang and rang. I scared him off. I'm proud of that. Told him the detective was Jake's and that he knew all about him and Jermaine. He rang me months later. From Brighton. He has vans now and Albanians working for him. I remember you saying he'll end up in a mock Tudor mansion, with a jacuzzi and two Alsatians. I was thinking how funny you could be, walking past The Castle, wondering where the junk shop had gone. Another bloody new croissant parlour, you used to say. But you threw away the glass head. That killed me.

I guessed what they were planning – we'd done it before, me getting to know someone, they'd come in months later, do the business with the cards, the identity fraud on the computer. Jermaine had started us off, given us the idea, the contacts, but he got more and more fucked. But this time I didn't want to. I told them. There was something special between us. But you asked them in. I did think about telling you but then, that was betraying them, landing myself in the shit. And anyhow, it was Jake's money, not yours. I never thought he'd actually go through with it, Carl. But that night he came back all wild-eyed, I knew. But he did it all weirdly, not as he usually operates – he was close to the edge. He must have spiked you. I still don't know because sometimes I think you were willing it all on in your weird way. Living by proxy, stealing from yourself. You'll be glad to hear I stole Carl's stash. I figured he'd put it back in the old house again, away from yours, after that night he took you out. I rang Big Mack, he hates Carl, so he bought it off me; paid me under but then, three grand's not bad. Carl never suspected, with the cops buzzing around. He'd never suspect me anyway.

So why am I writing to you now? That day. It was the same as always in the Park, gloomy. Those houses looking on, shrinking everything down to dainty proportions as you'd say. Dinky, you'd say, curling your lip, I remember a lot of what you said; your voice crops up in my dreams. Even now. That's what used to happen in those months after the accident. I'd think of you, see you, at the edges of my eyes. I suppose I was conjuring you up, out of everybody. And I'd start talking like you again. And now, in tutorials, at the Courtauld, I hear you in me all the time. I'm on my last year there, by the way. I'll always be grateful for that, you changed my life. I remember us in that house, so lovely at first and then it began to feel like that Von Hoogstraten peepshow, with both of us there, flattened, distorted, being watched by some unseen, outside eye. Well, we were, I suppose. As you always said, just because something's a fantasy doesn't mean it isn't real.

They all felt sorry for you, pregnant with a dead man's child. And thank God you never told Suzy about the money and the pendant. I saw through her; she's dangerous. It might have incriminated you, us, telling the police about all the thefts, the money. Thanks to me, it was an accident in everyone's eyes. You owe me that. Although that detective out there, he knows everything about us. Knows what the police didn't know. So I don't feel too bad about that diamond pendant. I do feel bad about the book – the Panofsky. I still don't know why I took it; maybe I was angry. You can have them back if you like.

I recall you saying if you think about someone enough they tend to appear. Anyhow, the other day hurt me. It may be why I might send this one, after all those letters in the past I never sent you. I was walking up the path, at one end of the Park, the animal farm to my left. There were a few people scattered around. Two women sat at a bench, one dark, one fair, a little girl running around before them. I knew it was you. Your shoulders are imprinted in my memory. We always recognize the ones we can't forget. Your shoulders, narrow and elegant, the slight stoop when you got excited talking, leaning forward. Still skinny. I walked on, nearer, head down, my heart thumping. The girl beside you was young, a nanny or something. I laugh to think of it now, I thought, oh yeah, another me. As I passed, I could barely look. So I looked straight ahead. It had been a good three years. You'd moved, what were you doing there? It meant something, both of us there at the same time. The synchronicity. Suddenly, light footsteps, little trots. The little girl was almost in front of me, her chubby tiny fists tight with excitement, smiling, swaying. I looked at her. White-blonde hair, wide green eyes. Not like you at all. Or Jake for that matter. A beautiful big smiley mouth, looking at me with no shame, as children do. What do they want, what did she want? She was trying to say something. I stopped still, bent down. 'Iris darling, come here.' That voice said it all, that cut-glass tone of yours. I turned; you looked, as the cliché goes, straight through me.

I wonder if you know about me and Paddy. His wife doesn't know yet. You never did go back to work with him. Well, you have enough money now. You didn't stop. But you weren't going for me. I knew then, in an instant, what I had to do. What you wanted. It was simple, pre-planned in a way. Remember how you used to talk about answering the call, the calculation of some other? *The Death of Actaeon*. I knew, the way you were looking at it, after seeing Jake in Moroni's knight just before. I knew what was going on in your head. What you didn't know, but I did, was that Jake was spying, just like Actaeon. We both did it – just like in the myth. He fell, of course. You didn't tell them that I pushed him. Just as I haven't told anyone about you speeding up to hit him, even though you saw him falling. Or about Richie. But once Jake knew about that – well. He did have to go. The thing is, we're the same. I knew it, the night I set it up, created that row with Carl on the street, when I saw you watching me. But even if I don't send you this (incriminating evidence, after all), we need to talk. That detective's phoned me after all this time. He wants to take me out for a drink. You need to know, we need to think what to do. But also, I must tell you, I hated it when you looked right through me.

Acknowledgements

I'd like to thank the following for their help, advice and contribution: Juliet Annan, Maria Aristodemou, Sue Armstrong, Helen Campbell, Clare Conville, Carly Cook, Vincent Dachy, Anouchka Grose, Anthony Hanania, Daryl Higginson, Mary Horlock, Sarah Hulbert, Darian Leader, James Le Fanu, Jenny Lord, David Luard, Sophie Luard, Jane Muir, Sam North, Hugo Ray, Mandana Ruane, Amanda Schiff, Dyan Sheldon.

He just wanted a decent book to read ...

Not too much to ask, is it? It was in 1935 when Allen Lane, Managing Director of Bodley Head Publishers, stood on a platform at Exeter railway station looking for something good to read on his journey back to London. His choice was limited to popular magazines and poor-quality paperbacks – the same choice faced every day by the vast majority of readers, few of whom could afford hardbacks. Lane's disappointment and subsequent anger at the range of books generally available led him to found a company – and change the world.

'We believed in the existence in this country of a vast reading public for intelligent books at a low price, and staked everything on it'
Sir Allen Lane, 1902–1970, founder of Penguin Books

The quality paperback had arrived – and not just in bookshops. Lane was adamant that his Penguins should appear in chain stores and tobacconists, and should cost no more than a packet of cigarettes.

Reading habits (and cigarette prices) have changed since 1935, but Penguin still believes in publishing the best books for everybody to enjoy. We still believe that good design costs no more than bad design, and we still believe that quality books published passionately and responsibly make the world a better place.

So wherever you see the little bird – whether it's on a piece of prize-winning literary fiction or a celebrity autobiography, political tour de force or historical masterpiece, a serial-killer thriller, reference book, world classic or a piece of pure escapism – you can bet that it represents the very best that the genre has to offer.

Whatever you like to read – trust Penguin.